Kyle glared at Zane. "You and I have never been friends, but take a little friendly advice—Don't do anything that will harm Mica."

Zane smiled. "Me? I don't know what you're talking about. She came over, she had a drink, she left. So what?"

"You know exactly what I'm talking about. I have a pretty good idea what happened when you were on location in Georgia last year, but don't let it happen here."

"That dame yelled rape in order to sue me. It happens all the time. I figured Mica was looking for a ticket to Hollywood. Most women are."

"She's not. And you'd damned well better not cause any trouble for her." Kyle turned and walked toward the door, then stopped. "I mean it, Zane. Watch your step with Mica." He closed the door behind him. Loud.

Dear Reader,

The popularity of our Women Who Dare titles has convinced us that you love our stories about Superromance heroines who do not back away from challenges. So, we're delighted to offer you three more!

For October's Women Who Dare title, Lynn Leslie has created another trademark emotional drama in *Courage, My Love.* Diane Maxwell is fighting the fight of her life. To Brad Kingsley, she is a tremendously courageous woman of the nineties, and as his love for her grows, so does his commitment to her victory.

Evelyn A. Crowe's legion of fans will be delighted to learn that she has penned our Women Who Dare title for November. In *Reunited,* gutsy investigative reporter Sydney Tanner learns way more than she bargained for about rising young congressman J.D. Fowler. Generational family feuds, a long-ago murder and a touch of blackmail are only a few of the surprises in store for Sydney—and you—as the significance of the heroine's discoveries begins to shape this riveting tale.

Popular Superromance author Sharon Brondos has contributed our final Woman Who Dare title for 1993. In *Doc Wyoming,* taciturn sheriff Hal Blane wants nothing to do with a citified female doctor. But Dixie Sheldon becomes involved with Blane's infamous family in spite of herself, and her "sentence" in Wyoming is commuted to a romance of the American West.

Please enjoy our upcoming Women Who Dare titles, as well as the other fine Superromance novels we've lined up for your fall reading pleasure!

Marsha Zinberg,
Senior Editor

# Lynda Trent

# St★rlit ★ Tomorrow

## Harlequin Books

TORONTO • NEW YORK • LONDON
AMSTERDAM • PARIS • SYDNEY • HAMBURG
STOCKHOLM • ATHENS • TOKYO • MILAN
MADRID • WARSAW • BUDAPEST • AUCKLAND

Published October 1993

ISBN 0-373-70569-7

STARLIT TOMORROW

## ABOUT THE AUTHOR

Dan and Lynda Trent have charmed readers all over the world with their colorful characters and "down-home" stories. But *Starlit Tomorrow* has a special place in their hearts. About three years ago, a movie was supposed to be filmed in their own town of Henderson, Texas. The movie was never made, but the idea sparked a lot of "what ifs" in their fertile imaginations. The result is a wonderful romp full of misunderstandings and the confusion that results when Hollywood meets small-town America.

Dan and Lynda enjoy hearing from their readers and will answer all letters personally. Please write them at the following address:

Dan and Lynda Trent
P.O. Box 1782
Henderson, TX 75653

## Books by Lynda Trent

### HARLEQUIN SUPERROMANCE

348—THE GIFT OF SUMMER
430—WORDS TO TREASURE
504—JORDAN'S WIFE
536—REFLECTIONS OF BECCA

# CHAPTER ONE

MICA HAD RARELY FELT so ill at ease and overwhelmed, but she refused to be intimidated. "I agree that *The Grapes of Wrath, The Catcher in the Rye* and *Huckleberry Finn* are excellent classics. No one would deny that."

"Then why ask for a change to our curriculum?" Arlen Hubbard, head of the Sedalia, Texas, school board, said with a frown as he steepled his fingers over the polished wood conference table. "Frankly, you've been a bit of a problem ever since you began teaching here, Miss Haldane."

"I had no intention of causing a problem." Mica kept her voice calm. She hadn't expected this issue to become so controversial. "The books I'm proposing as alternatives are also excellent. I taught them in Dallas. I chose *The Mayor of Casterbridge* because I thought the students would benefit from reading Thomas Hardy. I picked *Tom Jones* because of its color and richness of characters. And although *Gone with the Wind* was more recently written than the others, most people consider it to be a classic because it's been so widely read. The students in my Dallas classes loved them."

Hubbard sighed as if he thought she was being tediously obstinate. "The first two books are by British authors, according to our school librarian. Not American."

"I know, but the description of the senior literature course doesn't specify American authors only. The sole criterion is that the books had to have been originally published in the English language."

The members of the school board exchanged glances. Miss Farley, who sat on Hubbard's right, said in frigid tones, "In *The Mayor of Casterbridge,* the man about whom the book is written has sold his wife and child. *Sold* them, Miss Haldane. I, as a woman, am offended by that."

The man seated across from Miss Farley chimed in, "*Gone With the Wind* advocates slavery. We could have a real problem there."

"It doesn't advocate it," Mica protested. "The book is merely set during the time period of the Civil War. I've heard *Huckleberry Finn* objected to for the same reason, yet you're insisting that I teach it."

Hubbard added, "I tried to read *Tom Jones.* But I couldn't make heads or tails of it. If I can't understand it, I'm sure none of our students will, either."

Mica was having a hard time keeping her temper in check. Without thinking, she said, "The idea is to make them stretch mentally. If a senior can't understand a book written in plain English, then that student has no right to graduate." Too late, she realized she had made a huge blunder and tried to correct it by adding, "Maybe you found the book difficult because your mind was preoccupied with something else."

Hubbard was not appeased by her attempt to cover her faux pas. His face bright red from contained anger, he said through clenched teeth, "You're to stick with the curriculum as it is. That's all there is to it."

"But those books have been taught here for as long as anyone can remember. I want to challenge my students with something new. Won't you at least consider it? I don't need an answer now. I'm not scheduled to teach in summer school. I only need to know in time to order the books for the fall. Please. Won't you at least take a few weeks to consider the merit in my request?''

With a sigh, Hubbard looked up and down the table at his fellow board members. ''All right, Miss Haldane. We'll think about it.''

''Thank you.'' She suppressed a triumphant smile and nodded a farewell to the board as she left the meeting. Teachers in Sedalia weren't encouraged to remain for other issues of business after their own was finished. She didn't know if her arguments had swayed anyone, but she wasn't discouraged. She had taken a stand and brought this issue up through the ranks to the school board itself, despite several veteran teachers' advice not to make waves. And with three months of summer for them to think about this, she felt confident that they would see it her way.

Mica had only to finish a bit of paperwork the following day and her time would be her own for the summer. She hadn't had a free summer since her high school graduation, and she was looking forward to the peace and quiet. Now that her two-year probationary period as a new teacher in the district was completed and her renewal contract for the next year signed, she was eligible for pay raises and eventually retirement benefits. Her life lay ahead of her, perfectly planned, neatly ordered—except for the fact that she hadn't planned on still being single.

The next afternoon at a quarter past four, Mica shifted the precarious load of books and personal belongings she was bringing home for the summer and struggled to unlock the front door of her house. Finally successful, she pushed her way in and unceremoniously deposited her burden on the hall table. She straightened, rubbing her aching arm where the books had rested, and closed the door, drawing a deep, relaxing breath. It was then she noticed the smell of cigarette smoke.

At once she was alert. She didn't smoke and neither did any of her friends. Not for the first time she wished she had had the door locks changed, but she had never been sure that it was allowed, since she was only renting.

On several previous occasions, she had suspected that someone had been in the house without her knowledge, because one or two of her things seemed to be out of place, but she had discounted the notion since nothing was ever missing.

Slowly she edged down the entry hall and peeped into the living room. It was empty and silent. Other than the hum of the refrigerator coming from the kitchen, she heard nothing at all. "Is anybody here?" she called out tentatively, but got no response. As she eased toward the kitchen, she told herself that asking such a question had been foolish. If a burglar was in the house, he certainly wouldn't answer.

Her hand closed around her cordless phone, and she clutched it like a weapon. If she found someone and dialed 911, how long would it take for the police to arrive? The smoke smell was even stronger in the kitchen, and when she looked into the wastebasket, she found a water-soaked cigarette butt. In her sink was a saucer that had been used as an ashtray. No burglar would be so careful of her floors. She put the phone down. "Mrs. Mobley, are you in here?" she demanded.

Now confident that she had correctly deduced the identity of the intruder, she strode down the short hall, past the bathroom, and looked into the two small bedrooms. "Mrs. Mobley?" She found no one. Exasperated, Mica sat on her bed and kicked off her shoes. Ever since she had moved into this place, Mica had suspected her landlady of making unannounced inspections while she was teaching school. She had always guarded her privacy, and it bothered her to think someone had been in her house without permission. Even though the soggy cigarette was virtual proof that the intruder had been her landlady, Mica thought it best to be sure.

Barefoot, she went to the phone by her bed and punched in Norma Mobley's number. "Mrs. Mobley? This is Mica Haldane. Have you been in my house today?"

Norma replied, "Yes, I was."

"I wish you'd asked my permission first. I smelled cigarette smoke and thought I had interrupted a burglar."

"It was just a routine check. I try to make them when I won't disturb you." The woman offered no apology.

Mica gripped the phone tighter. "I don't allow anyone to smoke in here. I've told you I'm allergic to tobacco smoke."

"I was only in there for a short while and you weren't home. Say, have you heard about the movie they're fixing to film here?" Her voice was tinged with contempt.

"Yes, everybody in town's talking about it." She was angry with her landlady and didn't want to get tied up in one of the woman's long-winded conversations. "I have to go now. I just got in from school and I'm worn-out."

"I'm against having all those Hollywood people come here. There's no telling what corruption they'll be teaching our youngsters while they're here."

"I'm sure they're no more corrupt than anyone else." She bent closer to the cradle of the phone, preparing to hang up.

Mrs. Mobley chuckled, but in that annoyingly nasal way Mica had come to recognize as the woman's expression of contempt. "Sure. Right. You must have been born yesterday. Everybody knows what Hollywood people are like. We have a clean, drug-free town, and I for one don't want to see that change."

Mica wasn't entirely sure she agreed with Mrs. Mobley's assessment that Sedalia was drug-free. She had seen more than one high school student who looked as if he was on something. "I have to get off the phone, Mrs. Mobley."

"Brother Malcolm said he's calling a special prayer vigil to ask that the movie deal fall through. Would you like to go with me?"

"No, thank you." Mica knew of Brother Malcolm Stout's self-styled church and wanted to stay as far away from it as possible. He and his congregation espoused that their church and their beliefs were the only true beliefs and that anyone who differed from them was doomed. Mica privately thought Brother Malcolm was no more than a troublemaker. "I have someone at the door," she lied. "Goodbye, Mrs. Mobley." She hung up, weary from her efforts to keep her thoughts about Mrs. Mobley and Brother Malcolm to herself, and lay back on the bed. This house was in an ideal location, being on the same block as the school, but she was beginning to think it would be worth moving, and driving to school, in order to avoid having to deal with this particular landlady. Sedalia wasn't large, and no place in town really would be too inconvenient.

When the phone rang, Mica started, then groaned. Surely it wasn't Mrs. Mobley calling back. Quickly she sat up and took a deep breath, then answered it.

"Mica? This is Carrie. You sound upset."

"I just finished talking to Mrs. Mobley. I was right. She *has* been coming in here while I'm gone."

"I wouldn't put up with her if I were you. Have you heard the news?"

"About the movie? I haven't heard anything else."

"Then you know they're auditioning to fill several small parts. I'm going to try out. Are you?"

"I don't know. I don't know anything about being in a movie."

"Nonsense. You've been in plays here in the Little Theater. You're as qualified as anyone else in town."

"I know about stage plays. Movies are entirely different."

"I'm going to the first audition, tonight. Come with me."

Mica hesitated. She wasn't scheduled to teach English classes in summer school, so she would have the time, but a person needed more than time. And she wasn't sure that having performed onstage in their community theater was sufficient training.

"Zane Morgan has been cast," Carrie said temptingly. "It's been confirmed. Can you imagine Zane Morgan here in Sedalia? Remember how we used to fantasize about him when we were in high school?"

"That was twelve years ago."

"Just think about actually seeing him in person. Maybe even talking to him! If we get parts, we'll see him every day! Please come with me. I'll be too embarrassed to go alone."

"Okay, I'll go with you. But I'm not saying that I'll try out. I'm just going along to watch."

"Great! I'll pick you up at seven."

"I'll see you then." Mica hung up the phone and lay back again on the bed. She was tempted to try out. The opportunity to be in a movie didn't come to Sedalia every day. It would certainly be an interesting way to spend the summer.

THE AUDITIONS WERE HELD in the high school auditorium, a place as familiar to Mica as her own home. The casting director, a pudgy man with thick glasses and almost no hair on his head, gave everyone a synopsis of the movie and handed out the passages to be read. Mica had expected something different. This was the same way their local group did auditions for a stage play. As she felt familiar with the routine, she decided to add her name to the list of those intending to read for a part. Carrie grinned and poked her in the ribs. When it was Mica's turn, she was asked to try out for the part of Angie Dillon, the best friend of Dawn Bennet. She already knew Dawn would be played by Diane King, an actress she particularly liked. Mica had always been good at cold readings, and she gave what she felt was a credible performance. The casting director, however, didn't comment one way or another, but she saw him jot something down on the clipboard he carried.

When auditions were over, Carrie drove Mica home, bubbling all the way. "Wasn't that exciting? And can you believe all the people who came to audition? I even saw Miss Nelly Franklin! She's eighty if she's a day."

"The director said there would be bit parts for people of all ages. I thought she gave a good reading."

"So did I. But who would guess Miss Nelly would want to act? And did you see Buford and Birdine Ponder? They read as well as she did."

"I seldom see Miss Nelly without Birdine, and Buford takes every step Birdine takes." Mica looked out at the darkness beyond the car window. "It would be nice to have someone that devoted to you for half a century or more."

"Marriage is hard. I'm amazed anyone makes it work."

"You're still hurt over the divorce, aren't you?" Mica glanced at her friend. "It's been two years."

"I know. Marvin has remarried, and they have a baby, I hear. I wish the friends Marvin and I have in common wouldn't tell me so much about him. I just want to put it all behind me." Carrie wrinkled her nose. "How could I ever have fallen in love with a man named Marvin Stubs?"

"At least he was better looking than his name suggests."

"I was glad to take my maiden name back. Carrie Graham is better than Carrie Stubs any day."

"Graham means something here in Sedalia. I'd have taken it back, too."

"Daddy would have been upset if I hadn't. He's running for reelection again next year. Did I tell you?"

"No, but I figured he would." Harrison Graham had been mayor of Sedalia for more years than Mica could remember. "I couldn't imagine Sedalia without him as mayor.

By the way, how is Jake? I haven't seen him in several weeks."

Carrie smiled. "He's fine. And we're getting along pretty well. Things might have been different if I had married him instead of Marvin. But who knows? I don't even remember why I picked Marvin in the first place."

Mica nodded. "At the time you were more interested in moving away from Sedalia than anything else."

"And now here I am, home again." She turned onto Mica's street. "I only hope I can stay. Jobs are pretty scarce here for drama majors and it bothers me I haven't worked since I moved back to Sedalia. I don't want to live in my parents' house indefinitely."

"Maybe you could move in with Jake," Mica said in obvious jest.

"Right. And have every busybody in town talking about the loose morals of the mayor's daughter. You know as well as I do that we'd have to get married first, and I'm not going to rush into another marriage. If you ask me, Marvin remarried on the rebound." Carrie stopped in front of Mica's house. "When do you think we'll hear if we've been cast?"

"I have no idea. Filming starts soon. I guess we'll know in a day or so."

"You did a great reading. I can see you as Angie."

"Thanks. You did, too. I hope we both get parts, but it all depends on how the director sees things."

Carrie nodded. "Just the fact that they're making a movie here is exciting. I can hardly wait for the stars to get here. Jake's excited, too, even if he won't admit it."

Mica opened the car door and got out. "Thanks for talking me into going with you tonight. I'll see you later." As Carrie drove away, Mica made her way up her walk to her front door. Before putting her key in the lock, she paused and looked around.

The neighborhood where Mica had lived as a child was across town and nothing like this one. Coming from a low-income family, she had been the first in her family to go to college and one of the few to even finish high school. That was why it had been so important for her to return to Sedalia to teach. She wanted to inspire other children of poor families to persevere and get an education. She could offer herself as proof that it could be done.

To herself she whispered, "Someday I'll be able to look back and think, 'I made a difference.' How many people can do that?" She unlocked her door and went inside.

BY THE END of the week, Mica and Carrie had both been notified that they had been cast. Mica had been chosen for the part of Angie, the shy best friend of the movie's leading lady, who is also falling in love with the leading man. Carrie had been given a smaller part, but she was thrilled nonetheless.

By Tuesday of the next week, the stars began arriving in Sedalia, along with all the crews and equipment needed to film the picture. Sedalia was buzzing with more interest than it had exhibited since the last world war.

The moment Zane Morgan arrived at the county airport, a bevy of Sedalia's women immediately began dogging his footsteps. He tossed them a smile from time to time, and if he drank coffee from a plastic cup or wiped his mouth on a paper napkin, the object instantly became a souvenir and was snatched up by an adoring fan as soon as he moved away. Zane accepted the adulation as his due.

Shelley Doyle came the following day. All the men in town swore she was even more beautiful in person than she was on the screen, but the ladies gossiped among themselves that she was starting to age and that her skin might look good on film, but that it was more like tanned leather in person. Shelley didn't smile or show any interest at all in her fans;

instead, she ignored them as if they were pesky insects. This didn't go unnoticed by the people of Sedalia.

"I can't believe how stuck-up she acts," Carrie said to Mica as they sat on Mica's back porch drinking lemonade. "You'd think she was royalty by the way she struts around. All she needs is a long black cigarette holder and a matched pair of Russian wolfhounds to complete the picture!"

Mica laughed. "She does seem a bit full of herself. Maybe she's just shy off camera. Or maybe she doesn't have much personality of her own. I've heard that some actors don't."

"You'd make excuses for Jack the Ripper."

"He probably had an unhappy childhood," Mica teased.

"I wonder when Diane King will get here. I'd rather meet her than Shelley."

"I heard she's finishing a film somewhere in Europe and going through a real-life divorce in Hollywood. I guess they'll film her scenes last. They don't do them in order, you know."

"I know. I went to the library and read up on filmmaking. You should see Daddy getting ready for all this to start. He's beside himself. He says Sedalia's going to be famous."

"That's probably true. Especially if they use the town's real name in the movie. Are they?"

"I don't know. I never thought of that. I'll bet Daddy hasn't, either." Carrie took another sip of her lemonade. "Daddy's trying to get as many people as possible to paint their houses and fix up their yards."

"I wish Mrs. Mobley would paint this house." Mica reached out and peeled off a bit of flaking paint from the trim around her back door. "I ought to look for another place to live. She's the pits as a landlady. I think she was here again yesterday while I was shopping, even though I told her not to."

"You know how she is. She has to have her nose in everything." Carrie propped her foot up on the porch rail. "Kyle Spensor is supposed to be here tomorrow."

"I wonder what he'll be like. I love his movies."

"Me, too. I can't wait to meet him. Some of my lines are opposite him."

"And Angie winds up with him in the end. I don't know why they thought I could do this. I hope they're right. It's only now starting to sink in that we're going to be working with some really big-name stars."

"Did I tell you both Zane and Shelley are staying in the Brookridge Arms Apartments?" Carrie asked.

"Together? I hadn't heard that."

"No, no. Not together. Two separate apartments. The rent on those places will be sky-high after they move out. Everyone in town will be wanting to live there."

"I wouldn't move just for that reason, but I guess some would."

"And Kyle Spensor rented a house."

"I wonder why he didn't get an apartment at Brookridge Arms, too."

"I don't know. Maybe he doesn't like apartments."

"It's the little cottage-style house over on Maple. The one that had a new roof put on last fall."

"I know the one. I've always liked that house."

"The rent will probably go up on that, too. Who knows? The price of everything here in Sedalia may go up." Carrie's eyes glistened. "But it'll be worth it. Can you imagine going to the store for milk and running into Zane Morgan at the checkout line? I can't picture him shopping at all."

"He has to eat just like the rest of us." Mica put down her frosty glass and gazed out at her small backyard. "It's going to be a hot summer. We're already overdue on rain."

"I know. I wonder how people survived before air-conditioning." Carrie pulled a strand of her honey blond hair around and squinted at it. "Maybe I should dye my hair. It's such a mousy color."

"Don't you do any such thing. You were cast exactly as you are. You can't change your appearance until after the filming is finished. It says so in the contract you signed."

"You're right. I'd forgotten. But at least your hair is a good color. In the right light it's dark auburn."

"If you ask me, it's just plain brown." Mica had never been all that concerned with the color of her hair. She wore it smoothly curved under in a page boy style so it would be easy to wash daily and care for. Her eyes matched the shade of her hair. Not a fascinating blue or green, but just brown.

"Maybe I could get Lawanda to put some 'sun streaks' in my hair. Filming hasn't started yet," Carrie said thoughtfully. "It's such an uninteresting color."

"Jake likes it."

"Jake's easy to please. I think I'll have it lightened just a bit. The director will never notice."

"I'd check with him first. Have you started memorizing your lines?"

"Are you kidding? I have them almost all memorized. Of course, there're not that many."

"Did you bring your script?"

"Does a bear sleep in the woods? Sure I did. It's in the car."

"Let's go over lines together." Mica went inside to get hers as Carrie headed for her car.

KYLE SPENSOR AMBLED down the steep steps of the commuter plane that had brought him on the last leg of his trip from Dallas to Sedalia. As he reached the tarmac, he paused to look around. It was a sunny afternoon, with only a hint of the scorching heat that would likely come in a matter of weeks. The tiny air strip, dubbed Malcolm W. Graham Field, was bounded by tall pines, and through a break in the trees he could glimpse rolling pastures dotted with brown cattle. He smiled. He had always liked Texas, though it wasn't his home state. Especially East Texas, with its piney woods and rolling hills. For years, every time a contract dispute left him feeling disenchanted with the film business, he had fantasized about moving to one of the small towns here in East Texas and spending the rest of his life more or less incognito. But the disenchantment never had lasted long enough, and it was just as well, for he loved his work. It was all he'd ever done.

He shifted his bag of carry-on luggage and headed for the terminal. Glancing back, he noticed a crew of airport personnel starting to unload the belly of the small plane, and among those bags already on the cart were the ones belonging to him. He was more than a little pleased that this time, at least, his luggage had arrived with him.

At the gate he was met by Harve Giacono. Kyle nodded to him as if it were no more unlikely to be met by Harve in this small out-of-the-way airport than it was in Los Angeles. "How's it going, Harve?"

"Not bad. Shelley's already in a snit, and Zane brought his current bimbo after all. Greenberg's already fuming and glaring. I'd say we're pretty much on schedule." He grinned up at Kyle.

Kyle smiled and nodded. "It's always the same with Lance Greenberg. He's a damned fine director, though. I have to admire the man, even if I don't particularly like him."

"Yeah. I know what you mean."

"What's the town like?"

Harve shrugged. "It's like any small burg anywhere. I still don't see why we couldn't shoot this one on the back lot."

"It's too hard to find extras with the right accent. You know what a stickler Greenberg is for authenticity."

Harve grinned. "There's one old lady you're going to love. Her name is *Miss* Nelly Franklin. The 'Miss' is important. Everybody calls her 'Miss Nelly.' She could be straight off the set of *Driving Miss Daisy* or *Cocoon*. She's going to add color to the film like crazy—if she doesn't drive Greenberg mad first."

Kyle and Harve found the spot where all the baggage was being piled, and as no one around seemed interested in checking his claim stubs, Kyle shrugged and stuffed the claim checks back in his pocket and sorted out what belonged to him. He traveled relatively light compared to Shelley, but he had brought enough for a three-month stay. "Did you get a house rented?"

"Yeah. There wasn't much to pick from, but I think you'll like it. It's small, but it's comfortable."

"I don't know what I'd do without you, Harve. We were supposed to have everything in Dublin wrapped up two weeks ago, but you know how that is. You'd think that by now I'd know better than to agree to do back-to-back films." He shouldered the leather strap of a bag and lifted one in each hand. "How are Janet and the girls?"

"They're fine. Janet says I'm to bring you over to supper if we're ever in Burbank at the same time. The girls said to tell you hello."

"You've got a great family. Makes me envious."

Harve laughed. "Right. Who wouldn't trade fame and fortune for a home-cooked casserole? I just wish I were there more often. But a cameraman, like an actor, has to go where the work is, I guess."

Kyle smiled, but he didn't answer.

Harve showed Kyle the way to the car he had rented for him, as well, and offered to drive him into town, since he already knew the way. Kyle was tired from his trip and more than pleased to let Harve drive. He curled his long body into the vehicle as Harve went around to the driver's side.

Kyle's height was sometimes a problem since he was always cast as second lead. At six-two, he tended to tower over most of the leading men. But because of his popularity and talent, directors were willing to work around the problem of his height. On this film, for instance, he was several inches taller than Zane's five-eleven and would spend a number of scenes standing in a hole or next to a platform beneath Zane's feet. Hollywood was positive that American women wanted their heartthrobs on the silver screen to be taller than anyone else in the film.

The airport was several miles from Sedalia, and on the way to town Kyle enjoyed the view of peaceful farms and of mixed-breed cattle grazing. High above them, a jet traced a contrail across the cloudless, blue sky. There was no place even near Sedalia for a jet of any size to land. Only smaller planes serviced the area between Dallas and Shreveport.

"I like this place," Kyle said as much to himself as to Harve.

"What? Here?" Harve glanced at him to see if he was joking. "Give me LA any day. Wait until you see what passes for a restaurant around here!"

Kyle made no comment. He didn't know Sedalia firsthand, but he knew a dozen other towns just like it. He was still looking forward to spending some time here. That was one reason he always rented a house instead of an apartment. He liked to feel he belonged, at least for a little while.

"Wait until you meet the locals," Harve continued. "They watch us like we're alien life forms. The other day when I bought gas, the man behind the counter asked me more questions about Hollywood than the FBI."

"In trouble with the FBI again, are you?" This was an old joke with them. Harve was given to exaggerations and to drawing odd parallels. Kyle had teased him about this for years.

Harve grinned. "Just wait. You'll see what I mean."

The nearer they got to town, the closer together the farms became; then the small pastures yielded first to large yards, then smaller ones. They were in Sedalia before Kyle knew it.

The town was old as Texas towns went, and it had the settled look of a place that had seen prosperity come and then go again. Several working pump jacks, dotted here and there in pastures and yards, attested to the fact that Sedalia was a part of the famed East Texas oil field. But silent wells, far more plentiful than those being pumped, attested to the fact that the oil was running out. Sedalia was gracefully going to seed. It was perfect for the setting of *The Last Wildcat*.

Kyle idly wondered if anyone had given thought to the fact that the title sounded more like a nature film than a film about a "wildcat" driller—a man who drilled wells by the seat of his pants and who hoped someday to find a gusher that would make him rich for life. Kyle had almost turned the script down. He wasn't particularly fond of oil field stories, but when he learned it was to be shot on location, he had agreed. He would always choose doing a film on location over shooting on the back lot, especially if it meant a trip to East Texas.

The houses they passed were framed by carefully trimmed lawns and flower beds that, from the looks of them, had been established long before Kyle was born. A predominance of crepe myrtles, blooming in all colors, bordered the streets. He could already feel Sedalia's easy tempo and its measured way of life. Housewives in housedresses visited with each other over fences, and down the block ahead of them, a group of young boys on bicycles hurried across the street. "It's a nice town," he commented.

"It's okay. But I already miss Janet and the girls. I wanted to bring them with me this time, but Kathy is on a Little League team and she'd probably have a fit at missing baseball season."

"I'll bet you anything they have a baseball team right here in Sedalia that she could join. I never saw a town that didn't."

Harve was thoughtful for a minute. "I don't think Kathy would go for it. And besides, she knows all the kids back home and it would be hard on her to have to make new friends. I hate being away from them so much. The girls will be grown before they see me without a suitcase in my hand."

At the next corner, Harve turned onto Maple, and half-way down the quiet street, he pulled into a driveway. "This is it," Harve said. "Home sweet home."

Kyle leaned forward for a better look at the house. It was small and unpretentious, built of cream-colored brick, and it had a swaging roof over the porch that reminded him of cottages he had seen in picture books. Several of the ever-popular crepe myrtles lent color to the yard with a profusion of pink, rose and white blooms. "Perfect."

"I'm glad to hear you say that, because I've already signed your name on the dotted line. You have it for the duration of the filming. The owner wanted to sell it to me, but I told her movies don't take that long."

Trying not to show too much enthusiasm, Kyle got out first, and Harve helped him carry his luggage into the house. He turned on the nearest switch to be sure the electricity was on, then looked around. The rooms were large, and filled with sunshine from the many windows.

"It has central air, you'll be glad to hear. You don't have to roast like we did in Bogotá that time."

Kyle laughed. He knew exactly which film Harve meant. Both had sworn that if they ever saw an air conditioner again, they would never leave it. "The house is larger than I expected from what I could see out front."

"Yeah, it goes way back on the lot. It has two or three bedrooms. One might be a den. It's hard to tell from the layout."

"I've seen worse." He sat in a chair. "It's comfortable." He stood and went looking for the bedrooms. "You did good, Harve."

"Have I ever let you down?" Harve pretended amazement that his skills would be questioned. "We're to meet at the town square tomorrow to go over the first scene. I left the shooting schedule on the kitchen table."

Kyle nodded. "I'll be there."

"I hope we can say the same for Shelley. She's already moaning about the primitive conditions here and how this is the end of the earth and how no one could possibly expect her to stay here for three months."

"That's Shelley. She took the Amazon with better grace than she shows in small-town locales."

"She was the only blonde in the Amazon. You haven't seen the extras that are cast in this film. Sedalia may not look special on the outside, but there's something in the water here that turns out gorgeous babes!"

"Go call Janet. Your motor's starting to rev up."

Kyle walked his friend to the door and waved as he went to his own rental car, parked at the curb. Two women walking down the street stared at Kyle in open interest. Kyle didn't mind. That was part of the job. He went back inside and started to get better acquainted with his new, though temporary, home.

# CHAPTER TWO

HARRISON GRAHAM was proud of his town. He had been mayor of Sedalia, Texas, for the past two decades, and considered every alley, shop and lamppost to be a part of his personal domain. Therefore, he had no qualms about confronting the town's worst eyesore, Daws Air Conditioner Shop, in a head-on battle. With Jack Murray, the city manager, at his heels, Graham strode into the offending shop as soon as the doors were open for business.

Neville Daws, the owner of the shop, met him at the scarred and battered counter. He wiped grease from his hand as he waited for Graham to speak. They had known and disliked each other since grade school, and Daws didn't particularly care why the mayor was paying him a visit. He already knew his answer would be no.

"I've come to see you about that trash out back, Neville," Graham began. "You were told to clean that up months ago."

"It's real hard to work on air conditioners and the like without winding up with extra parts. They have to go somewhere." He didn't bother to look up from the greasy rag he held.

"You were given the option of cleaning it up yourself or having the city council order you to do it. If you refuse, the city council has the right to hire to get the job done and send you the bill."

"I wouldn't do it if I was them," Daws said, finally looking Graham in the eye. "I wouldn't take kindly to having my belongings hauled off."

Graham stood his ground, but Murray edged back a step. "That junk heap is a breeding ground for rats and mosquitoes. It's creating a health problem."

"It ain't creatin' nothin' it ain't created for the past dozen years. You've just got a bee under your bonnet about them shooting a movie here."

"Well, damn it, Neville, don't you want your town to look good on film? Do you want everyone in the United States to know you have an unsightly pile of junk behind your shop?"

"It don't matter none to me. That pile of extra parts is a pile of money in my pockets. Any repairman will tell you the same."

"And while we're on the subject, you should paint the outside of your building. Judging by the 'pile of money in your pockets,' you can afford to. You can barely tell what color it was to start with. Your sign is nearly illegible!"

"Everybody knows where I am. There ain't no reason to go to the expense of paintin' my sign back the way it was. Besides, when old Clyde Jones painted it, he misspelled 'conditioner.' Put an *o* in front of the *r*. I'm glad it finally chipped off, to tell you the honest truth."

"That's not the point."

"Is the city council willing to pay me to paint that sign and my building?"

"Certainly not. If we pay you, we'd have to pay every other business in town. It's out of the question." Graham was shocked that Daws would even suggest such a thing. "You've always been a hard man to deal with, Neville. I had hoped you had some civic pride, however."

"Can't afford it. My wife spends every penny before it gets to the house. The building and sign stay just like they are."

Graham drew himself up and threw a glare at Jack Murray, who had remained silent the whole time. He had hoped Murray would have enough backbone to help him argue with Daws.

Murray halfheartedly said, "Neville, think how proud you'd be of a freshly painted shop. And if you can't clear away the junk in back, maybe you could put a privacy fence around it."

Graham frowned at his city manager. "That wouldn't do anything for the rodent and insect problem. No, the trash has to go."

"If that's all you wanted with me," Daws said, "I have to get back to work. I'm taking an old air conditioner apart for the parts." He cast a maddening grin at Graham and disappeared through the door that separated his front counter and showroom from his shop.

Graham looked around in frustration. There was nothing he could do except take the problem back before the city council, and Daws knew it.

"At least he keeps the showroom fairly neat," Murray said as he walked over to one of the rebuilt air conditioners on display. He bent to look at the price on the reverse side of the tag marked Cheap. "Not a bad price."

Graham grimaced and snapped, "Come on." He should have known Murray would be less than useless.

They headed on foot back across the downtown area to city hall, for Graham liked to stay visible and, with Sedalia so small, walking made more sense. Graham played his role as a politician to the hilt. Several times he stopped to chat with people on the sidewalk, and always he asked about their families and commented on the growth and promise of their children or the adorableness of their grandchildren.

Murray followed him like a faithful dog, nodding and smiling and, thankfully, keeping his mouth shut.

Except for Daws's obstinacy, he had ample reason to be proud of his town. Once he had spread the news of the movie filming, civic pride had kicked in, especially among the downtown merchants, and he had had to do little else to encourage them to spruce things up. In only a month, the town had done more toward beautification than in the past decade. Many merchants had been busy painting, and a few had gone to considerable effort and expense to redecorate their storefronts. Even though not all the improvements were finished, for a month's time was terribly short notice, Graham was sure the movie people would understand and be accommodating. The city council had even authorized the purchase of new streetlights to replace the hopelessly outdated ones now in use. Whit Rodgers, owner of the town's best clothing store, the Chic Boutique, had even put up aluminum siding to hide the old-fashioned front of his building. His competitor, Buttons and Bows, was responding by replacing their rather small display windows with larger ones. That work was to be finished any day now. Yes, his town was making him proud.

He hadn't gone far before he saw the movie's director, Lance Greenberg, and the producer, Howard Jankowski, wandering down the sidewalk, staring at the newly spruced-up buildings and looking puzzled. Graham put on his best politician's smile. "'Morning, Mr. Greenberg, Mr. Jankowski. Fine day, isn't it?"

"Where did it go?" Greenberg demanded. "What did you do with the town I saw last month?"

Graham chuckled. "I knew you'd be pleased. When the people heard about the movie, they started fixing up and modernizing to beat the band."

"It's all wrong now," Greenberg said with a stunned expression. "You've ruined my movie set!"

Graham kept his smile in place. "Nonsense. Now it looks better than ever. Why, look what Whit Rodgers has done with his shop. I hear several more owners have ordered aluminum fronts for their buildings, as well. Of course, those changes won't be made for a few weeks yet, but I guess you can shoot around the construction work until they're finished." He was proud of being able to use an insider's phrase that he had learned from watching television movies.

"Shoot around it!" Greenberg looked as if he was about to have an apoplectic seizure.

With his palms outstretched, the producer made a settling-down motion toward Greenberg, then turned back to Graham. "What he means is that we wanted the town exactly the way it was. We wanted the buildings as they were—rustic, you know."

"But nearly all of them needed paint. Buttons and Bows had such small windows you had to get real close before you could see what was inside. When they are through, they'll have the largest plate-glass windows in town."

"You tell them to stop," Greenberg growled, clearly unable to contain himself. "Tell them to put the town back the way it was!"

"I'll do no such thing!" Graham was scandalized at the suggestion.

Jankowski reached out and took hold of Greenberg's arm to stop his progress toward the mayor. In a frustrated voice, he said to Greenberg, "He can't do that. These people can't duplicate peeling paint. I guess we'll have to fly in a special paint crew from the studio."

"I don't have any room in the budget for that. I'll have a hard enough time keeping the cost of this film in line as it is. And if we do that, look at all the time we'll lose. You know this picture has to be shot in the summer. I've got a schedule to keep."

Jankowski ignored him. To Graham he said, "At least call off any further improvements. You can do that, can't you?"

"I suppose I could ask them, but I don't think we should. We want the town to look its best."

Greenberg was starting to mumble to himself. "I knew I should have come in a few days early, but even if I had, it would have been too late to find another town and stay on schedule. I have the cast and crew ready to start shooting this morning at ten. How can I manage to shoot around every building in town?"

"Not all the buildings have been changed," Jankowski soothed. "See? The bank and the drugstore are the same."

Mayor Graham proudly raised his head. "Not for long. The drugstore has ordered a new sign. It ought to be hung by tomorrow."

Greenberg's face turned bright red, and he looked as if he was about to go for the mayor's throat. "If that drugstore gets altered in any way, I'm going to alter whoever is responsible! Half my scenes are planned around that drugstore!"

Graham took a step back. A glance told him that Murray was looking at his watch and probably fabricating an excuse to leave. "I won't have my town looking seedy. It's out of the question."

"That's why we picked it! Because it looked seedy!" Greenberg was practically shouting. People as far as a block away were stopping on the sidewalk to see what was going on. "Your city council signed a contract for us to use the town 'as is.' That meant you were not supposed to make any significant changes."

Graham drew himself up. "I leave the details of such matters to our city attorney, but I'm not aware of any such clause in the contract. We'll have to discuss this at another time. I have an important appointment in less than ten minutes. Good day." He walked away as briskly as his dignity would permit. How dared those Hollywood people come to his town and talk to him so rudely? he silently fumed. For a moment he considered forbidding his daughter Carrie from being in the film, then remembered she was an adult and he no longer had any say as to what she did or did not do.

No, it wouldn't do for him to say anything to her about his unpleasantness with the director. For days all he had heard from her was how exciting it was for her to get a part in this movie. At least the filming would keep her in town through the summer, and maybe that would give Jake Farrell time to convince her to marry him. Jake would be good for her, and maybe he could help keep her feet on the ground. She was a sweet girl and he dearly loved her, but she was so bullheaded. He could not imagine where she had gotten such a trait.

"I'M GOING to kill him!" Greenberg growled at Howard Jankowski as the mayor walked away from them without agreeing to do something to stop the "beautification" that was threatening to ruin the background setting for his movie. "If I find him in a dark alley, I'll—"

Jankowski cut him off. "Lance, you won't do a damned thing. Get hold of yourself, man. Let's think about this." Jankowski swiveled his head around, regarding the town and completely ignoring the gathering crowd. "I wouldn't have hired you for this picture if I hadn't thought I was getting the best. I'm sure you can find a way to set up the camera angles and screen out the improvements. Like you said, most of the action takes place in front of the drugstore. And that office building across the way there can be made to look like a clothing store if we change the sign."

Greenberg took a deep breath and made an effort to see what Jankowski was showing him. "I guess it's possible.

Damn! Why did they break the contract like that? You know it's in the contract that they can't change anything until after the film is finished!''

Jankowski put his arm around Greenberg's shoulder and escorted him a few feet away, where they would not be overheard. "Yeah, and you and I both know that that clause is unenforceable in a court of law. The city doesn't own these businesses.''

"I know, but it's always worked for us before. Even the city manager gave me his word that nothing would be changed. I'll have a talk with him later today when the mayor's not around and see what I can do. Meantime, do the best you can with what we have left to work with.''

Greenberg gave downtown Sedalia another disgusted glare and stalked away.

MICA WAS in the beauty shop, waiting for Carrie to finish having her hair streaked, when Bernice Mobley, Norma Mobley's sister-in-law and the owner of Buttons and Bows, rushed in. Hardly pausing for a breath, Bernice began relating the details of the shouting match between the mayor and the movie director that had occurred in the town square not ten minutes before. Even as she talked, Sally Mae Randolph, owner of the Curl Up and Dye Salon, whisked Bernice into a waiting chair and covered her with a shampoo cape.

"That man has no right coming here to our town and telling us what we can and can't do with our own property,'' Bernice fumed as her head was lowered into the shampoo sink. "The nerve of him!''

Fannie Rodgers, who was seated in the chair next to Bernice, nodded emphatically. "We've had our differences in the past, Bernice, but you're right on this. Why, that aluminum siding makes our building look brand-new! And your plate-glass windows must have cost a pretty penny!''

Lawanda Stewart, one of the two beauticians who worked for Sally Mae, said, "You'll have to hold your head still, Fannie, or I'll never get your hair done."

Fannie frowned at Lawanda's reflection in the mirror, but stopped bobbing her head. When Lawanda removed the towel from Fannie's head, Mica was amazed to see bright blond where gray hair had been the day before. She tried not to stare but could not resist several glances.

Bernice, who had been talking with her eyes closed as her hair was being shampooed, wiped her eyes with the corner of the towel Sally Mae was wrapping around her wet hair. When she turned in Fannie's direction to continue her conversation, her jaw dropped. "You've gone blond?"

Fannie tried to look nonchalant. "I always was, you know. Lately I've noticed a few gray hairs, so I decided to help things a bit."

"Not a bad idea," Bernice agreed with a raised eyebrow. "Sally Mae, I think I'll go back to my natural color, as well."

Mica saw Sally Mae's face grow still. Bernice had been gray so long that even her longtime beautician apparently had forgotten what color her hair had once been.

"Red," Bernice said with satisfaction. "My hair was the loveliest shade of red."

Sally Mae nodded and tried to hide her relief. "I've got the very color. It's called Irish Sunset."

"We'll do it, then." Bernice beamed.

Mica glanced at Carrie and swallowed hard, trying to suppress a chuckle but instead causing herself to cough and having to clear her throat. The mental image of the matronly Bernice Mobley with red hair caught her off guard. She buried her face in the magazine she was reading, hoping to become inconspicuous.

"Mica, I didn't see you over there," Bernice observed, her smile now more of a simpering grin. "I hear you've been cast for a part in the movie."

Mica was not sure what Bernice was up to. The woman was known for her sarcasm. "Yes, I have a small role."

"Small role? The article in the newspaper said it was the biggest role given to any of us locals. I, for one, am glad you got the part. After all, you've done so well in all the little theater plays you've been in, I'm sure you'll be able to tell those movie people everything they do that's wrong." For an instant, Mica thought she had been insulted, but then Bernice laughed at her reflection in the mirror and said, "Telling us we can't fix up our town, indeed. We'll set those Hollywood people straight, won't we?"

Fannie laughed along with her as Sally Mae started to roll Fannie's wet hair. "You bet we will."

Mica disagreed, but did not say so, even though she wished she had. She felt uncomfortable that she was being included with those who thought the movie people needed to be set straight. With her several years of experience working with the community theater, Mica knew the necessity for creating the proper stage set for a given play. She sympathized with the film company's desire that the buildings they'd chosen in Sedalia as a backdrop to their film remain unchanged until the film was finished.

A glance at her watch told Mica she needed to be going. "Is it okay if I blow-dry Carrie's hair, Sally Mae? We're supposed to be at the makeup trailer in a few minutes."

"Sure, go ahead. Lawanda's through with her. You can use that dryer there on the table in front of her. I didn't expect to get so busy today."

"That's okay." Mica turned on the dryer and started running her fingers through Carrie's hair to fluff it. Sally Mae was bad about overbooking her appointments, but she was the best hairstylist in town. Mica had been unable to convince Carrie that having her hair color changed at the last minute was a bad idea, so she was relieved to see that the finished effort looked natural.

Fifteen minutes later, they left the beauty shop and ran down the street to where a crowd was gathering. Mica could hear a man shouting directions for people not to block the view of the drugstore. "Are we late?" she whispered to Carrie as they neared the silver trailer parked in the vacant lot beside the bank.

"I don't think so." Carrie pointed at a man going into the trailer. "Look! There's Kyle Spensor! He's much taller than I expected. I thought all actors were short."

"Zane must be a giant. I've seen them together in films before, and Zane is several inches taller." Kyle Spensor was not only tall, but was much more handsome in person than Mica had expected. His crisp, wavy hair was reddish brown in the sunlight. She found herself wondering if he had had freckles as a boy.

"He looks so friendly. Don't you think he looks friendly, Mica?"

"Yes, I suppose so," she answered rather absently as she stared at the actor's handsome features.

"On my way to pick you up, I saw him outside Haney's Café. He was signing autographs right and left. He's much better looking than I had thought he'd be. Why do you suppose he never plays the leading man?"

Carrie's question broke Mica's reverie. "What? Oh, I don't know." Then, pulling herself back to the task at hand, Mica said, "We'd better hurry."

As they neared the trailer, the door opened and she saw Zane Morgan emerge with a smile for the crowd. There was a smattering of applause. Close by his side was an attractive young woman, who immediately draped herself all over him. Mica wondered who she was.

The main room of the trailer was full of activity. Several chairs and mirrors were permanently mounted at makeup stations. A tall, extremely pale man was back-combing a woman's hair. An ebony-skinned woman bedecked with exotic jewelry was reigning over the cosmetics tables. When she saw Mica and Carrie she motioned for them to come to her.

"Leon, do this blonde next," she said to the tall man after hearing their names and consulting her list. "Angie, let me start on you."

It took Mica a moment to realize that the black woman was talking to her. Quickly she slid into the empty chair.

"Not that lipstick," the woman said to one of her assistants. "We're back in the sixties for this one, remember?"

Mica wondered how the woman kept it all straight. She seemed to be able to watch the entire roomful of people and miss no details. She noticed Kyle Spensor was nowhere in sight and assumed he must have gone into one of the back rooms.

"I'm Calula," the woman told Mica by way of introduction. "I want you here earlier after this. Be here at seven. You can come even earlier if you like, but not later."

"No problem." Mica tried not to stare at the woman over her shoulder in the mirror. To say Calula was interesting would have been an understatement.

Mica guessed the tall, graceful woman was Afro-Asian in origin, but she wasn't sure. Her loose-fitting dress was a blend of brilliant yellows, oranges and reds. Her black hair was pulled up in a French braid that accentuated her slender neck. At her neck, wrists and ears she wore silver jewelry that jangled and bobbed with each of the woman's quick movements.

Calula looked at Mica's reflection in the mirror, lifted a hank of her hair and said, "Tease it, Leon. Joan, put her in this base and use the pale green eye shadow. I have to start on Kyle."

Joan called out her agreement; Leon acknowledged with a mere flick of his eye. Calula sailed away toward the back rooms. Mica stared at herself in the mirror. Was she going to fit into this world, even for the summer? She watched Carrie lean forward to peer after Calula. Sedalia had not had this much rushing and bustling about for as long as Mica could remember.

The makeup and hairstyling were quickly accomplished. Mica and Carrie left the trailer, each looking as if a time warp had brought them straight from the sixties. A man they had never seen before frowned at them. "You haven't been to wardrobe? Over there and step on it! And don't mess up your makeup!" They hurried to comply.

At wardrobe, they were given appropriate dresses and orders to come by after the filming for a fitting of their costumes for the final scene.

"I feel like I've landed in Wonderland," Carrie whispered as she pressed her full skirt closer to her hips. "Have you seen a white rabbit running loose around here?"

"We'd better get out there and see where we're supposed to be. Tomorrow I'm getting here at dawn!"

They left wardrobe and went out onto the street. Mica tried not to appear as awkward as she felt in the unaccustomed garb.

A strong male voice amplified by a power megaphone rent the clear morning air. Half a block down the street, they saw a small, wiry man who moved with quick jerks, as if he had more energy than his body could contain, barking instructions left and right, his face red with anger. Mica was sure he was the director, Lance Greenberg. "I want all you people to behave as you normally would. Go into stores. Shop. Walk down the street naturally. Forget the cameras are there. Got it?"

Several in the crowd surrounding him nodded enthusiastically, but no one made a move to do as he had said.

Greenberg shouted, "Move it!"

The crowd slowly came to life, but instead of following his instructions, most people simply shifted to the other side of the street. A few tried to do as he had asked, but most could not resist the urge to glance back to see if they were still being filmed. Two small boys ran out in front of one of the cameras and jumped up and down and waved and made silly faces until the camera crew corralled them and hauled them out of sight.

Greenberg looked as if he was controlling himself only with the greatest of effort. On the fourth try, he managed to get the extras to move up and down the street in a normal manner. Every time he shouted, "Cut," the surrounding spectators clapped in appreciation of his having filmed their neighbors engaged in everyday activities.

Mica drifted away from Carrie and the cast and crew and went to a wooden bench not far from where the street scene was being shot. Her palms were wet, and she was so nervous she was not sure she could remember her name, let alone her lines. What would she do if Greenberg yelled at her the way he did at the cameramen? She was sure she would forget everything she knew.

"Going over your lines?" an oddly familiar voice asked.

She looked up to find Kyle Spensor standing beside her. Her mouth dropped open, and she could only stare.

"Mind if I sit by you?"

Mica shook her head. She couldn't stop staring at him. His eyes were a greenish hazel, and he looked genuinely friendly.

"I'm Kyle Spensor," he said. "You're Mica Haldane. Right?"

She managed to nod. "How do you know my name?"

"I asked Greenberg about you. We're doing a scene together today, and I wanted to meet you before we start filming. You know, sort of break the ice. Are you all right?"

Mica tried to get herself under control. "Yes. Yes, I'm fine. I'm sorry for staring like that, but I've never met anyone famous before." Kyle Spensor was known all over the country, probably all over the world, and here he sat, talking to her as naturally as anyone she had ever met.

"Perhaps we could go over our lines for this scene a time or two. Would that help you to be more at ease?"

"Yes, I'd like to do that." She put her script aside, and in the role of Angie, she said, "I wish you'd pay attention to me, Ryan Colby! Why can't you see that Dawn doesn't care anything about you?"

Instantly Kyle's smile vanished as he shifted into his role. "That isn't true," he snapped. As he frowned, a muscle tightened in his jaw. "She does care for me. I know it! I just have to convince her of it!" He waited for her next line.

Mica realized she was staring again. Dropping character, she said, "I'm sorry. The anger in your voice startled me." She ran a hand through her hair, pushing it back from her face.

"You see, Ryan is upset in this scene. I have to raise my voice."

"I know. It just surprised me." She felt completely foolish. "I'm just nervous, that's all." She looked back down the street toward Greenberg, who was supervising the placement of ropes to keep the curious spectators out of the way of the filming. "Does he always yell that way?"

"He's not yelling," Kyle said with a lighthearted chuckle. "At least, not for him. When he yells, he gets right in your face. The authoritarian tone he's using now is the one he reserves for crowd control."

"I'd be scared half to death if he shouted at me. I'm too edgy as it is." She looked back at Kyle and found him smiling at her.

"Greenberg is one of the most talented directors in the business. He never yells at someone if he thinks it'll hurt his performance. He's a real genius at bringing out talent in an actor. Even nervous ones."

"Right," she scoffed. "I'm sure there are nervous actors all over Hollywood."

"You'd be surprised."

Mica studied his face. "Do you get nervous?"

He shook his head. "No, but I grew up in front of a camera. I started making films when I was a toddler."

"Why, that's true. I remember you as a child star." She tried to relax. "Your last movie was *Night and Day,* and the one before that was . . . *Jessie.* That's right, isn't it?"

He nodded and grinned. "We all nearly froze making *Jessie.* The director never admitted why he wanted it shot in Montana in the winter, even though the story takes place in the summer. I guess we were lucky that we didn't have all that many outdoor shots, because the script called for us to be wearing short sleeves and it was well below freezing even on the warm days. Before it was over, everyone on the set had a cold or the flu."

Mica smiled up at him. "It was a good movie. I thought you should have won an Oscar for your supporting role."

"Thanks. But the competition in this business is tough. I saw the performance Reinholt was nominated for, and I didn't mind losing to him. He had a great part, and he played it well. I'll have another chance."

"Just having been nominated must have been a great honor. Or at least, it seems to me it would be."

"Yeah, it is. Sometimes those of us who do a lot of films become a little jaded. It gets to be a job. Then that really special role comes along and you know you've got a chance to shine, to stand out in the crowd. And then, if it all comes together, it's an Oscar nomination. If you're lucky, you realize that all the hard work is paying off after all."

"I suppose it does get tiring doing one film right after another."

"Don't get me wrong—I enjoy my work. But acting isn't what one would call a steady job. Sometimes I have a lot of spare time between films. Other times I don't. I try not to go directly from one project to the next without a breather, but that's what I've done this time."

"At least an actor as talented as you are must not have to worry about competition."

"Thanks for the vote of confidence, but keeping an eye on those other guys who would love to have the roles I'm getting keeps me on my toes. Actually, the fear that your career may suddenly go down the tubes is generally truer of those who play leading roles, where youth and beauty are essential. For me it's a bit different—the pressure is not so intense. As I get older, I'll gradually switch from supporting roles to character roles. I'm not as likely to get typecast and age myself out of a career that way." He studied her face and his interest seemed genuine. "What about you? What do you do here in Sedalia?"

"Well, for fun we've got a movie theater and a bowling alley, and a very active community theater group. I've had roles in several plays. To make a living, I teach English at the high school and sometimes substitute for the drama instructor."

Kyle's friendly grin returned. "Don't tell Greenberg."

"That I've acted in our community theater?"

"No. I mean the part about teaching drama."

"What's wrong with that?"

"Take my word for it. He prides himself on being a self-made man who never needed a drama teacher."

Mica frowned. "Oh, dear. I put that on my audition application. I thought..."

He chuckled, but again she was sure his amusement was not at her expense. "Actually, I'm exaggerating his feelings, I suppose. He wouldn't refuse to cast someone he thought was qualified because of that. But he did have a rather loud argument with a drama coach on the set once. He's touchy about anyone trying to tell him what to do. Maybe that's why he never married. The cameras are his mistresses and never talk back."

"Is that a line from a movie?" she asked. She was fascinated by Kyle. He was so much easier to talk to than she had expected him to be.

"No, I made it up." He looked amused. "Do you want to go over our lines again?"

"Look! It's Zane Morgan!" She lifted her chin for a better view. Zane was emerging from the wardrobe trailer, his face aglow with his world-famous grin.

"Really? I heard he was going to be in this film!"

Mica looked back at Kyle, suddenly aware of her gush of enthusiasm, and more than a little embarrassed. "I'm sorry. I must have sounded like a star-struck schoolgirl. It's just that I've loved watching Zane Morgan in movies since I was in middle school."

Kyle winced. "That's another thing you don't want to say. Zane worries about aging. If his looks go, there may be nothing left."

"Oh, that's not true." Mica laughed. "I love his acting."

When she turned back to Kyle, his smile was thin and he averted his eyes.

"You sound as though you've gotten over a bit of your nervousness," he said, bringing their conversation back to the original subject, his warm smile returning in the process. "Do you feel more confident about going in front of the cameras now?"

"At least more than before. Thank you for helping me."

"It was my pleasure." He glanced at his watch. "I need to check on a costume change for tomorrow."

"Thanks again."

"See you later," he said as he sauntered away toward the wardrobe trailer.

For a moment, she thought she had committed a faux pas by praising Zane's talent in Kyle's presence, but decided she was reading too much into Kyle's brief change of expressions. She often jumped to the wrong conclusion and had to be careful of that. She had heard that actors had fragile egos and were self-centered, but obviously that was wrong. Out of the blue, Kyle Spensor apparently had noticed the nervousness of a newcomer and had reached out to make her feel welcome. Anyone as kind and thoughtful as he was wouldn't have a jealous bone in his body, professional or otherwise.

Turning her attention away from Kyle, she watched as Zane walked briskly toward the cameras, ignoring the autograph pads thrust across the rope toward him. He was every inch a star, and he was selling it with every smile. But his smile wasn't as open or as guileless as Kyle's. Oddly, Mica found herself thinking Zane was neither as tall nor as handsome as she had expected.

Greenberg shouted over his power megaphone for the actors to take their places for the scene about to be filmed, and all Mica's thoughts skittered away. This was her call to set. In only a matter of minutes, she would be face-to-face with Zane Morgan, moviedom's heartthrob *extraordinaire*. All the confidence she had gained by talking with the easygoing Kyle Spensor had vanished, and she was trying hard not to tremble. Her heart was pounding so hard she was having trouble breathing. When Carrie came up behind her and touched her elbow without speaking, Mica jumped.

"Carrie! Don't sneak up on me like that! You scared me to death!"

"He looks like he just stepped off Mount Olympus!" Carrie whispered, not taking her eyes off Zane.

As Zane reached the director and started talking, Mica strained to hear what he was saying, wondering if he was as soft-spoken as Kyle had been—and thus less intimidating than he appeared to be. But because of the noise from the crowd and the distance between them, she couldn't make out a word. "He's shorter than I thought he would be. I don't think he's even six feet tall. I expected him to tower over everyone."

"He's tall enough for me," Carrie said as she touched her skirts to be sure they were in place. "You have all the luck. You get to do a scene with him."

"Yes, and I'm so nervous I know I'll never remember my lines." Mica clasped her hands and drew a deep breath she hoped would calm her.

"Just pretend that you're on the stage at our little theater and that Zane is...oh, I don't know, maybe James Peschel or Doug Randolph. You've never been uneasy on-stage with either of them. You know, I noticed that Zane didn't sign any autographs the way Kyle Spensor did this morning when he came out of makeup. Do you suppose he's stuck-up? It couldn't possibly be because he's shy. A man with that much charisma wouldn't have a shy bone in his body."

"Maybe he was afraid he'd be late for the filming."

"I don't think so. Shelley isn't out yet. By the way, I saw you talking to Kyle. What's he like?"

"He's nice. Really friendly. I found myself forgetting how famous he is." Mica glanced back toward the trailer and found Kyle standing outside near the rope, talking to several spectators. As she watched him, he laughed and casually hooked one thumb in the pocket of his jeans. Everything about him was so natural. "He's really nice." Her voice faded away as she recalled their conversation.

The director caught her eye and motioned for her to join his conversation with Zane. With knees wobbling like jelly, she obeyed, moving to the director's side opposite Zane. Greenberg pointed at the drugstore and her eyes followed his finger. "This is scene number seventy-eight, and you both have your lines down and understand what we're trying to do here, right?"

Mica nodded, and out of the corner of her eye she looked for Zane's reaction but saw none. The veteran actor merely stood there, appearing somewhat impatient.

Greenberg ignored Zane and said to Mica, "I want you over there where that young woman with the clipboard is standing on the sidewalk, and on my signal for action, I want you to start walking toward the door. Zane, you stop her before she gets her hand on the doorknob and do the line about looking for Deborah. Angie," he said to Mica, using the name of her character, "you act as if you're surprised she isn't with him as you deliver your response."

Mica nodded. She had expected at least to be introduced to Zane before playing the scene, but apparently there wasn't time. She went to the sidewalk as instructed and took the place of the director's assistant, and when the director called for action, she started walking toward the drugstore. Behind her she heard hurrying footsteps, and as she reached for the doorknob, Zane's hand closed on her wrist. She found herself looking up into his eyes with surprise as he said his line, and when he paused, she said nothing, for she had forgotten every word of her carefully memorized part.

"Cut!" Greenberg barked as he glared at her. "What's going on? I thought you said you knew your lines."

"Sorry," Mica said. "Can we do it again?"

Greenberg made a motion that implied an affirmative response, but one that also conveyed his annoyance.

Before Mica could move back into position, Zane looked down at her, making eye contact and grinning with the same expression that had won women's hearts all across the country. "Don't worry if I startled you. It happens all the time," he said. "Next time will be better."

He grinned broader and winked.

Somehow, on the next take, Mica was able to play the scene to please Greenberg, but even as she was delivering her lines, she was aware of Kyle, who was watching the scene with an enigmatic expression in his eyes.

# CHAPTER THREE

As was their custom, Mica and Carrie sat on Mica's back porch, this time going over their lines in preparation for the next day's filming. A pitcher of iced tea and a plate of chocolate-chip cookies sat between them on a small table. "You know," Mica said as she sipped her tea, "I'm surprised how easy it is to learn these lines. Just having been in front of the cameras several times this week seems to have made it easier."

"Speak for yourself. Doing the scenes out of sequence confuses me."

Mica cocked her head. "Did you hear something?"

"No, I was talking."

Mica listened. "I think someone's knocking at the front door. I'll be right back." She put down her script and hurried to see who it was, but even before she reached the front door, she heard the sound of a key in the lock and then the door started to open.

For an instant Mica was startled, then anger welled up inside her. There was only one person it could be. She stopped and waited for her landlady to come in. "Well, Mrs. Mobley. What a surprise."

The woman jumped and paled. "Mica! You scared the life out of me! I thought you weren't home when you didn't answer."

"You didn't give me time. Carrie Graham and I were sitting on the back porch when I heard you knock. And besides, what are you doing letting yourself into my house?

I've already asked you not to come in here when I'm not at home."

Norma was immediately on the defensive. "It's *my* house, not yours. I have a right to make inspections."

"Not every week and not without giving me notice. I looked it up in our rental agreement. You have to give me twenty-four hours' notice."

Norma waved her hand in dismissal. "This is a small town. We don't go by all that folderol. Did you say Carrie Graham was here? I haven't seen her in weeks." Without waiting for an invitation, she stepped past Mica and made her way to the back porch. "Hi, Carrie."

"Hello, Mrs. Mobley." Carrie glanced at Mica and smiled. "What a surprise to see you here."

"I was just driving by," Norma said as she sat in the only available chair. "Whew! This is a hot day. Mind if I have a cookie?"

"Help yourself," Mica said coolly. She was still angry that her landlady was continuing to come into her house unannounced. "We were quite busy going over our lines for tomorrow," she said, hoping the woman would take the hint that she had disturbed what they were doing and leave without having to be told.

"I've been downtown a time or two to watch the shooting," Norma said as nonchalantly as if she had grown up around movie sets. "I can't say as I like the story."

Mica was instantly offended. "Have you read the script? We aren't filming it in sequence, you know. If you haven't read the script, you can't possibly know the entire story."

Norma shrugged. "I know enough. And I saw enough. The public behavior of those movie people is shameful. There was a skinny young redheaded woman, wearing hardly enough to cover her body, crawling all over Zane Morgan between shots. It's no wonder Brother Malcolm is so upset. Thank goodness the women of our community don't behave that way! By the way, what part is she playing in this movie?"

"You must mean Wendy Valentine," Carrie said. "She's not in this film. She just one of Zane's actress friends."

Norma snorted her disdain as she fished around in her bag for a cigarette. "She's nothing but a tramp. Even her looks could tell you that."

"Mrs. Mobley, you haven't even met the woman. How can you say such a thing about her?" Mica thought that if there was anything shameful going on, it was Norma Mobley's prejudice. In Mica's opinion, Wendy was pretty. She had fluffy red hair and a wide smile. And although Mica assumed Wendy's brilliant blue eyes were the direct result of tinted contacts, since Shelley's eyes were the exact same shade, and her clothes were skimpier than Mica would have chosen for herself, none of these things had anything to do with what sort of person Wendy was.

Carrie added, "I don't know her well, but I have met her and she seems friendly."

Mrs. Mobley lit her cigarette, took a deep drag and exhaled the smoke through her nose. Fortunately, the light breeze took the smoke away from Mica. "Well, you can think what you want, but in my opinion, she's a tramp, and so is Shelley Doyle," Norma firmly retorted. "Have you seen the way she eyes men as if she wants to eat them up? All those movie stars are alike. They're all phonies."

From behind Norma Mobley's back, Carrie looked at Mica and rolled her eyes.

As Mica leaned against the porch rail, she said, "I don't know about the others, but I've had a chance to talk with Kyle Spensor, and I can assure you he's genuine and is as nice as anyone I've ever met."

"Well, I wouldn't want to contradict you," she said with thinly veiled sarcasm. "I suppose there could be an exception here and there. Can you believe he's forty years old? He looks thirty. I read an article on him in *Star Glow*—you know, the movie magazine—and it said he's just turned forty. Why, I can remember when he was just a little boy." Abruptly, she stopped. "Of course, I saw those old movies of his on late-night reruns." She held out her hand and examined her multitude of rings, as if she was waiting for Carrie or Mica to agree with her that she could not possibly be old enough to have seen the first run of Spensor's early films in a movie theater.

Mica could not bring herself to falsely flatter the woman. Norma Mobley was fifty-five if she was a day, and she looked older, thanks to her sun-damaged skin and her bleached hair. "Iced tea?" Mica said as the silence grew awkward.

"No, I have to be going. Brother Malcolm is having a special service today, and I'm on my way there." She dropped what was left of her cigarette and ground it out on the concrete porch.

"On Saturday?" Carrie said.

"I said it was special. Brother Malcolm says we shouldn't have church just on Sunday and Wednesday nights. He says we ought to have a service whenever we need one. He's calling for special Saturday-afternoon services from now until the filming is finished."

Mica didn't dare meet Carrie's eyes. Norma was apparently happy with her religion, even if it was more extreme than any other that Mica had ever heard of.

Norma stood up and looked at them expectantly. "Wouldn't you girls rather go to church with me than sit here memorizing lines to serve Satan?"

Carrie groaned, and Mica hurriedly stood up and began ushering Norma back through the house. "Thank you for the invitation, but we have to memorize our lines."

At the front door, Norma stopped and said, "When you girls see the error of your ways, you know where the church is."

"We are women, not girls, Mrs. Mobley. And thank you for the invitation." Mica closed the door firmly behind her.

On her way back through the house, Mica stopped to make a quick phone call, then rejoined Carrie on the porch.

"I don't know how you can be polite to that woman," Carrie said. " 'Serve Satan,' indeed."

"I know, but she seems sincere in her beliefs and she's entitled to them, even if some of the things that church gets into are too radical for me. At least now she won't be leaving any more of those religious pamphlets from Brother Malcolm's church all over my house and making unannounced property inspections."

"Oh? How's that?"

"I just made an appointment for a locksmith to come by early next week and change the locks. And I won't be giving Mrs. Mobley a key."

"Good."

Mica sat down and took another sip of her iced tea. "I was curious about the reason for those Saturday services at Brother Malcolm's church, but with Mrs. Mobley's Satan reference, it seems pretty clear to me now."

"I think you're right. Only yesterday Daddy said there's been gossip around that Brother Malcolm is going to try to get the filming stopped. Seems he thinks the theme of the movie is immoral."

"Your daddy?"

"No, Brother Malcolm. Daddy thinks having the movie filmed here is great for the town." Quickly Carrie's smile faded, then she added, "It's a shame everyone doesn't agree with Daddy."

"I know," Mica commiserated. "Brother Malcolm could sure cause a lot of trouble."

"I meant Jake. I guess I was wrong about his feelings. He says we'd all have been better off if the movie company had picked some other town."

"Why is he siding with Brother Malcolm? He doesn't even go to that church."

"No, that's not it. He's got his own reasons. He says it was a mistake for me to take a part in this film because now I'm too busy for him. He doesn't seem to realize I have lines to learn and can't drop everything to go to a movie. If you ask me, I think he's jealous." She paused for a moment, then continued. "I care so much for Jake, and he says he feels the same about me. Do you think it's unreasonable of me to expect him to be happy for me because I've got a part in this movie?"

"No, but Zane and Kyle are enough to make any man jealous. If I were you, I'd—"

"Have you noticed the color of Zane's eyes?" Carrie asked, unaware that she had interrupted Mica. "They're blue, and with his black hair, I'd have expected his eyes to be brown."

"Maybe Jake's got a point."

"What do you mean?"

"You seem to be a bit preoccupied with Zane."

"Are you telling me you haven't paid any attention to his eyes?"

"No, not really."

"I'll bet you know what color Kyle's eyes are."

"Kyle's are green. Hazel, really, but more green than brown." Mica's thoughts turned easily to Kyle. "I've never seen anyone with so much expression in his eyes." Her thoughts centered on the intensity of his gaze, not only that first day of filming as he had watched Mica and Zane working together, but the way she'd noticed him looking at her on several occasions since.

"Now, what were you saying about preoccupation?"

Mica suddenly felt foolish for thinking any of the interest Kyle had shown in her had been personal. It was only that he was playing the part of a man in love with the character she was playing. She picked up her script. "I guess you're right. Let's get back to it."

KYLE HAD NEVER BEEN one to eavesdrop, but Zane's voice tended to carry so that sometimes hearing his private conversations was unavoidable. He put down the script he was studying. Apparently, Zane and Wendy were settling in for a long argument. With the day's makeup completed, he had hoped the stars' dressing rooms, which were in the same trailer, would be quiet. However, the walls were thin, and he could hear the conversation from Zane's adjacent room all too clearly.

"I don't want to go back to LA," Wendy was saying. "You promised I could be with you all summer, or until my agent got work for me."

"Look, I'm doing you a favor. If you don't stay visible in Hollywood, the movers and shakers will all forget you exist. I've seen careers destroyed by a lack of visibility."

"That's not what you said before we came here."

Kyle could hear the desperation in Wendy's voice, and he felt sorry for her. She was a sweet girl, if not one loaded with talent, and she deserved better than Zane. Kyle had come to know her, and he believed she really cared for Zane.

"I was wrong. Now I'm telling you to go."

"Back to your house, you mean?"

"Damn it, Wendy! We aren't married, you know!"

"But I sublet my apartment when you asked me to stay with you!"

Kyle heard the rustle of cloth and paper.

"Here. Take this and find another place."

"I don't want money. What do you take me for?" From the sound of her voice, she seemed close to tears.

Kyle closed his script and stood to leave. This discussion could go on for hours, and he had no desire to overhear any more of it.

"It's another woman, isn't it?" Wendy asked in an accusatory tone. "You've got your eye on another woman, and you want me out of the way."

"Next you'll be jealous of that old broad who sits under the beach umbrella watching the actors," Zane snapped peevishly.

"Knowing you, I may have reason to be," Wendy retorted. "I know you're not sending me away for my own good."

Kyle's muscles tensed. The day before, he had seen Zane watching Mica Haldane with the same intentness a cat has when stalking a canary. And Zane's affairs were legendary.

"Then don't take the money! Just leave!"

Kyle tamped down his mounting anger and left the trailer. He had already heard more than he'd wanted to hear.

Drawing a calming breath, he crossed the vacant lot to where his friend Harve was setting up the cameras for the afternoon's filming. Harve grinned in greeting. "How's it going?"

"Okay." As Kyle watched Harve adjusting the lens, he debated whether or not to say anything about what he had overheard.

Harve looked up at Kyle. "You don't sound okay. What's eating you?"

"Zane and Wendy are calling it quits. That's why I left the trailer."

"I knew it wouldn't last. She's too good for him."

"Nobody'd argue that. I just hate seeing her get hurt."

Harve nodded. "She couldn't have lasted, though. Maybe she'll give up trying to become an actress and go back to wherever she's from."

"I doubt it. You know how optimistic she is. No, I'm afraid she'll hang around LA and take whatever work she can get while she waits for her big break. Damned shame." It wasn't necessary for Kyle to tell Harve what her ultimate fate might be. Both of them had seen too many hopeful young women with beauty but no talent or common sense fall prey to Hollywood's subculture.

"I liked the kid, too."

Kyle looked back at the trailer as Wendy came out, tears on her cheeks, stuffing the money Zane had given her into her purse. At least, Kyle thought, she had plane fare. "She seemed to think Zane had another woman on his mind."

Harve glanced at him. "I'm sure he does. You know how he brags about making it with women. New location, new woman."

"Who do you think it is here in Sedalia?" Kyle asked.

"Beats me. The prettiest of the local women in my opinion is... what's her name... Mica Haldane."

"I think so, too."

Harve looked up from his work and grinned at Kyle. "Oh?"

"Don't give me that look. Zane is the scalp hunter, not me."

"She's got talent, too. I wondered about her being cast as Angie until I saw her in front of a camera. I mean, Greenberg's casting methods are different, to say the least, but she's a natural."

"But that doesn't mean she wouldn't be vulnerable to Zane. I've seen some pretty savvy women taken in by him."

"If you're interested in her, make your move before Zane does."

"I can't do that. No, it wouldn't be fair to her." He was remembering how soft her hair looked before Leon had gotten his brush into it, and how her lips curved up a bit just before she smiled. And how temporary his stay in Sedalia would be.

"What do you mean by 'not fair'? She's a grown woman, for Pete's sake! If you want to date her, do it. She knows you don't live here and will be leaving in a few months. What's not fair about that? Unless she's married. She's not married, is she?"

"Not that I know of. And you know I wouldn't try to date her if I thought she was."

"So you do want to date her?"

"That's not what I said. It's just that I'd hate to see her get hurt."

"My Janet gave me some good advice after you and Tamara split. She told me that when it came to you and women, I should mind my own business. So that's what I think I'd better do. I've got to go get some more cables. See you around."

As Harve walked away, Kyle headed in the direction Wendy had taken, hoping to get a chance to talk with her before she left for the airport.

WITH WENDY ABSENT, Kyle knew Zane might well shift his interest from her to Mica Haldane, and for a day he wrestled with whether he should tell her she was most likely to be singled out as Zane's next target or mind his own business. He had known Zane since Zane was only an extra hoping for the chance to get a speaking role, and he knew the man would be no more serious in his interest in Mica than he had been in any of his other conquests. Zane had once bragged to him that he always had an affair with a local woman in whatever location he was filming because it brought him luck. Kyle had little regard for Zane as a person because of his treatment of women, but he had said nothing about it in the past. He and Zane never had been friends, and Kyle had always thought his opinion of Zane's behavior was best kept to himself. But the idea of Zane going after Mica was causing him to reconsider his silence.

What was it about her that was affecting him so? He had asked himself that question often during the past week. She was beautiful, but so were scores of other women he knew. She had a pretty and easy smile, but so did others. For some reason thoughts of her kept returning to his mind despite his efforts to set them aside. He looked across the street at her. She and her friend Carrie Graham were in a scene being shot in front of the drugstore. He was too far away to hear more than an occasional syllable, but he knew Mica must be delivering a good performance. As Harve had said, she was a natural. She put herself into her part as if she had been born to be Angie Dillon. Just out of the camera's range, he saw Zane watching her every move. Kyle turned away.

Shelley was sitting in a folding chair a careful distance away from the area populated by the fans and sightseers. Kyle went over to her and pulled up a chair beside hers. He knew she avoided her fans for a reason different from Zane's. Shelley was past forty, and up close she was starting to show her age, despite the face- and fanny-lifts.

She glanced at him in welcome. "That Greenberg is a jerk," she said in disgust. "I don't know why I ever believe a word he says."

"What now?"

"He promised me. He *promised* me that I wouldn't have any outdoor shots. Now look where we're shooting! I think I'll refuse to do it."

"It's hard to film a street scene inside. It won't take long." He knew she avoided sunlight because it showed her small wrinkles, despite Calula's artful attempts to hide them. "It looks like he's only doing distance shots."

Shelley glared at him. "What's that supposed to mean? You think I can't handle close-ups?"

Kyle shook his head. "I didn't mean anything by it. You're looking great."

Shelley was mollified. "I should. I spent a fortune at that spa in France. I was looking great until I came to this god-forsaken place." She glared around at the town. "Why do you suppose people choose to live in such primitive, out-of-the-way places as this, when they could live in a big city with lots of convenient shopping and good restaurants?"

"Perhaps it's because they like it. I think I'd really enjoy living in a nice quiet town like this and not have to put up with traffic gridlock and air so thick you could cut it with a knife."

"You're welcome to it." She looked around the set. "I wonder where Wendy is. Zane is usually wearing her like a necklace."

"Haven't you heard? Wendy is history. Zane told her to pack her things and go back to LA. I talked to her before she left and she was pretty upset. She was crying."

"God, what a wimp." Shelley kept her voice low so the sightseers could not hear her words. "I've never seen anybody as dumb as Wendy Valentine."

"I wasn't talking about her intelligence—I was referring to her feelings. She was pretty broken up over it."

"Hell, girls like that don't feel much of anything," Shelley said with a snort. "All they think about is whether or not their hair roots are showing or if their nails are chipped."

Kyle thought her assessment of Wendy was a pretty fair description of Shelley herself, so he made no comment. He felt sorry that Shelley was so egocentric and had such low self-esteem that she had to constantly put down others in order to feel good about herself. Although he didn't partic-ularly like Shelley, he always tried to be friendly with all the cast members on a particular project. He would be eating, working and talking with all of them for the next three months. It only made sense to maintain friendly terms.

"Why do you suppose Zane sent her away?" he asked. He was watching Zane watch Mica and hoping he was wrong.

"What do you mean, why did he send her away? He's obviously trying to come on to me again." Shelley shifted in her chair and glared at Zane. "You know what an item we were a while back."

Kyle had almost forgotten. Shelley and Zane had made a movie together several years back, and during the filming they had had a blatant affair that had shocked even Hollywood. The affair had ended as soon as the movie was in the can.

"If he thinks I'm going to pick up where we left off, he has another think coming," Shelley said with cheerful malice. "I dropped him then, and I don't want him now."

"Maybe he has someone else in mind."

Shelley shot him an accusing glare. "Who else could he possibly be interested in? Diane King hasn't graced us with her company yet. As if *she* might be his type."

Kyle decided not to comment. Of the two women, he thought Zane would pick Diane over Shelley any day. Zane liked women who made him look good, and Diane was younger and prettier than Shelley was now. "This is an odd business we're in," he mused aloud. "In what other job, except modeling, would it matter if a person ages or if they gain a pound or two?"

Shelley gave him a withering look. "What's that supposed to mean?" She touched her flat stomach as if she was making sure she was still thin. Kyle knew she starved herself to the point of gauntness before she started a movie.

"Not a thing." He was tired of trying to be friendly with Shelley. She didn't take easily to friendships. He glanced toward the crowd of spectators and an elderly woman among them waved at him. "I'll be seeing you," he said to Shelley as he went over to the rope to see what the woman wanted.

"Will you sign your autograph for me?" she said. "I know you're awfully busy, but I've seen all your pictures and having your autograph would mean so much to me."

"Have you?" He grinned and reached for the pad she held out toward him.

"My favorite was *Jessie*. You should have won an Oscar."

"Thanks. Maybe next time." He handed the pad back with a grin. He never tired of meeting people. "Have you lived in Sedalia long?"

"All my life," the woman said with pride. "I guess it's not much to see after the places you've been."

"I wouldn't say that. I liked Sedalia the minute I saw it." He nodded toward the scene that was being filmed. "Do you know Mica Haldane?"

"Mica? Why, sure. She teaches my grandkids. Teaches English, she does. Yes, we're proud of Mica. Her parents moved away a while back, and she was gone, too, for a while, but she came back to us." The woman laughed. "I've seen her act before—you know, with our community theater bunch. I always thought she was really good. Now here she is a movie star!"

Kyle grinned. As he listened, he mentally stored the patterns and pronunciation of the woman's speech, automatically adding her accent to his repertoire as he had done with so many others over the years. He took special pride in the fan letters he got asking if he was from the region where a particular movie had been filmed, because he seemed to have the proper accent. "She has talent, all right."

"That she does. Yes, that she does." The woman seemed to suddenly realize she was chatting with a star, and she added, "I won't keep you. I know you're busy."

"It was good talking to you." Kyle was not really busy at all. He had come downtown because he knew Mica was going to be there and he wanted to watch her work. He had to remind himself several times a day that his interest in her was only professional. After all, it had to be, because when the shooting was over, he would be going back to the West Coast and Mica would be resuming her teaching.

Trying to get that lonely notion out of his head, Kyle strolled over to where an elderly woman and an equally elderly couple were sitting under a beach umbrella. The woman he knew as Miss Nelly motioned for him to come over.

"Have some candy," she offered. "Birdine and I made it last night." She opened a tin and offered him a piece of fudge.

"Thanks. I haven't had fudge in years." He bit into it. "This is great! Better than I remembered."

Miss Nelly nodded as if she had thought he might like it. "It's a recipe my mother gave me, so you can see how old it is." She laughed at her own joke. Birdine laughed with her.

Kyle squatted on his heels beside them. It was cooler under the umbrella, and he found it refreshing not to hear age spoken of as an enemy.

"I saw you talking to Ms. Doyle," Miss Nelly said. "She's hard to get to know, that one."

"True. I've known her for years, and I can't say I understand her." He looked back at Shelley, who was leaning her head back to tan her throat.

"I offered her some fudge, and from the way she looked at me, you'd have thought I was giving her a snake," Birdine said.

"Shelley never eats sweets," Kyle explained. "She has to watch her weight."

Birdine's husband, Buford, piped up. "If you ask me, she's too skinny now. A man don't like an armful of bones."

Birdine giggled and swatted at Buford. "You old rascal! Don't you talk like that!"

Kyle grinned. They reminded him of his grandparents. Although they had died when he was young, he could remember them laughing together that way. As always he yearned for a simple, steady affection such as Birdine and Buford Ponder shared.

"Birdine is right," Miss Nelly said primly. "If you're going to talk like that, you just go over to where the men are talking."

"Do you have a scene today?" Kyle asked. He knew Miss Nelly and her friends were only in a few shots.

"No, we just wanted to see what's happening. How about you?"

"Same here."

Miss Nelly looked at him thoughtfully. "Are you married?"

Birdine tapped her friend's arm. "What a nosy question! Between you and Buford, he'll think we're apt to say anything at all."

"No, I'm not married."

"You used to be, though," Buford said, as if he thought the fact must have slipped Kyle's mind. "You were married to Tamara Nolan."

"That's right. We were married for five years. In Hollywood that's a long time."

Buford nodded. "It's a long time anywhere these days." He shook his gray head. "My cousin Lerla named her youngest daughter Tamara. She was a real ring-tailed tooter."

Kyle smiled. "Tamara was her stage name. She was born Kathy Jean Nolan."

"She shoulda stayed with it. 'Kathy Jean' sounds friendly, like a name you could call a person by."

"Have some more fudge," Birdine said.

Kyle took another piece. "Mica Haldane isn't married, is she?" he asked casually.

Miss Nelly and Birdine exchanged a wink and a smile. "Why, no," Miss Nelly said with studied nonchalance. "She's a single woman."

"Can't understand what young men are thinking of these days," Buford rumbled in his deep voice. "In my day a girl as pretty as Mica would have been married straight out of high school."

"You didn't marry me straight out of high school," Birdine retorted. "What does that tell you?"

Buford grinned at her. "You were too pretty. I was scared to talk to you. Still am."

Birdine gave him a dismissing wave of her hand. "Get away with you. What a thing to say!" But she was smiling.

"Does Mica have a man she's particularly interested in?" Kyle pursued.

"Not at the moment," Miss Nelly said. "She was dating that Harris boy. What was his name?" she asked Birdine.

Birdine thought for a minute. "Lee. She was seeing Lee Harris."

"But not anymore?" Kyle asked. He couldn't imagine a local man not continuing to date a woman like Mica.

"No, he moved to Houston. His job took him away. Mica said she felt she had to stay here in Sedalia and continue teaching. Too many of our smart, young people are moving off to the cities. We're proud of Mica for coming back and planning on staying for good."

"I see."

"If I was you," Buford said, leaning forward to punctuate his words, "I'd go ask her to go for a walk or to get a hamburger."

"A hamburger!" Birdine said in disbelief. "Folks nowadays go to nicer places than a hamburger stand." She smiled at Kyle. "She'd like to go for a walk, I imagine. We don't have a real nice place to eat here in town, but I can recommend the Sassy Cow over in Tyler."

"The Sassy Cow?" Kyle repeated, thinking he must have misunderstood.

"Don't pay any attention to the name," Miss Nelly confirmed. "I've been there and the food is good."

"If I was you and if I had my eye on Mica Haldane, I'd ask her out pretty quick," Buford said. "Looks like somebody's trying to beat your time."

Kyle looked in Mica's direction and saw Zane walking across the street toward her. She looked as though she might be waiting for him, and she had a pleasant smile on her face. Instantly the fine hairs on the back of his neck stood up and he felt an odd flush on his face. Was this a twinge of jealousy? Even Tamara's constant flirting with men during their brief courtship and marriage had not made him jealous.

A commanding male voice from behind him drew Kyle's attention and he turned around to find Lance Greenberg striding toward him.

"Spensor, we've been trying to reach you by phone for half an hour. The damned schedule is being changed again, and we need to shoot scene 37B this afternoon at two instead of tomorrow. No script changes. Can you be ready?"

"Sure. No problem."

"Great. The new schedule is being posted just outside the makeup trailer door. Better check it daily. The way things are going around here with the mayor and his beautification program, there's no way of knowing what we'll have to change next. All this is about to drive the writers crazy. By the way, have you seen Angie, I mean... What's her name? Mica Haldane?"

"Yes. She's over there," Kyle said, turning back to where Mica had been, only she was gone—and so was Zane. "She was there only a moment ago."

"Well, it doesn't matter. She's not in 37B. I just needed to ask her something. I'll catch her later. See you at two."

"Right." Kyle looked again but found no sight of either Mica or Zane. Taking a step closer to Miss Nelly and the Ponders, he said to Buford, "I think I'll take your advice."

"Her number's in the phone book," Buford said as he sat back in his chair. He and the ladies looked pleased with themselves and their matchmaking.

## CHAPTER FOUR

THE LOCKSMITH ARRIVED at Mica's house the next day as scheduled. As she sat on the front porch, watching the man rekey the locks, she noticed Kyle Spensor walking along the sidewalk out front of her house, headed toward downtown, she assumed. Mica was startled to see the famous face in her own neighborhood, but she waved, and he came across the lawn to her.

"Hi. What's going on?" he said as he climbed the porch steps.

"I'm having my locks changed. Mr. Newsome, this is Kyle Spensor, the actor," she said to the locksmith. "Mr. Newsome is helping me take care of a problem."

Newsome glanced at Kyle and nodded but didn't speak. Mica thought nothing of it. She had known the man all her life and had never heard him say more than was absolutely necessary.

"Have you been robbed?" Kyle asked with concern. "I wouldn't have thought there'd be much crime here in Sedalia."

"No, no, nothing like that."

Newsome stood up and handed her two keys. "Check 'em," he said.

She tried each key in the lock and both turned it smoothly. "Thank you, Mr. Newsome. Do you want a check now?"

"You can pay next time you're over my way." He bundled up his tools and, with a nod to Kyle, left the porch.

"He doesn't say much, does he?" Kyle commented when the man was well out of hearing range. "Is he one of the people who are so upset about the filming?"

"No, Mr. Newsome just isn't long on conversation." She looked up at him and motioned for him to sit down. "I gather you've heard the gossip, too."

Kyle sat on the nearest chair. "I don't know who's behind it, but Greenberg got a letter yesterday warning him about staying in town. It was signed 'Concerned Citizens.'"

"That wouldn't be Mr. Newsome. He keeps pretty much to himself." She frowned. "It does, however, sound like something my landlady may be involved in. I didn't want to say anything in front of Mr. Newsome, because he and my landlady are cousins of some sort, but she's the reason I'm having my locks rekeyed."

"Your landlady?"

"She has a bad habit of coming into my house when I'm not here. I don't have anything to hide, of course, but I don't think she has a right to do that."

"Of course not. Have you told the police?"

Mica laughed. "The police? In Sedalia? They'd think I was crazy. I've been told more than once that since I returned from college, my ways have been a bit peculiar."

"You're saying Sedalia isn't exactly a progressive town?"

"Right. Not in any sense of the word. I know several people who still don't bother locking their doors when they go to the store."

"You're kidding! I feel like I've stumbled onto the set for *Mayberry*."

"It's more like *Stepford Wives* in some sense."

"Don't you like it here?"

"I love it, but that doesn't mean that I don't see its shortcomings. Don't you feel that way about Hollywood?"

"I don't actually live in Hollywood. My house is in Burbank. Of course, out there in the LA area, the only distinction between one town and another is which side of the city-limits sign you're standing on."

"Do you like living there? I don't think I could ever adjust to a big city. I lived in Dallas for four years after graduating from college and couldn't wait to move back to the peace and quiet of Sedalia."

"I'm seldom home. Not since my divorce. When I'm not on location, I'm visiting friends or just traveling around. I've been told I'm part gypsy. I think I've always been looking for something."

"Oh?" She smiled across at him and put the porch swing into motion with her toe. "What are you looking for?"

"I'll know when I find it." His hazel eyes met hers and held.

Suddenly Mica was aware of a warm glow in the center of her being that spread rapidly throughout her body. Kyle hadn't moved; his words had been spoken quietly. But his penetrating gaze and the resonance in his deep voice had a profound impact on her. Startled at her reaction, she stood. "I just remembered you were on your way toward downtown when I flagged you down. Am I keeping you from something?"

"No. Actually, I was coming to see you. I tried calling you yesterday afternoon and evening, but I got no answer, so I thought I'd come by."

"I must have forgotten to turn on my phone answering machine. Carrie and I went shopping in Tyler. I'm sorry I missed your call."

Although his smile stayed on his lips, it left his eyes, and she wondered what he was thinking. He remained silent and looked a bit uncomfortable. "Greenberg is trying to get word to everyone that he's having to make schedule changes he hadn't anticipated and wants us all to check the schedule board outside the makeup trailer every day."

"Thanks."

Again an awkward silence hung between them. Then, with inspired enthusiasm, she asked him, "How long has it been since you've had a real ice-cream soda?"

His eyes smiled again as he thought for a minute. "It was on the set of *Sycamore Alley,* year before last."

"Well, that was too long ago. Come on. I'll buy you a soda, any flavor as long as it's strawberry, vanilla or chocolate."

Kyle uncoiled his length from the chair and went down the steps with her. "Where's your car?"

"Let's walk. It's only a few blocks."

Kyle fell in beside her and matched his longer stride to hers. Mica was aware of him with every nerve ending in her body. What was happening to her? She had dated Lee Harris for months prior to his move, and he had never affected her like this. She tried to tell herself it was only because he was *the* Kyle Spensor, but she knew that wasn't it.

Dubois' Drugstore, on the corner of Main and Elm, hadn't appreciably changed since the fifties. Kyle grinned as he gazed at the anachronism. "I see the mayor's campaign for beautification hasn't reached here yet."

"Not yet. Mr. Dubois probably won't care if it does. He votes for anyone who runs against Mr. Graham. Incidentally, the mayor is Carrie Graham's father. She's quite protective of him."

"Thanks for the warning." They went inside and were instantly enveloped by cool air. "I hadn't realized how hot it's getting."

"Just wait. Summers here are terrible. This part of Texas is humid, and it's nothing for the temperature to top 100 degrees in August."

Kyle groaned. "I can hardly wait."

Mica sat on a stool at the marble-topped counter and the boy working as the soda jerk smiled shyly at her. "Hi, Miss Haldane."

"Why, hello, Jimmy. I didn't know you were working here."

"I just started when school was out. I'm saving money for college."

Mica said, "Kyle, this is Jimmy Dubois, one of my best students this past year."

Kyle held out his hand. After a pause, Jimmy shook it. He grinned and blushed all the way down to his collar. "You're here making that movie, aren't you?" the boy asked.

"That's right. Have you learned to make an old-fashioned ice-cream soda yet?"

Jimmy laughed. "I've been making them all my life. My father owns this place."

"I'll have chocolate," Mica said decisively.

"Same for me," Kyle echoed. As he viewed his surroundings, he said, "It's a shame Greenberg's not doing any filming in here. This would be great for the showdown scene between Shelley and Diane."

"I know the one you're talking about. He's not going to shoot it in here?"

"No. He's changed his mind. A lot of the inside shots are being done back in Hollywood. He has a crew building the set now, I expect. He says it'll give him better control that way. You know, I've always wanted to try my hand at directing. I'd do some things differently from Greenberg. He's a good director, mind you. Maybe even one of the great ones. But I have some ideas that I'd like to try out."

"Why don't you do that? I think you'd be good. You've certainly had enough experience."

"True. I've spent more of my life in front of a camera than not."

Mica looked at him closely. "Do you mind that? That you never had a regular childhood?"

Kyle thought for a minute. "I don't know. All the kids I grew up with had childhoods exactly like mine. We were tutored on location or at the studio between shots. For me that *was* a regular childhood."

"Do you always rent a house when you're on location?" As Jimmy put two chocolate sodas in front of them, she reached into her jeans pocket and got the money to pay for their drinks, waving away Kyle's protest.

"Every chance I get. I like the feeling of belonging to a particular area, even if only for a while. Besides, this is as close as I get to permanence. My friends say my house in California is just a storeroom with a street address and that I really live in a suitcase."

"There'll be a waiting list to rent that house once you're gone."

Kyle laughed and tasted the soda. "Not as long as the line to rent Zane's and Shelley's apartments."

Mica smiled. "This movie has set Sedalia on its ear." She paused, debating whether to ask Kyle about something that had been bothering her. Deciding this was the only way she would get the information, she asked, "Kyle, what's Zane like?"

"Zane?"

"I mean, what sort of person is he?" Gossip of Zane's reputation had preceded him, and Mica was concerned that Carrie's fascination with him might leave her vulnerable.

"I guess he's pretty much like anyone else," Kyle answered, a bit vaguely.

Mica laughed. "Maybe where you come from!" She caught her breath and hoped he wouldn't think she was some star-struck woman trying to flirt. In her opinion, Kyle was more handsome than Zane, and he was by far more professional. Her scenes with Kyle had flowed easily. The ones with Zane had had to be shot over and over.

Kyle studied her face, and she wondered what he was thinking.

"Well, Zane's been married several times—I forget the exact count. I'm not sure I know what you're asking."

"I don't know. I was just curious about him. Have you known him long?" Mica wished she could be less circumspect and simply ask if Carrie should be warned to stay away from him.

"Yes. For years."

"Are you two friends?" If they were, she could hardly ask him if Zane was as promiscuous as she had heard.

"More acquaintances, I'd say."

She ran her finger down the frosty side of the soda glass. Kyle certainly wasn't given to volunteering information. "I've heard he, well, has affairs."

"Wendy wasn't his wife."

"I know. I meant, I've heard he has affairs with local women when he's on location." The silence grew long, and Mica glanced at Kyle to see if he intended to answer.

"So I hear." His voice was cooler than before, and she saw a muscle tighten in his jaw.

"Oh. I just wondered." She could see he didn't want to discuss Zane, and she had heard enough. Carrie needed to be told that the rumors were true.

Kyle drank the chocolate soda, but didn't taste it. It appeared that Mica might have more than a passing interest in Zane. He felt a keen disappointment. What would she say if he told her Zane was worthless, in his opinion, and that she should stay away from him? More than likely, she would tell him to mind his own business. After all, he had no legitimate reason to care if she wanted to have a fling with Zane.

Or did he?

Kyle glanced at her. She seemed to be deep in thought and unaware he was looking at her, so he took the opportunity to study her profile. She was a beautiful woman, and with her bone structure, she would be attractive well into her elderly years. Yet there was something special about Mica that set her apart from other women he'd known—something that transcended her physical appearance. It was as if there was unfinished—and compelling—business between them. Almost as if she held some key he had been searching for all his life.

"I'd better be going," he said abruptly. He pulled money from his pocket to cover the cost of the sodas and put it on the counter, even though she had paid. If she didn't want it, the boy behind the soda fountain would get a generous tip.

"I'll go with you," she said.

Kyle got off the stool and waited for her to do the same. At the door, he leaned forward, holding it open for her, and she passed easily beneath his arm. Kyle was quiet on the walk back to her house.

"Is something wrong?" she asked.

"No, no, I was just thinking. About tomorrow's schedule," he added.

"I know what you mean. Tomorrow is Sunday. If Brother Malcolm's church is behind the 'Concerned Citizens,' as I suspect, they may try to stop Greenberg from filming tomorrow."

"They won't have any luck. Greenberg has to meet a schedule. He can't afford to take Sundays off."

"I understand that, but Brother Malcolm won't."

Kyle looked at her. His thoughts had nothing to do with any local group's protest. He had been trying to decide whether her questions about Zane's rumored affairs with local women were due to idle curiosity or because of Mica's personal interest in Zane.

He thought wryly that it would be just his luck to be attracted to a woman who found the leading man more interesting than himself.

He was used to the fact that most women preferred getting to know the star of a movie rather than the second lead. Usually this was fine with Kyle. But this time the star was Zane, and Kyle knew more about Zane's escapades than the press had discovered. Zane wanted to go to bed with every attractive woman he saw, but only to add to his absurdly high score of lovers. With AIDS so great a threat, Kyle was amazed that Zane dared the risk. Obviously Zane thought AIDS was something that only happened only to other people.

He breathed in the warm air to calm his growing resentment and forced his thoughts in a more pleasant direction. The air here was clean and sweet with the scent of newly cut grass and the more subtle fragrances of summer flowers. In an odd way, Sedalia smelled like home to him, but not a home from his own childhood—for that had been movie sets and apartments filled with his mother's cigarette smoke. Sedalia smelled the way he thought home should smell. Here there was no pollution problem, at least none that was noticeable, and Kyle appreciated that. In the distance he could hear the shouts and squeals of children at play. On one lawn a sprinkler whirled with a monotonous tapping sound. The only litter in the streets was leaves.

"You don't know how lucky you are to live here," he said to break the silence. He didn't want Mica to know how disappointed he was that her interest was in Zane and not in him.

"I agree. That's one of the reasons I came back to Sedalia to teach. As I said earlier, I taught in Dallas for a while, but I got tired of the crowd and the frantic pace of city life."

"Have you taught long?"

"Six years altogether. Four in Dallas, and I've just finished my two-year probationary period here. Most Texas schools require only one year to evaluate new teachers, but here in Sedalia it's two." She tilted her head back as if she was enjoying the earthy scents and warm breeze. He wondered what she would say if he asked her to go out with him. They walked in silence for a few minutes.

"I'm thinking of getting a cat," she said unexpectedly. "Do you like cats?"

"Sure. I like all animals. I've never had one of my own, though. I travel too much for pets."

"You've never had one? Not even a dog?"

He shook his head. "Not really."

"How can you 'not really' have had a dog? Either you did or you didn't."

"I was in a picture when I was about eight with a brown-and-white dog named Butch. At least, that was his name in the show. His real name, the one the trainer had given him, was Rex." He smiled at the memory. "I always called him 'Butch.' He was that sort of a dog. I used to pretend he belonged to me. You know how boys are, and I wanted a dog really bad."

"Why didn't your mother let you have one?" Mica asked softly.

"She couldn't. Our apartment owner didn't allow animals, and besides, I was traveling as much then as I am now."

Mica made no comment, apparently waiting to hear more.

"Anyway, Butch seemed to be as fond of me as I was of him. He used to whine and jump up and down every time he saw me. He became fonder of me than he was of his trainer. That was the problem. The trainer complained that Butch wouldn't obey him if he considered me to be his main person. They shot all the scenes with Butch as quickly as possible, then took him away.''

''You never saw him again?''

Kyle felt a muscle tighten in his jaw. ''They told me he had been run over and that he had died. I was heartbroken, of course.''

''That's terrible!''

''It got the emotion the director wanted for the remaining segment of the movie, the part where my dog was lost, and I was grieving.'' Kyle walked a few steps in silence, lost in the refreshed pain of the memory. ''I believed it until about five years later when I accidentally saw Butch, alive and well, in another picture.''

Mica brushed at her cheek, and he wondered if she had been pushing back a tear. ''I didn't mean to upset you. You asked if I had ever owned a dog and that was the answer.''

''That was so cruel! Why did your mother let them do that to you?''

''I don't know. Maybe she thought Butch was dead, too. I never asked her. Sometimes it's best not to know the answer. In those days, it was considered fair to do whatever was necessary to get a child actor to do his part the way the director wished. I've heard of other stories not too different from that one with other child stars.''

''I hope it's not still so heartless!''

''I don't think so. I haven't worked with a child actor in years.''

''Where are your parents now?''

''Mother is dead. She's been gone several years. I never knew my father. She said he deserted us when he heard I was on the way. I don't know if that's true. She used to get letters from a man, and from the way she acted when they arrived, he was someone important to her in a negative sort of a way. I don't remember his name or where the letters came from, however, so I can't check it out. He may be dead, too.

He stopped writing her several years before she died." He glanced over at Mica. "What about your parents?"

"They live in Dallas. The company Dad worked for went out of business, and Dad couldn't find other work here." Her expression became closed, as if she didn't want to discuss her family. "We don't see each other very often since I moved back."

He wondered what she wasn't telling him.

They were within sight of her house now, and Kyle knew there was no excuse for him to linger. She probably had things to do. When they were even with her house, he said, "I'll see you tomorrow."

"At the shooting. Yes."

Mica watched him go, then crossed the street to her own yard. She wished he hadn't left so soon. She had been trying to think of some way to ask him over for dinner. Kyle was one of the nicest people she had ever met, and she wanted to spend more time with him. But all things considered, she decided she was being foolish. She was just an East Texas schoolteacher and he was a Hollywood star. His only reason for coming to see her had been to deliver the message from Greenberg.

As she crossed her yard, she paused to pull up some of the nettle that was determined to invade her lawn. The grass needed cutting, but it was too hot. Perhaps later in the day, she told herself, when it would be cooler.

She put her new key in the lock and opened her door. Her house seemed unusually empty, she reflected as she closed the door to keep in the air-conditioning. Lately, more than ever, she had noticed how lonely it was.

She glanced through the morning's mail, which she had left on the table nearest the front door. There was the usual mix of Occupant mail and a bill or two, and a letter from Lee was at the bottom of the stack. She sat and opened it.

The letter was typical for Lee, chatty but not terribly interesting. He said he was enjoying his job and that Houston was the place for him. He hinted that he might be home to see his parents for a weekend in July, but made no mention that he wanted to see her again. She was pleased that he was moving on with his life without her.

He had been disappointed by her refusal to marry him, and it hadn't been easy for her, either. Only days before he proposed, he had taken a job with an oil company in Houston. He expected Mica to give up her personal commitment to teaching in Sedalia and to move to Houston with him. She had thought she was in love with him, but realized she wasn't when staying in Sedalia won out. At first she had thought he might not take no for an answer, because he called her every day for a week, trying to convince her to change her mind. But then the calls abruptly stopped, and by the end of the next week he was packed and gone.

She had not dated anyone on a regular basis since Lee and often thought how lucky she was that she had learned that the feelings she'd thought were love were not.

A knock at her back door drew her attention. It was Carrie.

"It's hot out there!" Carrie said as she breezed past Mica and collapsed in a kitchen chair. "Do you have any tea made?"

Mica smiled. They had been friends for so long there was no need for formalities between them. "It's in the refrigerator. Help yourself."

Carrie got out the pitcher of iced tea and put it on the counter while she got herself a glass. "Want some?"

"No, thanks. I just had an ice-cream soda."

"Shoot! If I had sodas as often as you do, I wouldn't be able to fit through that door." Carrie frowned at the tea. "Was it chocolate? Don't tell me it was chocolate."

Mica only smiled at her.

"It was! If I wasn't trying to lose weight, I'd head straight for Dubois'. And I'll bet you weren't alone, were you?"

"Kyle Spensor came by and we went together. Since you're on a diet, I decided to try to addict him."

"Dubois' sodas could do it." She poured the tea and put ice cubes in her glass before sitting back down at the table. "Kyle?" she said as she jerked her head around and looked at Mica, as if she had only then become aware of what Mica had said. "Kyle Spensor came here to see you?"

"Well, actually, he came to give me a message from Greenberg. We're all supposed to check the schedule board outside the makeup trailer every day for last-minute changes."

"Kyle came here just to tell you that? In person? I got word from my mother. She said Greenberg's assistant called."

"Kyle said he'd tried to call last night. It must have been while we were in Tyler shopping."

"So he came by and then invited you to go to Dubois' for sodas?"

"No. The sodas were my idea."

"But he accepted the invitation. And what does that tell you? I wish I could get close enough to Zane to see if he's friendly. He speaks to me on the set, but we haven't really talked."

Mica changed her mind and poured herself some tea. "I don't know that I'd want to know Zane better. I think the rumors about him having all those affairs may be true."

"I don't. People can say anything at all about stars. It has something to do with them being public figures or in the public domain. Something like that. Do you have any lemon?"

Mica opened the refrigerator and took out a covered bowl. She offered the lemon wedges to Carrie, then took one herself.

"You know," Carrie said as they went into the living room, "I sometimes get a little jealous of you."

"Me?" Mica asked with a laugh.

"You have a job, for one thing," Carrie said with a grimace. "I still don't. I'm not qualified to do one single thing but teach drama in high school. And unless Betty Andrews quits her job or dies, I won't be teaching it here. I guess I could substitute for her now and then, like you do, but I need a full-time job."

"You took electives in office skills. You can operate a computer."

"Apparently so can everyone else who's looking for a job. Maybe I should try a larger town."

"Is that what you want?"

"I wouldn't mind leaving here. My roots aren't as deep as yours, I guess. And now that Mom's health is better, I wouldn't worry about leaving if I can't find work here."

"What about Jake?"

Carrie curled her feet under her in the armchair. "In a way, Jake is the biggest problem of all."

"He loves you. Anyone can see it."

"I know he does. But I went from living with my parents to a college dorm to Marvin. Now I'm back with my parents. Here I am, thirty years old, and I've never been on my own the way you are. Now Jake's getting serious and dropping hints about us getting married, and I'm not sure I want to be married again. I care so much for Jake, but if I marry him, I'll be here in Sedalia all the rest of my life."

"It's true that Jake isn't likely to move away. All his family still live here, and he owns the best hardware store in town."

"And if I marry him, I'll turn into my mother!"

"Pardon?" Mica said with a laugh.

"I love Mom, but her life seems so boring! She still belongs to the same clubs and groups that she was in when we were kids. She shops at the same stores and sees the same friends. When she and Dad go on vacation, they always rent the same beach house at Galveston!''

"There are worse fates. Loneliness, for instance."

"I think I'm falling in love with Jake, and it scares me. I can see years of grocery shopping and mopping floors ahead of me. And kids and parent-teacher meetings and Little League ball games."

Mica smiled. "You just described my idea of happiness."

Carrie leaned forward. "I'm not saying those things are bad, only that I want to taste life first."

"I'd say that being in a movie should qualify as tasting life."

"Maybe all drama majors dream of being discovered. Of giving up their ordinary lives in exchange for the bright lights."

"Is that what you want?"

"I don't know! I only want a chance to decide. How can I be completely happy with Jake if I always wonder if I could have had, say, Zane Morgan?"

Mica laughed. "Zane Morgan? From the stories I hear, he's not that difficult to be had. Kyle said that, more or less, this afternoon."

"He talked to you about Zane?"

"Among other things." She sipped her tea. "In a way, I know what you mean. I like my life here, and I don't want to change it, but there's something about Kyle…" Her voice trailed off.

"Oh?" Carrie's interest was piqued.

Mica shook her head. "I know I'm not his type, except maybe as a friend. He hasn't asked me out or even given any hint that he'd like to."

"But you'd like it, wouldn't you?"

"Yes. I'd like it. I can't explain it, not really, but when I talk to him, it's as if everything he says is important to me. He told me something sad about his childhood today, and I wanted to put my arms around him and comfort him."

"Maybe you should have."

"Right, Carrie. And have him think I'm like all the other women who must constantly throw themselves at him. As handsome as he is, I'm sure he has to fight them off."

"I've never heard any gossip about him. He didn't have a Wendy in tow."

"No, I don't think he's like that."

"I wonder what Zane is really like."

"I don't think you should find out. We've been friends all our lives, and you should listen to me. It's good advice."

"How do you know? Have you talked with Zane? Personally, I mean?"

"No, only about the movie." She shook her head again. "He just doesn't seem as open as, say, Kyle."

"Maybe he's simply more difficult to get to know."

"Maybe." Mica doubted it, however.

"I think I'll try to make friends with him. After all, he's a stranger in town. Maybe he's lonely."

"What's Jake going to think?"

Carrie laughed. "I said make friends with him, not seduce him. It's not like Jake and I are engaged. We have sort of an understanding about having other friends. It's okay for you and Jake to be friends. Everyone knows there's nothing serious between you two. Jake will understand about me being friends with Zane. You'll see."

Mica wasn't so sure about that. For all of Jake's fine qualities, Mica had seen him as being somewhat possessive of Carrie's time. And she could also see how a man like Zane might undermine Carrie's interest in Jake. Knowing how stubborn Carrie could be, Mica decided it would be better to say nothing now and instead take the initiative to get to know Zane better. Carrie wasn't likely to accept a warning about Zane based on hearsay, but if Mica spoke of Zane from her personal knowledge, Carrie might listen.

"I know it's silly," Carrie said, "but sometimes I find myself daydreaming that I'll catch some producer or director's eye because of this film." She laughed self-consciously. "That I'll be asked to be in another one. That I'll be discovered."

"It happens." Mica shook her head in concern. "But it doesn't happen very often. I've heard it takes hard work to break into the movies. No, this is just a passing thing for us."

"You sound like Jake."

"Listen to him. He's right." Mica leaned forward. "I don't want you to set your mind on doing something drastic. This movie is only temporary. In two and a half months they'll all be gone, and we'll be back to things as usual."

"I know all that." Carrie rubbed her finger down the sweating side of her glass.

"You and Jake are falling in love, and you were happy about that before the movie came to town. I hate to see you unhappy now."

"What about your friendship with Kyle? Is that a mistake, Mica?"

Mica paused for a moment to think. "I guess it sounds silly—I've known him only a few days—but I'll miss him when he's gone."

Carrie nodded. "But that won't happen for two and a half months. In the meantime, we shouldn't pass up the chance to make the most of it. The opportunity to rub elbows with the stars won't come again to Sedalia. No matter what Daddy may think, no movie company is going to think of this town as another back lot. Why would they? Enjoy it while you can."

"Maybe you're right. You know, Carrie, I really like Kyle. I like him a lot." She was thinking of Kyle's touching story about the dog. Although he had tried to make it sound as if it hadn't mattered too much to him how it came out in the end, she could still feel his pain. She had a notion that he hadn't told that story often. It had too much emotion attached to it. "I think I'll miss Kyle for a long time," she said softly.

# CHAPTER FIVE

HARVE SPREAD his playing cards and sighed. "Who shuffled this deck?"

"It had to be me if it wasn't you," Kyle cheerfully responded as he moved one of his cards to a different place in his hand. "We're the only ones here. Your move."

Harve put a six of spades on the discard pile.

Kyle grabbed it up. "Thanks. Gin." Kyle laid out his cards faceup.

With a groan, Harve displayed his cards and wrote down Kyle's score on the notepad at his elbow. "That's three hands in a row for you. Whose idea was it to play gin?"

"Yours, originally. Mine, tonight." He and Harve had played gin rummy for years and in many places around the world. Usually they were evenly matched. "Is something bothering you?"

"Yeah. Kathy's first baseball game of the season is next week, and Suzy is playing T-ball. I'll miss all that."

"Suzy? Already? Seems as if she should still be a toddler." Kyle pushed the cards toward Harve. "Your deal."

Harve gathered the cards and straightened them into a single deck. "They'll be grown before I know it. I'm missing out on all the fun. You know how kids are. What if they think I'm out of town because I'd rather be here than with them?"

"Janet would tell them it's not true."

Harve sighed and shuffled the cards. "That's another thing. I miss Janet like hell. Maybe I ought to find some other job."

"I know what you mean." As Harve dealt the cards, Kyle picked up his and arranged them according to number and suit. "If I never saw another airplane boarding pass, it would be just fine with me." He glanced at his friend. "Mica Haldane is doing a good job with her part, don't you think?"

"Mica? How did she get into this conversation?"

"We were talking about missing people."

Harve's hand paused over the cards he was placing in his other hand. "How's that?"

Kyle discarded a six of diamonds. "She's someone I want to know better. That's the problem with this sort of work. We only get to know other people in the business. Once this film is history, I'll probably never see her again."

"That'll bother you, won't it?"

"Yes, it will. It bothers me already."

"So get to know her. What's stopping you? You usually take some time off between films. Stay here an extra month or so."

"I can't do that."

"Why not?"

Kyle watched Harve draw the next card. "If I were to stay longer, I might not ever want to leave."

Harve whistled as he selected his discard. "That sounds serious."

"I'm not saying it is—just that it could get that way. Damn it, Harve, I think about her all the time. I'm having trouble learning my own lines because my mind keeps wandering back to her."

"That sounds to me as if it's already serious."

Kyle drew a card from the stack, realizing too late the one Harve had discarded was one he needed. "You know how romances flare up during the making of a film. After it's over, the two people have nothing in common—they were just reacting to their roles. You've seen it dozens of times.'' He put the card he had just drawn on the discard pile.

"Yes, but not with you."

"It's your play."

Harve drew a new card and added one to the discard pile. "It's a good thing Janet isn't hearing this. You know how she's hoping you'll find someone. Despite her advice for me to stay out of your business, she's convinced you're too lonely."

"Janet's a perceptive lady."

"You *are* lonesome? You never told me that. The last I heard, you were enjoying your freedom." Harve stared at him.

"It's called acting, Harve. That's what I get paid to do. I even thought I could convince myself I wasn't lonely if I pretended. It didn't work. I've often wondered if things would have been different if Tamara and I hadn't been apart so much of the time. We didn't have years together, like you and Janet, to build a solid foundation for our marriage. She had her acting career, I had mine. It wasn't that we grew apart. We were never together long enough to really get to know each other. I guess that's why I've never missed her. But it is lonesome not having anyone to go home to."

"All the more reason to make friends with Mica. She's not always on the move like Tamara was."

"That's one of the reasons I can't get too interested in her. She's not a career actress, and she doesn't know the rules."

"What's another?"

"I think she's more interested in Zane."

"Bull," Harve barked with a laugh. "I don't believe it. Not Mica. I've seen Carrie Graham staring at him, but not Mica. No way."

"She was asking me about him."

Harve gave him a quick glance. "She was?"

"Zane's the star. You know how that goes."

"Zane's a horse's rear. I think you're wrong."

"Whether I am or not doesn't matter. I can't let Mica think there's any hope of a real relationship between us. It's impossible. I'm based in LA, and she's committed to being a teacher here."

"I've known actors who've moved from LA and still worked," Harve said with studied nonchalance. "Some even to small towns about the size of this one. And I've known women to move to LA. If she's that important, don't lose her."

"I'm not saying I'm falling in love with her," Kyle said quickly. He wondered if it was true.

"I wouldn't have let Janet go." Harve grinned and lay a card facedown on the discard stack. "Gin. Finally."

"I can't lead her on and then just pack up and leave when the film's over. That's Zane's trick."

"I said I ginned. Put your cards down so I can count the points."

Kyle dropped them on the table. "I've always thought love at first sight was ridiculous. Seemed to me such a quick romance was more a case of raging hormones than love."

"Hormones are good. Did you deal last?"

"I don't remember." Kyle pushed the cards toward Harve. "I just don't think it's good for people to fall in love too quickly."

"Live and learn. All I know is that when I first met Janet—I guess I had seen her a time or two, but we hadn't talked—I knew she was the one I was going to marry."

"You did? Just like that?"

"Pretty close. Janet said she knew she was in love with me even before we talked. I guess that was her falling in love at first sight. And for me it was at, like, third or fourth sight." He grinned at Kyle.

"I'm not in love with her. I'm just interested. That's all."

"Keep telling yourself that. Meanwhile, I'm going back to my place and call Janet. All this talk about not being in love is making me homesick."

Kyle nodded, his thoughts far away. "See you tomorrow."

As Harve let himself out, Kyle slowly gathered up the cards and put them back in the box. He wasn't falling in love with Mica. He couldn't be. He wouldn't let himself.

Despite his efforts to the contrary, he reflected on the idea that LA had schools and also might need an English teacher—one with laughing brown eyes and a soft Texas drawl. He shook his head to put the thoughts away. Falling in love was the last thing he wanted to do.

MICA WAS SURPRISED when Zane motioned for her to come to him. She glanced around to be sure he was not gesturing to someone else, then crossed the lot to where he was waiting.

"I've been meaning to talk to you," he said. "You show a lot of promise."

She smiled. "Thanks. The only other acting I've done is with our amateur theater group here in town. I was a bit afraid to try out for this part."

Zane swung his body around so it blocked her view of the filming and her back was against a tree. "I should have known you'd done this sort of thing before."

"No, plays are entirely different." She had given a lot of thought to the rumors about Zane and had concluded that it wasn't right for her to base her opinion of him on hearsay. She had always hated for people to judge her for having come from a poor family, and she was determined to be objective.

He shrugged and his eyes darkened. It seemed as if he was excited at her nearness, but that was surely just the charisma that made him such a popular actor with the ladies. His famous half smile lifted the corner of his mouth. "Acting is acting. At times I'd like to give it all up and find a place to settle down and a woman—the right woman, not some starlet—to settle down with."

"You would?" Mica couldn't have been more amazed if the tree itself had spoken. "You? Give up acting?"

He gave her a look that implied he was struggling to keep hidden a mountain of pain and hurt. "Yeah, but I can't do it. This is the only life I know." He looked past her at the tree-lined street. "What wouldn't I give to be able to settle down in a place like this."

Mica turned her head to see if he was seeing the same thing she was. "Here? In Sedalia?"

"Maybe not Sedalia, but someplace like this. You don't get to meet real people in Hollywood. They're all after something. Especially when you're a star. I can't tell you how often my heart has been broken when I think a woman cares about me and I find out all she really wanted was a ticket to Hollywood or a part in one of my films."

"Not me. I don't want to live in Hollywood." She shook her head. "That came out all wrong. I don't mean to imply that there's anything wrong with Hollywood, but—"

"I know. I feel the same way. Unfortunately, that's where I work." Zane looked down the shady street as if it were Mecca and he were one of the faithful.

"Where did you grow up?" she asked. "Maybe you'll be able to return there someday."

Zane shot her a glance, but then shook his head. "You can never go back home. I forget who said that. Somebody a lot smarter than me."

Reflexively, Mica started to identify the author of the quotation and correct his grammatically incorrect usage of the pronoun *me,* but she caught herself in time. Zane wasn't one of her students. "The people in your hometown must be awfully proud of you."

"Yeah, I guess." Mica couldn't help but notice that the way he said that sounded as if he had no idea if it was true. "Say, I don't suppose you'd like to come over and see me sometime? At my apartment, that is. We could rehearse some of the scenes we have together. Maybe I could give you some pointers."

"I suppose I could do that." She couldn't believe she had heard him correctly. She wanted to ask him if she could bring Carrie along, but thought better of that before she spoke. This would be the perfect opportunity for her to get to know him better, so she would know for herself whether she should be steering Carrie away from him. Before Zane had a chance to say more, she heard Greenberg's assistant calling for her scene. "I have to go," she said as she dashed away.

Across the way Kyle was also watching the exchange between Mica and Zane, but his expression was guarded. He wasn't fooled by Morgan's smile. Mica didn't seem to be terribly naive, but he didn't know her well enough to judge that. Zane had tremendous charisma and influence over his fans, especially the women. Again, he deliberated whether he should warn her that the man's intentions were likely dishonorable, or stay out of it. And again, he shook his head and looked away. Surely Mica had the good sense to recognize the purpose of Zane's flirtations.

All that aside, Kyle had no claim on Mica, and it was none of his business if she chose to become Zane Morgan's latest lover. Kyle began walking to put more distance between himself and Mica.

Carrie was waiting for Mica by the trees where the upcoming scene was to take place. "I saw you talking to Zane," she said under her breath. "I'm impressed. Can I have your autograph?'' Although her tone was light, her eyes weren't smiling.

"We were just talking," Mica said as nonchalantly as she could, though she was feeling a bit guilty for stepping into what was really Carrie's own business. After all, Carrie was a grown woman and could take care of herself. "He asked me to come by his apartment for some extra rehearsal. Do you want to come? I could—"

"No, thanks. Zane didn't invite me." Again Carrie's voice sounded as if she was joking, but Mica sensed an underlying strain.

Before Mica could respond, Greenberg's assistant stepped between them, shooing Carrie away. After he looked back at Greenberg, he pointed to a spot on the ground two feet to Mica's left and motioned for her to move there. As Mica waited for the signal for action, she tried to tell herself she was reading more into Carrie's words than had been meant, but Carrie's marriage to Marvin and the subsequent divorce had changed her friend in subtle ways. At times like this, Mica was no longer sure she knew Carrie as well as she used to. When the boards smacked together, Mica's thoughts snapped back to the character she was playing and she started her lines.

Hours later, after the day's work was finished, Mica was more than ready to go home. It had been an emotionally exhausting scene, and she wanted to wash off the stage makeup and brush her hair into its usual style. However, instead of rushing off, she lingered, looking around for Kyle. Unfortunately, he was nowhere to be seen.

Often, of late, she found herself looking for him and hoping to see his heartwarming smile. Immediately, she cautioned herself against such behavior, because she knew she couldn't have him.

As she was passing the striped umbrella where Miss Nelly and her friends held court, Mica was called over by Miss Nelly herself.

"I saw you talking to that Morgan fellow a while ago," Miss Nelly said after the briefest of greetings.

"Yes, he was offering to help me with my lines."

Miss Nelly grunted her disapproval. "I know it's none of my business, but your grandmother was one of my dearest friends, God rest her, and I feel that gives me the right to say this to you. That man is no good."

"Pardon?"

"I've seen his type before. He's too slick." She turned to Birdine. "He reminds me of that man over in Tyler that used to sell used cars on TV. What was his name?"

Birdine tipped her head in order to think better. "I don't recall. He married Essie Hopkins's middle daughter. Remember her? The one with puffy yellow hair."

"That's the one." Miss Nelly turned back to Mica. "I don't trust the man. He's not friendly except to you pretty young girls."

Mica smiled. She hadn't thought of herself as a girl in years, but from Miss Nelly's vantage point, she must seem so. "We have no interest in each other. I'm sure he meant nothing by the offer."

"Meant nothing, my foot! You watch him close, girl."

"I will, Miss Nelly." For as long as Mica could remember, Miss Nelly had been handing out advice to everyone in town. However, she had seldom heard her put any advice so strongly.

Mica had thought Miss Nelly was through, but she had only stopped to catch her breath. "If I was you," she continued, "I'd set my cap for that other fellow. That Spensor fella."

"Kyle? I'm not setting my cap for anyone. They'll only be in town for the summer. After that, I'll never see any of them again." She cast a sideways glance at Miss Nelly. "Why Kyle?"

"I like him. He always takes time to talk to us."

Birdine nodded, her chin jerking in staccato motions. "You can always tell about a person by noticing how he treats people that can't do anything for him. And he always eats my fudge or cookies and says how much he appreciates me making them."

"Exactly," Miss Nelly seconded. "He has manners. You don't see much of that these days."

"I always eat a cookie or two," Mica objected. "I'm going to have to let out my dresses if I eat any more."

Birdie gave Mica a toothy grin. "You've always been a good girl. That Zane hasn't tasted but one cookie, and he didn't even thank me for it." Birdine pursed her lips. "He's not like us." For Birdine this was strong criticism.

"Just keep it in mind," Miss Nelly said. "Don't be rude to the man, but keep your feet under you."

Mica swallowed her smile. "Thank you for the warning. I'll keep an eye on him." She took a piece of fudge from the plate to be polite, told Birdine how good it was and walked away. She held no resentment for the elderly women's intrusion into what was, after all, her own business. In Sedalia, the older folks had always kept an eye on the younger ones, and Mica had known these ladies all her life. She also knew Miss Nelly sometimes had an uncanny perceptiveness when it came to people. Although she was already forewarned, she appreciated Miss Nelly's concern for her welfare.

Up ahead, she noticed Kyle round a corner and head off in the direction of his house. She increased her pace to catch up with him. "Hi," she called out. "I thought you'd already gone home."

"I stopped to talk to Harve Giacono," he said as he continued walking.

"The cameraman with the bald spot and dark-rimmed glasses?"

"That's the one. We've been friends for years. He was just telling me what he'd heard about his oldest daughter's baseball game. She hit her first home run yesterday."

"That's great, but he must miss them when you all are gone from Los Angeles for so long at a time."

Kyle nodded. "That's the problem with this business. It's hard on families." He glanced at her. "Earlier today I saw you talking to Zane."

"Yes, that was the first actual conversation I've had with him."

Kyle was stoically silent.

"He says he's tired of all the Hollywood glitz. Do you think he meant it?"

A growling sort of noise rumbled from Kyle's chest. "How should I know? I really don't want to talk about Zane."

"You don't like him, either?"

Kyle jerked his head around to face Mica. "What do you mean, 'either'?"

"Miss Nelly and Birdine warned me about him. Miss Nelly says he's too slick, like some used-car salesman she used to know."

Kyle turned his head back in the direction they were walking. "There's a lot to be said for the wisdom of the elderly."

"Are you saying Miss Nelly is right?"

"Look," Kyle barked with growing irritation, "it's none of my business what you or anyone else thinks about Zane."

Mica stopped walking. "You don't have to snap my head off."

Kyle stopped and ran his hand through his wavy hair. "I'm sorry. I guess I'm having a rough day." He glanced back at her. "Okay?"

"Sure. I have bad days, too." She tried to get him to smile. "I used to say it was my evil twin coming out."

Kyle finally smiled. "I like that." His face brightened even more. "Would you like to go with me to a movie?" he asked as they resumed walking.

"I'd think your fans would be a problem."

He looked around. "Do you see swarms of fans following us? I've been in town long enough that I'm not news anymore."

"I guess I'm just surprised you'd want to go see a movie. I'd have thought going to a movie on your time off would have been like a busman's holiday for you."

"I like keeping up with what's going on in the business. Not going to see movies would be like a writer not reading books or an artist never examining other exhibits. Do you want to go or not?"

She smiled. "Okay. When?"

"How about tomorrow night? You and I don't have to be on the set early the next day."

"I'd like that. Do you want to go to the theater here or drive to Tyler?"

"This one is fine. *House of Four Seasons* is showing. It's a ghost story. Have you already seen it?"

"Not yet, but that sounds good to me."

"How about if I come by at seven? Will that give us time? I forgot to ask when the evening show starts."

"On a weeknight there is only one showing, which starts at seven. If you come by at six forty-five, we'll have plenty of time." She veered off down the street that led to her house. Kyle waved and continued on toward his own place.

As Mica walked down the familiar sidewalk, the reality of what had just happened suddenly hit her. Kyle Spensor had asked her out on a date. He was so easy to be around, she had temporarily forgotten how famous he was. The idea of her dating a movie star brought a smile to her face.

She looked back over her shoulder at Kyle. He had stopped to pet a neighborhood dog, and that reminded her of the story he had told her about the dog named Butch, and her heart went out to him. She liked Kyle more than she had liked anyone in a long time.

GREENBERG COULD HARDLY wait to finish filming so he could have a talk with the downtown merchants. He had heard a rumor that a plan was under way to dig up the sidewalks in front of each store along the main street and put in permanent flower beds. As yet, nothing had been done, and he felt sure he could prevent it.

"You can't do this," he explained to the owner of the Chic Boutique. "If there are changes in the appearance of the street, it'll destroy the continuity of the movie."

Fannie Rodgers nodded as if she was considering all he had said. "All I know is that Mayor Graham's trying to get the city council's okay."

Greenberg tried to control his temper. He had heard this story in every store. "I understand. But can't you and the other merchants talk sense into him? Can't you all see how this will ruin what I'm trying to accomplish?"

"Sure I can. I can't speak for the others, but we want our town to look really good in the movie, and Mayor Graham says these flower beds will give the street class."

"Give it class after I leave."

"Well, I don't hardly see how I can do that. I mean, if the other merchants agree to the flower beds, I'll look bad not to do it, too. I can't have my business fall off just because you don't like flowers."

"I love flowers. I adore them. But the street's appearance can't be changed."

"I don't know what to tell you. Looks like you and Mayor Graham should have worked all this out before you got started."

"I thought we had. Apparently I was wrong."

"Well," Fannie said, "as far as that goes, I'm about to change my window display, too. The new fall clothes have come in."

"No! You can't do that!"

"I have to. Buttons and Bows orders from the same place we do, and I saw the salesman over there just before he came here. I can't let them advertise fall things and me stick with summer dresses. I'll lose customers."

"I'm not saying that you shouldn't get new merchandise. I just want you to leave your window display as it is. I'm asking all the stores on Main Street to do that."

Fannie nodded thoughtfully. "I could talk it over with Whit. That's my husband. He makes all the marketing decisions."

"Is he here?" Greenberg felt as if he were trapped in one of those dreams where it was impossible to move forward.

"Sure is." She went to where a red curtain blocked the view of the back room. "Whit? Can you come in here a minute?"

Greenberg tried to resolve himself to repeating his speech all over again. Why hadn't the woman told him from the beginning that her husband made most of the decisions?

Whit came out and stood by his wife. His expression was the bewildered one of a man who knows one thing well and isn't in his element with change. Fannie looked at him in consternation. "Mr. Greenberg says we can't put our fall clothes in the windows, and that we have to tell Mayor Graham not to put in that flower bed out front of our store."

Whit looked more confused than ever. Greenberg drew a deep breath and started from the beginning.

After Greenberg left, Whit looked at Fannie. "Did you make sense out of what he wants?"

"Not much. I reckon he doesn't have much knowledge about how a business is run. You'd think at his age he would."

"Are you wanting to go to that downtown-merchants meeting tonight? There's a ball game on."

"I guess we ought to. You know what Bernice Mobley said about us the last time we missed."

"I guess we ought to talk about those flower beds and the window displays," Whit said uncertainly. "He seemed real upset."

"Mayor Graham will be, too. You know how important it has become to him to fix up the town."

"I sure do. He's the best mayor we ever had."

Fannie watched out the window as Greenberg negotiated the street. "He seems like an unhappy man, don't he? I'll bet he's not in a happy marriage."

"Could be." Whit joined her and they both watched as Greenberg went into the Buttons and Bows opposite them. "Or it could be he's got an ulcer. You saw how he kept chewing those tablets? He's working himself to a frazzle."

Fannie shook her head sadly. "He ought to take it easy. Enjoy life."

Whit put his hand affectionately on her shoulder. "Not many have it as good as we do."

She patted it. "I know. Do you want me to help you with that window display?"

"Might as well. We don't have any customers right now." Companionably they went into the back room to decide on new dresses for the mannequins.

# CHAPTER SIX

THE FOLLOWING DAY, the filming began at dawn. Carrie had never been an early riser and was self-conscious about the stumbling around she'd done in the makeup trailer before downing several cups of Calula's thick black coffee. Calula and the several veteran film-crew members, on the other hand, had arrived on the set alert and energetic, as if they required little, if any, sleep. Carrie wondered how they managed it.

The daybreak scene they had come so early to shoot had gone well, and as Carrie mingled with the crowd of actors awaiting the shooting of the drag-strip scene, her attention was focused on Zane. He held a fascination for her that defied even her own understanding. It was more than his handsome face or the charisma he exuded on-screen. He had been so many places, experienced so many things. He had lived a life that seemed brilliant in comparison with the dullness of her own.

At once she felt guilty. Jake wasn't dull. She hadn't meant that. But Jake would never be a movie star, with all the glamour and privileges that stardom entailed. Jake was dependable and sweet and sexy in his own way, but no one would ever gasp at the sight of him entering a room, or ask him for his autograph. His name was not now, and never would be, a household word. This didn't make her care for Jake any less, but it didn't make her care more, either.

She watched Zane and Mica exchange lines. Mica was good—better than Carrie had expected. She wondered if

Zane was only acting or if that heart-stopping smile of his was meant for Mica alone.

Carrie moved away. She and Mica had been friends all their lives nearly. She didn't like feeling jealous of her. She went to the far side of the crowd of extras so Zane and Mica were not in sight, and in doing so, she almost ran over Jake.

"What are you doing here?"

"I came to see what you're up to these days." He didn't sound pleased. "I seldom see you at night anymore."

"By the time we've filmed all day, I'm too tired to do anything other than go to bed at night."

"I miss you, Carrie, and you seem to be too busy these days to even talk to me. I love you and I want to see you more often."

Carrie glanced up at him. "Jake, this movie won't last forever. Aren't you glad I'm having this experience?"

"Of course I am. But I miss spending time with you."

"I wish you could understand how important it could be to my future for me to get to know these people and become friends with them."

"I had hoped you'd think it was important to your future for you to spend your time with me. What about us?"

"If you're starting to talk marriage again, I—"

"Hold on a minute, Carrie. I know you're skittish about that word. I didn't say it. I know you're afraid of rushing into anything, and I didn't bring it up. It's just that you don't seem to have any time for me since this movie thing started."

"Please be patient."

"I'm trying to be. But there aren't many men who wouldn't worry about having to compete with Zane Morgan."

"What are you talking about?"

"I've been here watching you for nearly an hour. I've seen the way you look at him."

Carrie playfully punched his arm. "Don't say things like that! Do you realize how foolish that sounds? He doesn't know I'm alive."

"I just don't want the woman I love to get her head stuck in the clouds. I know how much this movie means to you, and it worries me a lot."

"For heaven's sake, Jake! This is the only chance I'll ever have to do something exciting. Please don't ruin it for me. How can I do my next scene when you have me so upset?"

"I'm not trying to upset you, honey." He touched her arm in an awkward gesture of caring. "Just remember it's only for the summer."

She reached out and hugged him. After all, it wasn't Jake's fault that she felt such a compulsion to put some excitement into her life. "I've got to go." She stood on tiptoe and kissed him lightly.

"Don't go yet. Can't you talk a little longer?"

"A few minutes, but only a few."

Carrie hadn't told him—or anyone, for that matter—that for years she had secretly dreamed of moving to Hollywood and becoming an actress. The film company's selection of Sedalia as the site for a movie and her getting a speaking part couldn't have been stronger signals that she should follow through with her desires. Hollywood wasn't an impossible dream anymore. Her part in this movie would give her a credit. Doing a movie with stars like Zane Morgan, Shelley Doyle and Kyle Spensor had to count for a great deal. True, she had few lines compared with the stars, but it was amazing that she had any at all. If she actually got an agent, who could know where she might end up!

"Are you listening to me?"

"I was thinking about my lines," she lied.

"I asked if you have to be on the set this weekend. If not, we could spend the day together."

"I'd love to, but I'm not sure if I can."

Jake gave her a level look. "Not sure?"

"For goodness' sake, Jake. I just want to do a good job. Surely you can understand that."

Jake looked back at the set. "Sure, I can understand."

Carrie sighed. "I'm trying, Jake. I really am. I can't quite explain it, but when I'm in front of the camera, it's as if I can be someone else. Someone really important."

"Like I felt in high school when I used to hit home runs? I know that feeling. It's great, but it's not forever."

"I know that," she said a bit too quickly.

"I've known you all your life, Carrie, and I can tell when something is bothering you, when it's something really important."

She heard Greenberg's assistant shouting the call to set for the next scene. "I have to go." She didn't want to meet Jake's eyes. "I'll phone you tonight. I don't know when we'll be through. It could be late. Okay?"

"Okay."

As she ran away from Jake and toward the cameras, she felt a twinge of pain at not having been completely open with him. But she couldn't have been, because she didn't want to hurt him with her doubts. As she found her place, she went over her lines frantically and prayed she would remember them all.

MICA HURRIED to finish dressing for her date with Kyle, anxious to be looking her best by the time he arrived. The day's filming had taken longer than anyone had expected, and she was pressed for time. She had washed her hair in the shower and towel-dried it before putting on her makeup. But as she was buttoning her white silk dress and fastening the red belt, she noticed that her hair was still too damp to brush.

She glanced at the clock and groaned. He would be there at any moment. She dashed back into the bathroom to blow-dry her hair. Twice before she was finished, she thought she heard the doorbell, but she had been mistaken.

"Shoes," she mumbled to herself as she ran to her closet. "Where did I leave my red shoes?" Fortunately, they were on the shelf where they were supposed to be. Hopping on first one foot, then the other, she slid them on. "Purse!"

Just as she found the purse that matched her shoes, the doorbell rang. Unceremoniously, she dumped the contents of her everyday bag into the red one, then hurried to answer the door.

Kyle grinned when he saw her. "You look great!"

"So do you." It was true. He was wearing gray slacks and an open-collared oxford shirt, striped in gray, coral and white.

She stepped aside and motioned for him to come in. "I'll just get my purse and then we'd better go or we'll miss the beginning."

"We don't want to do that. Lily Hogan told me the first half hour is the setup for the rest of the movie."

Mica's mouth dropped open. "You know Lily Hogan? She's the star!"

Kyle laughed. "She's also my neighbor. You'd like her. She's much funnier off the screen than her scripts allow."

"Of course you'd know her. I don't know what I was thinking of." Again it came home to her that her date was far from the ordinary run of males available in Sedalia. She stepped out onto the porch and waited while Kyle pulled the door shut and checked to be sure it had locked.

As he drove them the short distance to the theater, they chatted about the day's filming. Mica shook her head in disbelief. "I can't believe I'm riding to the movies with you to see your neighbor's film while we talk about the movie we're in together. It doesn't feel real."

"Try not to believe it. That's how most people in the business adjust to the idea."

"Is that how you did it?"

"No, making movies has been a part of my life for almost as long as I can remember. Now if you were an astronaut—that would boggle my mind." He grinned at her. "It's all a matter of what you're used to."

Kyle parked in the closest available space, and as they walked to the ticket window, Mica couldn't help but notice the surprised glances from passersby. Apparently not everyone in Sedalia was accustomed to seeing Kyle Spensor around town. The teenage girl selling tickets almost swallowed her gum and tried to hand them two extra tickets. Kyle gave back the extras and opened the door for Mica.

Once they were seated in the dimly lit theater, Mica whispered, "Does it bother you to have people stare like that?"

"Sometimes. But I guess I'd be really worried if they stopped." He winked at her and smiled.

The lights faded to black, and the screen lit up with advertisements and previews of coming attractions. Mica pretended to be interested, but she was too aware of Kyle beside her in the dark.

When the feature started, she heard Kyle chuckle. "What's funny?" she asked.

"Lily is wearing a scarf she borrowed from me. I bought it in France and sent it to Tamara—we were still married at the time. When Tamara moved out, she left it conspicuously behind. Lily and I have a running joke about the scarf having run Tamara away."

"She must be a very close neighbor," Mica observed.

"She is. And she's happily married." He reached across and took her hand in his as if it were perfectly natural for him to do so.

His hand was warm, and although his skin was smooth and free of work calluses, it was decidedly masculine. With her senses keyed to Kyle, she had great trouble concentrating on the movie and had to struggle to follow the plot. It would not do for her to have to admit to him that she had no idea what the movie had been about because of her greater interest in him. When the ghost made his appearance, she jumped, then laughed as Kyle squeezed her hand to reassure her of his protective presence. She had never enjoyed a movie so much.

After it was over, she and Kyle walked out into the night air, still hand in hand. "That was creepy!" she managed to say.

"I know. I love a good ghost story."

"That surprises me. You do so much comedy."

He shrugged. "I guess I'm more complex than the characters I play."

"I'd say that was an understatement." When he released her hand to open the car door for her, she felt a twinge of disappointment. Once she was comfortably seated, he closed her door and went around and got in behind the wheel. As he started the engine, Mica continued with her train of thought. "You've lived such an exciting life."

"After a while it becomes a job. You lose sight of the excitement." He gazed at her. She was beautiful in this light. But then, she was beautiful in every light.

Her gaze met his, and Kyle felt a stirring inside. It was as if he could see her soul in the depths of her dark brown eyes. After a long moment, he realized he was staring, so he looked ahead and put the car in gear.

He was aware that Mica had glanced away at the same moment, as if she, too, had felt a need to break the spell. She ended the silence between them. "I was wondering if you could give me some pointers about my character. I'm afraid I'm not portraying her properly, and I don't know what I'm doing wrong."

"You're doing a great job. If you weren't, Greenberg would be yelling at you instead of Shelley."

"I guess I'm being supersensitive. I'm trying to do my best, but at times I'm not sure what Greenberg wants."

"I'm telling you that you're giving him what he wants or he'd let you know. Greenberg isn't one to pull any punches."

She smiled at last. "I've noticed. He certainly lambasted Shelley this morning."

"That was mild compared with what he may do by the end of summer. I've often wondered how it is that he can be so unpleasant and still get his actors to do exactly what he wants. If I were the director, I'd use a different technique. But then, I'm not one to yell."

All too soon, Kyle pulled into the driveway at Mica's house, wishing for the first time that Sedalia were a larger town. Once he was stopped, he said, "We'll have to do this again soon."

"Not too soon, I'm afraid. Not unless you want to drive to Tyler. Movies here don't change all that often."

"We could go to Tyler. I don't mind driving."

"Yes, but it's a bigger town. Won't you be swarmed by your fans?"

He grinned. "I could wear dark glasses and a fake mustache. So could you." Mica laughed as he had thought she would.

"That's one of the things I like best about you," she said.

"My fake mustache?"

"You make me laugh."

Kyle smiled. That was his best cover-up for his feelings. He had always been able to make people laugh, and that way no one ever delved too deeply into what he was really thinking and feeling. Now he wanted to put the protective mechanism aside, but he was unable to do so. "That's me. A laugh a minute." He kept the wryness from his voice, but not without great effort.

"I heard once that some people use laughter as a means of maintaining distance from others, as sort of a protection," she surprised him by saying.

"Who told you that?" He had the odd sensation that she was all but reading his mind. No one had ever come this close to seeing through his facade.

"I took a psychology course in college."

"Well, even if my humor wasn't useful for other reasons, I'd be between a rock and a hard place if I couldn't make people laugh. In some of my films it's essential."

"Then it does serve another purpose for you?"

Kyle studied her face. "I'm not used to people asking such intuitive questions."

"I'm sorry." She looked away. "That was rude of me."

"No, it wasn't. I meant that as a compliment."

"I have a bad habit of saying whatever pops into my mind."

"It's a shame there's not more honesty everywhere. Sometimes I get tired of the fence I put between me and the rest of the world. It would be a relief to be able to be simply myself."

"You don't have to put up a fence with me."

He had to smile. "I especially have to with you."

She looked as if she was about to ask him to explain, so he said, "Would you like to go somewhere and get a soft drink? It seems too early to end the evening."

"No, thanks. I have some inside. You could come in. I even have more than one flavor for you to choose from."

He studied her in the darkness and turned off the car's engine. "I'd like that."

They walked across the yard to her door in comfortable silence, and as she unlocked it, he studied her profile, wondering not for the first time what it was about Mica that made her so irresistible to him. Part of it, he had come to realize, was her genuineness, her almost total lack of pretense. But it was something much more elemental that sparked a fire in his soul every time she crossed his mind.

He followed her into the kitchen, and as she looked into her refrigerator for soft drinks, he bent over her shoulder and selected one for himself. Inadvertently, his thigh brushed against her backside, and the intimacy of the contact shot through him like an electric charge. As quickly as he could move without being obvious, he backed away. It wouldn't do to become so physically aroused. Mica could never be more to him than a good friend.

"It's such a nice evening. Let's go out back and sit on the porch," she suggested.

"Wonderful idea."

Following Mica's lead, he sat next to her on the top porch step. As his eyes adjusted to the inky blackness, he noticed the flickering glow of lightning bugs dancing across her yard, and in the distance he heard a chorus of insect sounds. "Crickets?"

"And tree frogs. On a still night you can even hear the whistle from a train, and we're miles from the tracks. It brings back pleasant memories of my childhood. I love it. That's one reason I didn't like living in Dallas. Too much noise."

"What's another?" He studied her features in the dim light filtering through the glass panes in her kitchen door.

"My students," she surprised him by saying. "Sedalia never has had much of a school system. I think too much of the school's budget is spent on physical education and not enough on scholastics. Unfortunately, that seems to be all too common, especially in this part of the state. It's a good thing I don't know exactly what a coach's salary is here or I'd probably become depressed." She gave him a quick smile. "But scholastically, it's traditionally been a vacuum."

"You turned out okay."

"I read. For as long as I can remember, I've read every book I could find. By the time I finished middle school, I had read every book in the school library. Then I tackled the public library. By high school graduation, I had read them all twice."

"You went to a public school?"

"That's all there is in Sedalia. We also have the highest ratio of dropouts in the area." She paused, as if she was considering whether or not to go on. "I was one of the few in my family to finish high school and the first to go to college."

He waited, sensing there was more.

"My family is poor. Not lower middle class, but poor. My dad drove a truck now and then for an oil-field equipment company, but when the oil business went bust a while back, they moved to Dallas so he could look for work."

"You mentioned that earlier. I assume he found something there."

"Dad's working as a maintenance man at a school on the north side of town and Mom cleans house for a really nice family in Highland Park. We see each other when we can, but they don't have much free time."

"I see."

"Do you?" Mica turned to him. "How can you when we have so little in common?"

"I can empathize without having had the same experiences. You came back to give other kids who are in the same economic rut you were in a way out."

She nodded. "That's it exactly."

He reached out and took her hand. "Over the years, one of the things I've learned is that people are more or less the same wherever I go—the same hopes and fears and dreams. But there aren't many who are willing to shape their lives around the hopes, fears and dreams of others."

"I'm not as noble as you make it sound." She looked away with a short laugh. "I'm just doing my part."

"Have you ever considered doing your part somewhere else?"

She looked surprised as she glanced back at him. "Somewhere else? Not since I decided to come back to Sedalia. I belong here. My roots are here."

He was sorry her answer hadn't been different. "I understand." He laughed wryly and made a capitulating gesture. "Again, without the personal experience to back it up, I think I understand. I've traveled all my life, and at times I wish I had a place I could call a hometown. Being on the road so much definitely gets old. But that's the way it is in this business."

"You obviously enjoy your work, though, and that's important. We're both lucky in that way."

Kyle was beginning to see just how important Mica's teaching here in Sedalia was to her. Clearly, it would be best for him to put the notion of her ever leaving Sedalia out of his mind. Whatever relationship he had with Mica would be short-term, and he'd have to be content with that. He turned his eyes toward Mica and found her looking up into the night sky, as if her thoughts were far away.

Unexpectedly, Mica looked back at him and asked, "Am I your friend? I've never had to ask that of anyone before, but you're so different from everyone I've ever known. I hope I am."

"My friend?" he repeated carefully. "As in platonic?"

She smiled. "There are all kinds of friendships."

He wasn't sure how to respond. "What kind did you have in mind?"

"I don't know." Her eyes darkened and she looked a bit troubled or maybe confused. "If you lived here in Sedalia—permanently, I mean—I might know the answer. But you don't." Mica studied his face a moment, then said, "I guess I shouldn't have come right out and told you that I want to be your friend. That's something that ought to happen or not without being discussed. It's just that you're leaving at the end of the summer, and we don't have time to go through the usual rituals."

"Does my friendship mean that much to you?"

"Yes. It's very important to me." She let the words lie there between them without any further explanation.

Kyle reached out and touched her hair. It was as soft as it looked. "Mica, what exactly are you asking for?" He loved the feel of her name in his mouth.

She looked away. "I don't know. Maybe I've already said too much. I didn't mean to."

"It's the summer night. It inspires confidences." He put his arm around her shoulders. Her skin was soft and warm and seemed to invite his touch. Experimentally, he caressed her arm with his thumb. Mica didn't pull away.

Mica turned in his arms without pulling back. "I don't want you to get the wrong impression. I'm not trying to chase you into bed."

"I knew this was too good to be true," he said with a smile. "Are we back to platonic again?"

"No, I just want you to know that I want us to be...good friends. And then, well..."

"I can live with that." He didn't dare tell her that such close contact as this with her was physically driving him wild.

"Good," Mica said, easing out of his embrace. "In that case, I'm glad I brought up the subject. You know what? Friends feed friends, so would you like to come over for supper next Saturday? All I'm having is hamburgers, but I can be trusted not to burn them."

"Sounds good to me." Kyle was still a bit confused about whether Mica wanted a deeper relationship with him than friendship, but the one thing that was clear was that he should not hurry things with her and should let her be the one to initiate intimacy between them.

They got to their feet, and Kyle followed Mica through the house to the front door. She paused and looked up at him.

"I'm glad you came in and that we talked." Lightly she added, "I wondered what I would do with all that hamburger meat if I couldn't trap someone into helping me eat it."

Kyle laughed, enjoying her sense of humor. Before he realized what she was doing, she stood on tiptoe and put a light kiss on his lips, the sort of kiss one friend might give another. But she didn't step away, as he'd expected her to do. Hoping he was reading her nonverbal signals correctly, he drew her closer, bent his head and brought his lips fully against hers. As her lips parted and she swayed into him, his arms encircled her, bringing her body fully against his. The passion he had barely kept in check leaped to life, and he drank in her sweet kiss as a man dying of thirst longs for water.

Mica returned his ardent kiss with matching passion until Kyle felt drunk and hot. When he reluctantly let her go, they gazed into each other's eyes for a long moment, neither daring to speak. He knew she was feeling the same emotions he was, and the knowledge made him want her even more. Mica swayed toward him, but caught herself and stepped back. "I'll see you tomorrow," she said in a voice filled with longing.

He nodded, aching with desire for her, not trusting himself to speak, for he knew he might ask to stay, and he didn't want to do anything that might drive her away.

With great effort, he managed to leave her, but as he walked back to his car, every atom of his being pleaded with him to run back to her. Instead, he continued walking away, knowing he had to keep himself in check. Whatever he was feeling for her, it had to be transitory—he was only in Sedalia for the summer. One month of that was almost gone already.

Kyle got into his rental car and closed the door, wishing he were able to close away his thoughts as easily.

## CHAPTER SEVEN

MICA HAD KISSED many men, as had most women her age, yet no man's kiss had ever stirred her the way Kyle's had. All night her thoughts had been on the passion of that kiss, and even in the light of day, the memory of it made her blood run hot.

She had forgotten to set her alarm clock, but luckily had awakened on her own early enough that she wouldn't be late for her makeup call. She had skipped breakfast and dressed hurriedly, but as she combed her hair, her thoughts returned to Kyle, and her brush strokes slowed considerably. Studying her reflection in the mirror, she asked herself why she was letting her dreams about him overshadow reality. What could she, an English teacher in a small Texas town, offer a movie star? "Love," a voice inside her head murmured. She could offer him love. Mica tossed the brush aside and told herself not to be foolish. She couldn't allow herself to love Kyle, for the simple reason that she couldn't have him.

A glance at the clock brought reality back with a jolt. If she didn't hurry, she would be late, and Calula hated to be rushed because of the tardiness of others.

THAT AFTERNOON while they were finishing up the last filming for the day, Zane sauntered over to Mica. As she noticed him moving toward her, she studied his expression, looking for a leer or some other sign that she should be particularly guarded, as Miss Nelly had suggested. Instead, she found nothing but a pleasant smile, not unlike the one he often wore as part of his Zane Morgan-the-star image. She expected flirtation from him because that, too, was part of his trademark, and she was prepared.

"Are you avoiding me?" Zane asked, his voice professionally caressing.

"No, of course not. Why would you think that?"

"You accepted my invitation last week to do some extra rehearsing but never came by." With a wink, he asked, "Are you playing hard to get?"

She wasn't sure how to take his question because of the wink, but she decided to respond in kind. Sternly she answered, "No, I really *am* hard to get," then she smiled up at him.

He lifted an eyebrow as if he was surprised, then gave her his famous half grin. "What are you doing tonight?"

Days before, she had decided to heed Miss Nelly's warning and ignore his previous invitation to come alone to his apartment. Apparently he was going to renew the proposal. Prepared to turn him down this time, but feeling playfully confident, she said, "Me? Nothing special. I have some errands to run this afternoon, but I have nothing planned for tonight."

"I really would like you to come over to my place."

"No, I don't think—"

"It's a cast sort of thing, a get-together after-hours. To talk shop. We did it last week, but you weren't there."

"Oh?" So this wasn't just a personal invitation, it was a cast get-together. Mica was thankful he had cut her off before she had made a fool of herself. "Okay. What time?" It only made sense that Zane and the other members of the cast got together after work to discuss the progress of the film. She wondered who else would be there. Shelley, she supposed; Kyle, she hoped; and maybe a few of the others.

"Come about eight."

"Fine."

Zane winked at her again as he strolled away, and for a moment she thought he was signaling that he might have more than the film in mind. Then she put everything in context and realized how absurd that was. Setting all that aside, she turned her thoughts to Carrie and whether she should invite Carrie to join the group. But based on Carrie's reaction the last time she'd extended an invitation on Zane's behalf, she concluded it would be better for Carrie to get her invitation directly from Zane. She wasn't sure that Zane hadn't invited Carrie himself the week before. For all she knew, since she hadn't talked with Carrie lately, Carrie might have attended the get-together she had missed. Besides, she wasn't sure it was in Carrie's best interest, anyway, for her to be around Zane more than was necessary for the filming, because Carrie might take Zane's casual flirtations as an indication of serious interest and make a giant mistake. Again she reflected on how much Carrie had changed in the years since high school. In some ways, Carrie was a stranger now.

Mica got home earlier than usual and spent the remainder of the afternoon straightening her house in the hope that staying busy would help her keep her mind off Kyle. She was a neat person ordinarily, but the hectic schedule of the filming had left her little time to do housework. Soon the dust she was stirring up had her sneezing. Mica put up with it for a while, then gave in and took one of the sinus-medication tablets that she kept handy for her occasional bouts of hay fever, a combination of antihistamine and decongestant. By the time she was ready to go to Zane's apartment, the sneezing had subsided.

When she pulled her car into the visitors' parking area at Zane's apartment complex, she was surprised to find most of the parking spaces unoccupied. She checked her watch to see if she had come too early, but found she was right on time. As she was speculating on the reasons the other members of the cast might have for being late, she remembered that most of the actors hadn't bothered to rent cars. Kyle, of course, had a rental car, but he frequently walked wherever he went, and Shelley lived in this same apartment complex. Feeling better that she would not necessarily be the first to arrive, she got out of her car and began looking for apartment number 326. As she guessed, it was in the third building back from the busy street, and Zane's door, not unexpectedly, faced the outdoor swimming pool. As she waited for Zane to answer his bell, she thought how odd it was to have come to this apartment complex, one she had passed without particular notice for years, and to know Zane Morgan would soon be opening the door. Never in her wildest dreams had she ever thought she would even speak to him, let alone be acting with him in a movie and having the chance to socialize with him and his friends.

He opened the door and Mica looked in. No one else was in sight. "Am I early?"

"No, you're right on time." He grinned at her and motioned for her to come in.

She thought for a moment that she had made a mistake by accepting his invitation, but quickly put the idea aside. With the others due to arrive at any moment, she felt certain he would behave himself. If he did try to come on to her, she would simply say no, and if that didn't work, she would leave. Feeling more confident, Mica crossed the room for a closer look at a photograph of Zane and two actresses whose names were household words.

"Drink?" he asked as he stepped behind the wet bar.

"Sure." She never gave a thought to the medicine she had taken before leaving her house. "I can't stay long," she said to ensure a tactful exit if she felt a need to leave before the others arrived. When the others showed up, she could say she had changed her mind and stay longer.

"That's too bad. I was hoping you'd be able to stay quite a while."

She took the drink he offered her. It was far stronger than anything she was accustomed to, but she didn't comment. As he drank generously from his glass and she sipped at hers, she felt as awkward as she had the first time she had been in a man's apartment. The sensation was quite unpleasant. "Filming went smoothly today. Didn't you think so?"

Zane came closer. "Let's talk about us."

"Us? There is no us."

"I meant the parts we're playing in the film. What did you think I meant?"

Mica was in no mood to engage in word games. "That was one of my lines from the film," she lied coolly. It certainly sounded as if it could have been, and she was reasonably sure Zane wouldn't know. Already she had learned that most actors paid little attention to the dialogue in the script that did not pertain directly to them.

"How's your drink?"

"Strong. How's yours?"

He laughed. "I always mix them like this."

Mica compared the color of the liquor in her glass with his and found hers darker. He probably had put more bourbon in her glass, but whether that had been intentional was subject to speculation. She hadn't taken time to eat before coming, and the few sips she already had taken were warming her empty stomach. She reminded herself to go easy on the drink.

"Would you like to listen to music?" he asked as he turned up the volume on the radio and a soft, romantic melody filled the room.

"I thought we were going to run lines."

"We will. Later. Let's unwind first."

Mica sat on the front edge of an armchair and put her drink on the coffee table.

"When will the others be here?"

"The others? Oh, yes, the others. I never know who'll come or when," he said with a smile. "In the meantime, let's dance."

Mica wavered. If his intentions were innocent, she would feel foolish for making it clear to him that she mistrusted him. Besides, he'd only asked her to dance, not go to bed with him. He drew her to her feet. Mica felt his arms encircle her, and together they began moving to the music.

Mica had always loved to dance, and although Zane was reasonably good at it, he made unexpected moves from time to time that would have been hard for a less-experienced partner to follow. Smiling, she reminded herself that not everybody had had the good fortune to be taught to dance by Francine Dennis. Francine taught all the Sedalia children to dance as well as to twirl batons, and she was fanatical that all the boys learn to lead. She was sure Zane could have profited from some lessons from Francine.

"Why are you smiling?" he asked.

"I was just thinking. Nothing, really."

She looked up into his blue eyes. There was a sense of unreality in having Zane Morgan so close. She felt as if she were living in the close-up scenes of a movie, and she found herself wondering if he had always been blessed with good looks or if he had invested in plastic surgery in order to have his perfect nose and firm chin. "Do you look like your parents?" she asked.

"A little. Why do you ask?"

"I just wondered. I was trying to picture you growing up in some town and going to school like all the other kids. Where are you from?"

"Hollywood."

At first that struck her as odd. Hadn't she read some-where that he'd grown up in Brooklyn and had been coached to get rid of the accent? But then, she could be wrong. Hollywood was a city in addition to being the movie mecca, and it was only logical that some people were born and raised there. "I guess you wouldn't have been so amaz-ing in the Hollywood schools. I mean, I was trying to imag-ine you as one of my students, and I can't see how I would be able to teach the girls anything—they'd just be looking at you."

"I'll take that as a compliment." As they passed the cof-fee table, he scooped up her drink and handed it to her.

Mica sipped it, then sipped again. She was surprisingly thirsty, totally unaware of the effect the mixture of medi-cation and alcohol was having on her. "I grew up here," she said. "Right here in Sedalia."

"And you never left? I can't imagine that."

"Only long enough to attend college and work for a few years in Dallas. You never left your hometown, either, if you grew up in Hollywood," she countered. The room made an unexpected dip. She looked suspiciously at the glass. Had she drunk that much? She put it back in Zane's hand.

"Yes, but Hollywood is a destination, not a starting point."

"True," Mica agreed, but her thoughts were on how warm the room seemed to be. "Is your air-conditioning working?" She remembered the hay-fever medication and hazily recalled hearing something about antihistamines amplifying the effects of alcohol.

"Would you like for me to make it cooler?"

"If you don't mind. I guess it's the dancing. I feel hot all over."

Zane laughed and stepped away from her long enough to turn the dial on the thermostat. "That's how I like my women—hot all over."

Mica knew she should put him in his place, but her mouth was as dry as cotton and she wasn't sure she could speak. She moistened her mouth with another sip of her drink. "Could I have some water?"

Zane went into the kitchen and returned with a small glass. "Maybe you should sit down. The bourbon must have gone to your head."

"Evidently. I should have taken time to eat supper." As she drank the water, she eased herself onto his couch and wondered if she would be out of line to ask for some crackers or bread or just anything to put in her stomach besides bourbon.

"I like this song," Zane said as he settled beside her on the couch. Humming along with the tune, he put his arm around her and drew her closer. "Do you like it?"

The melody was lovely. "It's pretty," she said as she eased away and leaned her head back on the couch cushions, letting the music run through her.

"You're beautiful, you know that?"

She opened her eyes to find Zane much closer than she had thought he would be. "No, I'm not. Shelley is beautiful. I'm just average."

"Shelley's getting old. If she doesn't get a face-lift soon, she's going to age herself right out of her career."

"That's sad. Don't you think that's sad?" She had never noticed just how sad that was. "Everybody gets old, but in your business it's not allowed. That's so unfair."

"That's life." He stroked her hair back from her face. "We have all the time in the world, you and I. We have forever if we want it."

Mica shook her head. "I really should be going." But with the bourbon warming her, it seemed to be too much trouble to stand up and leave. She put down the glass and pushed it away with one finger.

"We can forget there's a world outside this door. It's only the two of us," he murmured.

*"When She Was Good,"* she stated triumphantly as she sat straight up.

Zane pulled back. "What?"

"It's the scene from *When She Was Good*. You and Marie Griffin were escaping from the Nazis and hiding in a bombed-out farm in France. Right?"

"I wasn't thinking about Marie Griffin."

"What's she like?"

"She likes other women."

Mica was shocked. "No! That can't be. I've seen her in so many movies! She always gets the man."

Zane chuckled and started nibbling at her neck.

Mica pushed him away. "I really do have to go. I can't do my lines like this. I took a sinus pill, you see, and I didn't eat supper, so now the bourbon has gone to my head." She pressed her fingers against her temples as the room twirled. "Oh, my!" She felt as if she were moving in slow motion. Was he? She was about to ask him, when the doorbell sounded. "The others are here," she announced.

"What others?" He scowled as the bell rang again.

Mica slid farther away from him. How had he come so close without her noticing? She automatically put up her hand to smooth her hair. The room was spinning faster. She glanced at her glass. It was almost empty. Had Zane drunk some of it? Surely she hadn't had that much. She tried to focus on the door.

Zane opened it and Shelley came in. "What are you doing here?" he demanded.

Shelley gave him a look that held no warmth. "I just thought I'd drop by."

"I'll bet she saw my car out front," Mica said. To Shelley she added, "I'm sorry you didn't get here sooner. I was about to leave."

Shelley came to the coffee table and picked up Mica's nearly empty glass. "I'd say that's a good idea if you're going to be able to act tomorrow."

"I don't understand it," Mica confided. "I've never had a drink hit me like this before. It's a good thing I don't have any scenes tomorrow. At least, I don't think I do."

"I think it's time you left anyway," Shelley said as she pulled Mica to her feet.

"What the hell are you doing?" Zane demanded. "This is none of your business."

"It is if I'm going to star opposite you. I don't want a repeat of what happened in Georgia to reflect on me." Shelley glared at Zane as she led Mica to the door and handed her purse to her.

Mica wanted to tell them she wasn't sure she could get home, but neither asked, and she hated to interrupt their argument. Before she knew it, she was out on the walk, trying to balance on her feet.

Carefully she made her way to her car. Then she paused. She was definitely too drunk to drive. Taking a deep breath, she left the car where it was and started walking in the direction of her house. At least, she hoped it was the right direction. All the streets seemed equally familiar. After having walked what she thought was quite a long way, she saw the sign for Maple Street. That was the street Kyle lived on, but that meant she was still a good mile from home. And her rubbery legs were growing more unsteady with each step. Halfway down the block, she stopped in front of a cottage-style house that she was sure was Kyle's. A light was burning in the front window. This wasn't home, but it was a safe haven, and it was as far as she could go.

She crossed the lawn that looked flat but was filled with what seemed like mountains and valleys, and climbed the steps. When she reached the door, she leaned on the door-bell.

When the door opened, she nearly fell into the house. Kyle's strong arms caught her.

"Mica! What in the hell ... What's happened to you?"

"It's that bourbon," she confided. "I think it had some-thing to do with the sinus pill, and I didn't have supper. Could I have a cracker, do you think? I feel a little funny."

Kyle picked her up and carried her into the living room. He sat down on the nearest chair with her in his lap. "Now, what did you say happened?"

"I had too much to drink over at Zane's, but not on pur-pose," she said in explanation. "I thought we were going to go over our lines, but Zane wanted to dance, instead, and—"

"Zane!" Kyle interrupted.

"Yeah, and before I knew it, I had drunk almost a whole glass of bourbon, and I can't understand it, because I never drink even enough to be light-headed, and we never did study our lines, and now I can't see my toes." She looked at him earnestly. "Understand?"

"I wish I did." Kyle could hardly see her through the red flash of anger he felt. How could she have led him to be-lieve she cared for him and have kissed him with such ear-nest passion one night and then have gone to Zane's apartment for drinks and dancing the next? And what was that about studying lines? Did she think him so naive as to believe she had gone to Zane's to rehearse scenes, and then she "accidentally" danced and drank with Zane until she was staggering drunk?

Even as the questions formed, he studied Mica's face for some sign of treachery or deceit, but he found none and his anger faded as quickly as it had come. Her eyes were pleading with him to understand. Surely, he thought, there would be answers to his unspoken questions and some reasonable explanation for this. Touched deeply by the vulnerability of the woman he held in his arms, he brushed the hair from her face and caressed her cheek. "I think you'd better sleep this off where I can keep an eye on you."

Mica nodded and nestled her head on his chest.

Kyle was overwhelmed with the protectiveness he felt for her. Even though Mica had gone to Zane's apartment of her own free will, if Zane had harmed her in any way, he would see to it that the bastard was arrested this time. He stood and carried Mica to his bedroom.

Balancing her on her feet, Kyle pulled down the bed covers, then sat Mica down and swung her feet onto the bed. As if she were at home, she curled into the place where he usually slept and burrowed her head into his pillow. He was torn between his desire to crawl into bed beside her and the disturbing thought that she had come to him from Zane. Had she gone to Zane's apartment innocently believing he was interested in going over lines, or was she wanting to be Zane's "friend," too? He wanted to believe the former, but he had not thought Mica could be so easily duped. On the other hand, Zane was a master at the art of seduction. Just the thought that Zane might have seduced Mica made Kyle want to punch out Zane's capped teeth.

Instead, Kyle redirected his attention to Mica. He slipped off her shoes, and so that she would be comfortable enough to sleep this off without waking, he loosened the waistband of her skirt and began carefully easing it down over her hips. Suddenly he stopped. He was no saint, and this was pushing himself too far. After the impassioned kiss they had shared the night before, he had fantasized about doing exactly this, but with Mica alert and willing. He left the skirt in place and pulled the cover over her. She would sleep just fine as she was.

He went to the kitchen and put on a pot of coffee. He had been awake most of the night before and was quite tired, but this had him too upset to sleep. Once the coffee was brewed, he poured himself a cup, returned to the bedroom and sat in the overstuffed chair beside the bed so he would be near Mica if she needed him.

As Kyle kept watch over her, sipping his coffee to be sure he stayed awake, she slept soundly, her breathing steady and calm. Time and again he thought back over what Mica had told him before going to sleep, but try as he might, he could make little sense of it. After having been at Zane's apartment, drinking and dancing, she had come to him instead of going home. But why? Mica had been in no shape to explain, and that had left him with only his own speculation—and that was driving him crazy.

When he was sure she was resting easily, he left the bedroom and went to the phone in the kitchen. He dialed Zane's number, and as he waited, he drummed his fingertips on the countertop. Zane answered, and from his tone of voice, Kyle had a feeling Zane had been expecting the caller to be Mica. "This is Kyle. What the hell happened over there?"

"I don't know what you're talking about."

"Don't play games with me. Mica showed up on my doorstep. She told me she'd been at your place, then she passed out."

"She drank too much," Zane said in a bored voice. "She'll sleep it off and be fine in the morning."

"I'll bet you told her other cast members would be there, too. And just what did happen over there that made her leave and come to me?" Kyle was gripping the receiver so tightly his fingers were growing numb and cold.

"That's none of your damned business. What are you, her father? I didn't touch her. She wanted me to, though," Zane added maliciously. "She was begging for it. She left right after Shelley showed up. Maybe you two can adopt her.''

''You'd better not be lying.''

''Go to hell!'' Zane snapped, then hung up.

Kyle slammed down the receiver and went back to his vigil in the bedroom. As he sat on the side of the bed next to Mica, she turned her head slightly, as if she was aware of his presence, though he was sure she was still sleeping. Gently he touched her cheek and she smiled. Kyle was unprepared for the tenderness he felt for her. He wanted to be angry with her, but he couldn't sustain it.

He had known many women, but none who had engendered such a strong sense of protectiveness in him. Mica touched his heart as no other woman ever had, not even Tamara. He had loved Tamara, or at least he thought he had, despite what everyone had thought. At least, he had in the beginning. Several people had suggested to him after the divorce that she had probably never been faithful to him. He didn't want to believe that was true, but it might have been. What he did know was that the long months of separation necessitated by their divergent careers had kept them from growing close enough to sustain their marriage. Now that he had met Mica, he was beginning to doubt if what he had felt for Tamara had been love after all.

He was also curious as to why Mica had never married. He had learned from Birdine Ponder that recently Mica had dated someone who had moved to Houston. She must not have loved him, however, or she would have gone with him. But then he recalled what Mica had said about having roots in Sedalia and feeling a need to be teaching here, to the exclusion of anywhere else. Maybe she had loved the man but couldn't give up teaching in Sedalia even for love.

Kyle stood and went back to the chair. He couldn't think in those terms. He didn't want to fall in love again, and especially not with someone who had a life of her own here in

Sedalia. He had to be reasonable about this and not go off on some tangent. She might not care for him at all.

But then he remembered the kiss they had shared the night before and how she had looked into his eyes as if she was trying to read what he was thinking and feeling. At the time he had been certain that it was not a casual kiss for her, either. Now he didn't know what to think.

Kyle ran his fingers through his hair and rubbed the back of his neck. Of all the people for him to be falling in love with, why did it have to be Mica?

# CHAPTER EIGHT

WHEN MICA AWOKE she was dizzy and disoriented and had no idea where she was. Her mouth still felt as though it were stuffed with cotton, and when she lifted her head, she instantly regretted it. Carefully she lay back down on the pillow. As she looked about the room, she finally remembered going to Zane's apartment and something about dancing. Then the glass of bourbon. She remembered that. Gently she sat up and put her feet on the floor before she looked down. She was fully clothed except for her shoes, but her skirt was loose and twisted around her. She pulled it into place. Now that she was awake and sitting up, her head hurt more than ever.

A clock on the dresser indicated it was nine-thirty, and judging by the light coming through the curtains, it had to be morning. As logic began to catch up with her, she concluded that she was in Zane Morgan's bedroom. A wave of embarrassment began to wash over her when she could not remember anything beyond the glass of bourbon. She had to get out of here and go home. How could she ever face Zane again? And Kyle! She wanted to go home to the safety of her own bed. Quickly she slipped her shoes on and crossed the room to the door.

Anxiety crept over her as she opened the door a crack and peeped out. She saw a short hall and a sunny kitchen at the opposite end. None of this looked familiar, but then, she could hardly remember anything of the evening before. Sounds coming from the direction of the kitchen suggested that Zane was in there. How could she get out without his seeing her? What would she say when he did? With no answers and no choice but to try to get out unnoticed, Mica picked up her purse from the chair by the door and made her way down the hall as quietly as she could. When she reached the kitchen, she risked a glimpse around the corner and, to her amazement, she saw Kyle, not Zane, standing at the stove. Her anxiety was suddenly replaced with intense curiosity.

Without turning around, he said, "I thought I heard you get up. How do you feel?"

Experimentally, she poked her head around the door. "Awful. Why are you here?"

"I don't have any scenes being shot until tomorrow, and neither do you. I thought I'd make breakfast." His tone was cool.

"No, I mean why are you *here?*"

He turned around with a perplexed look on his face and said, "Because I live here. You don't remember?"

Mica tilted her head suspiciously. "This is your house? How...I mean..."

"Perhaps I'd better fill you in. You went to see Zane last night and had too much to drink. You came here and passed out."

"Don't be silly." She sat down at the breakfast table and rubbed her aching head. "I don't do things like that." She wished he weren't cooking; the smell of frying bacon was making her mildly nauseated.

"You need to get some food in you. You'll feel better then."

"I'll never feel better," she said with morbid conviction. He hadn't cracked a smile and was more distant than she'd ever seen him. She was confused and embarrassed. Apparently Kyle was upset with her. After all, she had come to his house drunk and passed out. Her head throbbed, and the longer she was awake, the more it hurt. She tried to hold it level; it seemed to be less painful that way. "All I remember is that I went to Zane's apartment to run through some lines. I assumed you and the others would be there."

"I wasn't invited. It's my guess none of the others were, either. Zane wanted to get you alone."

Mica didn't want to think she'd let herself be deceived. She hadn't considered herself to be naive, not since her sophomore year in high school, at least. Defensively, Mica said, "He was polite. He offered me a drink and turned on some music."

"And you danced?"

"Yes, we danced. I remember thinking Francine Dennis could have given him some pointers."

Kyle looked confused. "Who?"

"Francine Dennis. She teaches dancing and baton twirling here in Sedalia."

Stoically, Kyle turned back to the frying bacon.

"Anyway, we danced." Mica frowned as she strained to recall the details of the evening before. Her memories were fuzzy at best, but she was ashamed to admit that to Kyle. He already thought she'd been foolish to go to Zane's apartment. And with twenty-twenty hindsight, she had to admit to herself that it was true. She couldn't hide the fact that she'd left Zane's apartment drunk, but maybe she could save face by recounting the details of the remainder of the evening. She stopped struggling to remember and the fog in her mind began to lift ever so slightly. Bit by bit things were coming back. "I remember being terribly thirsty. After we danced, we sat on the sofa and talked...about the movie he was in called *When She Was Good*. Then Shelley arrived and I left."

"Do you remember coming here?"

Suddenly panic hit. She had absolutely no recollection of *anything* beyond leaving Zane's apartment. She wanted to lie to him, but she couldn't. "No. I don't remember anything else."

Kyle turned back to her and stared for a moment, then the corners of his mouth turned up in a smile, as if he was relieved. "How do you like your eggs?"

What did he know that she didn't? "In the refrigerator. I'm going home!" Mica stood to leave, but she had to wait for the room to stop spinning.

"You need to eat first. Here. Start on this bacon while I scramble the eggs."

Mica felt a wave of sickness rising. "No, thank you," she said with great dignity. "I would rather be sick at my own house." She crossed the living room and opened the front door. She heard Kyle follow her. "Where's my car?"

"At Zane's, I assume. You apparently had the good sense to walk here."

Mica couldn't remember making the decision not to drive, how she had gotten to Kyle's house, anything at all—until she'd awakened in Kyle's bed. Fear seized her. Struggling to remain calm, she asked, "What happened here last night? It seems to me that I should be questioning you instead of you questioning me. After all, I woke up in your bed." She felt a blush rising but couldn't help it. She had never in her life been in a situation such as this.

"I was a perfect gentleman," Kyle said wryly. "You landed on my doorstep, passed out in my arms, and I didn't take advantage of you."

"Exactly what happened?"

"I opened the door and there you were. I put you to bed."

"My skirt was loose." She frowned up at him. "Are you sure nothing else happened?"

Kyle paused. His face grew dark and his eyes bored into 'hers with an intensity of emotion that rivaled the passion his kiss had stirred in her the last time she remembered being with him. "Mica, I don't take advantage of helpless women—or any women, for that matter. If I ever take you to bed, it will only be with you fully awake and willing. If I had done otherwise, you wouldn't have awakened this morning fully dressed.''

Mica was all the more embarrassed for having questioned his integrity, but at the same time, she was offended by his suggestion that she had been vulnerable. Her head hurt with a fury, and to compound matters, the smell of food cooking was making her stomach churn.

"I'm leaving. Goodbye, Kyle. Thank you for your hospitality." With sarcasm, she added, "And thanks for your insinuation that I can't take care of myself." Mica lifted her chin and stalked across the porch and down the steps. Her head hurt with every movement, but she refused to let it show.

When she was two houses away, she risked a glance back and found Kyle's door shut and no sign of him. She slackened her pace and rubbed her forehead. Now she understood the suffering her roommates at college had endured for drinking too much. Had she been rash to leave Kyle in anger? "No," she muttered, rationalizing that he'd had no business asking her all those questions and suggesting she hadn't used good judgment. But the bitter truth was that she hadn't been prudent. That she would never let such a thing happen again was little solace. Kyle had seen her at her worst, and she was embarrassed all over again at the thought.

She found her car parked in one of the visitor parking spaces in front of Zane's apartment complex in full view of the street. Anyone driving by could have seen it, and her car was well-known around town. She fumbled through her purse, looking for her keys for what seemed to be forever before finding them, then hurriedly got in the vehicle and started it. Had anyone seen her car here? Why hadn't she thought to park in a less obvious place? But she had never thought it would be here all night. As inconspicuously as possible, she drove away, her anger at Kyle melting as the minutes passed.

AFTER MICA LEFT, Kyle chastised himself for the way he'd handled the situation with her. He had no right to feel such jealousy. He'd never even told Mica that he was falling in love with her. And he probably shouldn't, especially now that it seemed that Mica had more than a passing interest in Zane. Just the thought of that made his blood boil. Zane cared about nothing but building his own ego and satisfying his sexual desires. Mica was clearly Zane's targeted prey, and Kyle cared too much for her to stand by idly and see her get hurt. Knowing Zane wouldn't respond to a subtle approach, Kyle decided to confront him. Less than ten minutes later, he was knocking on Zane's door.

Zane opened the door and his face registered surprise. "Come in," he said after a brief hesitation.

Kyle stepped into the apartment. He could picture Mica coming here, and he had to struggle to control his temper.

"Do you want a drink?" Zane said at last.

"It's not even noon. And I'd have thought you'd already outdone yourself offering drinks to your guests."

Zane poured himself a drink and sat on the couch. "What are you talking about?"

"Mica. I want you to leave her alone."

"Yeah. Right."

Kyle stepped forward menacingly and glared at Zane. "You and I have never been good friends, but take a little friendly advice. Don't do anything that will harm Mica."

Zane smiled as if he had never caused anyone harm in his life, and he spread his arms, palms up, to show how harmless he was. "Me? I don't know what you're talking about. She came over—she had a drink—she left. So what?"

"You know exactly what I'm talking about."

Kyle scowled at him until Zane's smile disappeared. "I have a pretty good idea what happened when you were on location in Georgia last year. Don't let it happen here."

"That broad yelled rape in order to sue me. Hell, I never put a hand on her by force. It's too damned easy for women to do that, especially if the man's rich and famous. I'm surprised it hasn't happened to you, too." He grimaced. "Or maybe you aren't interested in women after Tamara."

"Tamara has nothing to do with it, and you know it. I've never been accused of rape because I don't live the way you do. I don't know if you forced the woman in Georgia or not, but don't try any funny stuff with Mica. She's not like the women you hang out with." He didn't bother trying to hide the disgust he felt.

"So what are you? Her big brother?" Zane got up from the couch and crossed to where Kyle stood. He had to look up to meet Kyle's eyes.

"No, I'm her friend."

"I figured she was looking for a ticket to Hollywood." Zane turned away and went to the window. "Most women are."

"She's not! And you'd damned well better heed my advice and not cause trouble here." Kyle turned and walked back toward the door.

"Are you threatening me?" Zane started after Kyle, but stopped abruptly when Kyle wheeled around and glared at him.

With his voice rumbling deep in his chest, Kyle said, "You can take it any way you please. But I mean it, Zane. Watch your step with Mica." He went out and closed the door behind him, feeling good for what he'd done.

SHELLEY DOYLE WAS accustomed to being the center of attention, especially during the shooting of a picture. Thus, when Zane had sent Wendy Valentine away, she had assumed Zane had done so in order to have an affair with her. Zane, however, was not so predictable—as evidenced by the intimate situation she had interrupted at Zane's apartment two evenings before. She had intended on waiting for Zane to come to her, but a sixth sense had compelled her to go to Zane's apartment that night. And she was glad she'd paid attention. With little effort, she had sent Mica Haldane on her way, and once the little nobody was gone, she'd flirted with Zane just enough to get him hot, then she'd made her exit—leaving Zane wanting more. The ploy had worked well for her many times, and she was confident that it would be successful again.

She had once been quite fond of Zane, and she still found his body appealing. A smile crossed her face as she recalled the first time she had worked with Zane and how awed he had been at the mere chance of making love to her. They had been an item at the time. As quickly as the smile had come, it faded. Lately Zane had become obsessed with women younger than he was, and she was sure it was a sign of the insecurity he was feeling as the years slipped by.

Several years before, *The National Spyglass* had accused her of just such a concern, even going so far as to suggest that she was terrified of getting older. She had been careful to say in her next interview that nothing could have been farther from the truth, but she was afraid no one believed her. Besides, not everyone became unattractive as the years passed. She felt she was a prime example of that, and frequently she pointed that out to her friends. She was as great a star and sex symbol today as she ever had been. That was why she hated to have a nobody like Mica Haldane come in from nowhere and monopolize the attention of the only man on location whom Shelley found truly attractive. She wanted to have Zane Morgan for herself and was determined to get her way. That would relieve the boredom of an entire summer spent in this little backwater town, and if Mica was pursuing Zane, rather than the reverse, it would put Mica in her place.

Twenty minutes later, Shelley emerged from her trailer for the day's filming and looked around with casual interest. The woman she wanted to speak with was standing nearby, alone for once. She put a smile on her face, and as nonchalantly as she could, she closed the distance. "Nice day, isn't it, Mica?"

Mica looked up in surprise. "Yes, it is."

Shelley's smile broadened. "I've been meaning to speak with you for several days, but this is the first free moment I've had."

"Oh?"

"Yes, I've been noticing the way you move on camera. You're doing something all wrong, and I thought I should point it out before Greenberg shrieks at you. That little man can be so unpleasant."

Mica put down her script and said, "Thank you. What am I doing wrong?"

"For one thing, it's the way you walk. You seem to bound along. You should move more deliberately, as if you own the street. Take your time getting from place to place. After all, this is the only picture you'll ever be in, and you want to have as much exposure as possible."

"But I thought—"

"And then there's your voice."

"What's wrong with my voice? I don't have a strong accent. Not anymore. I got rid of most of it in college. Besides, I'm playing the part of a young Texas woman. I'm supposed to have an accent."

Shelley laughed as if she couldn't quite believe Mica could be so stupid. "You may have thought you got rid of it, but, honey, it's so thick you can cut it with a knife."

"I think you must be mistaken," Mica said calmly.

"Do you want my help or not? Now, when you deliver your lines today, make your voice whispery. It'll make you sound sexy. Like Marilyn Monroe. You must remember what she sounded like."

"I've seen some of her movies on TV."

Shelley had seen many of Marilyn Monroe's films as first runs at the movie theaters, and she had forgotten that Monroe must have died about the same year Mica was born. "So did I," she said with saccharine sweetness.

Out of the corner of her eye, she noticed Greenberg acknowledging the signal from his assistant that scene two for the day was set up and ready for the actors. To impress Mica, she nodded in Greenberg's direction, just in time to imply that she knew he was going to shout over his megaphone for the actors to take their places.

"We have to go. Remember to do what I told you. This is one of your scenes with me, and I want us both to look good."

Mica nodded, but with an uncertain expression.

Shelley moved into place. As soon as she heard "action" she put Deborah Stinson's smile on her face and started walking down the sidewalk. Mica came toward her from the opposite direction. As Shelley had instructed, Mica was moving slowly.

"Cut!" Greenberg barked with a frown aimed at Mica. "What's wrong with you today? Got cement in your shoes? Get the lead out."

As Shelley watched Mica blush all the way to her hair roots, she hid the pleasure she felt. Mica hadn't had her share of reprimands. Shelley intended to remedy that.

The second time through, Mica disregarded Shelley's suggestions, and Shelley was forced to drop a line to keep it from being a take. Before Greenberg could say anything, Shelley screwed her face into a grimace and headed straight for him. When she was close enough not to have to raise her voice, she said through clenched teeth, "I can't work with that woman."

"What? Why not?" He glared up at her. Shelley was taller than he was by several inches.

"She has no idea what she's doing. That walk she started off with, for instance. She hasn't moved like that until today. She was deliberately trying to throw off my timing and ruin my performance."

"No way. She doesn't know that much about acting in front of a camera."

"I want her replaced."

"Forget it. She's already been in several scenes. I'm not reshooting them. Mica's doing fine."

Shelley stuck out her lips in a pout. In her youth, this had worked with every director. "Then I won't be able to do my best."

"You will or I'll dock your pay."

Shelley jerked upright. "You can't do that! We have a contract."

"So sue me. I know your reputation for causing trouble and putting pictures over budget, and I'm not going to put up with it."

"*My* reputation? Zane's, you mean!"

"I'm keeping an eye on you both. Now, get back in position. I'm not going to stand here arguing with you while the payroll clock is ticking." Greenberg gave a departing glare and went back to his chair. "Places!" he ordered.

Shelley tossed her head and flounced away to her trailer, instead. She would show him!

Greenberg groaned and threw his clipboard on the ground. His assistant shouted, "Take five!"

Mica knew Shelley and the director had been discussing her, because Shelley had been glaring at her as she'd talked. She was embarrassed and wanted to crawl under something. She knew valuable time was being wasted and was afraid it was her fault.

"Don't look so glum," Zane said as he came to stand beside her. "Shelley's always pulling stunts like this. If I were you, I'd just ignore it."

Mica forced herself to smile at him. She was convinced that he had meant to take advantage of her in his apartment two nights earlier, and she had no interest in talking with him. She also didn't want anyone else on the set knowing that she'd been taken in by his trickery. "Thanks for the advice," she said coolly, then turned away.

"You looked great," he continued. When she turned back in his direction, his professional smile tilted his lips. "The only way you'd look better would be if you were in my dressing room. How about it? It'll take Greenberg longer than five minutes to pry Shelley back out of hers."

"What?" Mica was shocked that he would blatantly say such a thing. Trying to maintain a smile for the benefit of anyone watching them, she said through clenched teeth, "I have no intention of going to your dressing room now or ever!" She noticed Carrie watching them from a distance and was startled at the jealous expression on her friend's face. When their eyes met, Carrie turned away.

Mica didn't want Carrie to get the wrong idea, so she started to go to her, but Zane caught her wrist. "Stay with me," he said with his famous wink. "Give me a chance to make up with you about the other night."

Mica turned back to him. "Take your hand off my arm. I'm going to see if something is wrong with Carrie."

Zane glanced in the direction Mica was looking. "I'll see what's wrong with her while you're doing the next scene. Talk to me until then."

"You never give up, do you?" Mica jerked her arm away, but by then Carrie had disappeared into the nearby crowd. As Zane walked away, she was relieved. Whether Zane had meant for her to drink too much that night or not, she had to take responsibility for her own actions. But that didn't mean she was going to give him another chance. She had had time to think the evening over and knew that since she had passed out at Kyle's, Zane had had to know she was too drunk to reach home safely when she'd left. Yet he and Shelley did nothing to help. That had told her all she needed to know about the sort of person Zane was. And Shelley, too. She had been foolish to think Shelley was giving her good advice about this scene. Mica resolved not to trust either of them again.

ON THE SET that evening Mica was cool toward Zane, but Zane was friendlier than usual. Shelley glared at her every time they met off camera.

During a break between scenes, Carrie arrived on the set along with thirty or forty extras for the filming of a crowd scene. Quickly Mica made her way through the throng, hoping to talk with Carrie and avoid a misunderstanding. Mica also felt a need to warn Carrie about Zane, and even though this wasn't the best place to do so, she was afraid she might not have another opportunity. According to Carrie's parents, Carrie had been out every time Mica had called, and she hadn't called Mica back.

Carrie smiled at Mica, though somewhat thinly, as Mica joined her. "Carrie, can we talk? In private?"

"Here?" Carrie asked as she looked at all the people who had gathered around.

Mica tilted her head in the direction of the empty storefronts down the block, and together they moved out of earshot of the others and stopped in front of Buttons and Bows.

"What did you want to talk to me about?" Carrie asked with forced cheerfulness.

"Zane Morgan."

Carrie stiffened. "Yeah, I've noticed you've gotten rather chummy with him."

"Look, don't be upset with me. Let me explain."

"Upset? I'm not upset," Carrie said, then tried to laugh.

But Mica could see the hurt in her eyes. This was going to be harder than she'd expected, and she was getting a bit rattled. Carrie had been a close friend for a long time, and she didn't want anything to get in the way of that. Mica hesitated for a moment, then decided she'd better tell Carrie the whole story about Zane so Carrie would pay attention. "I went to Zane's apartment last Tuesday night, and I got drunk and—"

"Don't tell me any more," Carrie interjected. "I don't want to hear any more about you and Zane."

"Wait, Carrie. It's not like that. See, I only had one drink, but it went straight to my head. I hadn't eaten before I went over, and I'd taken a sinus pill. It was a bad combination." She looked around to be sure they were still alone. "I woke up in Kyle's bed."

Carrie looked understandably confused. "Wait a minute. I thought you said you went to Zane's apartment. Kyle was there, too?"

"No, no. Just Zane. No one else was there. I thought there would be others. Otherwise I wouldn't have gone. But—"

"You were alone in Zane Morgan's apartment?" Carrie's jaw dropped. "Alone? Together?"

"Hush. Someone might hear you."

Mica could see she was making matters worse and confusing the issue. Cutting directly to the point she was trying to make, Mica said, "Carrie, you should stay away from him. He's not trustworthy."

Carrie let out a short laugh. "Pardon?"

"He invited me to his apartment under false pretenses. He had no intention of us studying our lines."

"I can take care of myself," Carrie said with an edge of coolness. "So how did you end up with Kyle?"

"Apparently, I showed up at his house three sheets to the wind, and then I passed out."

"That's all?"

"Isn't that enough? I never intended for any of that to happen!"

"If that's all that happened, why are you so mad at Zane? You can't blame him for trying."

"Yes, I can! Haven't you ever heard of date rape?"

Carrie drew back. "I thought you said it wasn't a date, that you thought other members of the cast would be there."

"It wasn't!"

"I wish Zane had asked me to his apartment," Carrie said in a defensive voice. "It seems to me you should be at least as concerned about Kyle. After all, you said you spent the night at his place. Or maybe you want them both, and this is your way of turning me against Zane!"

Mica's mouth dropped open. "Carrie! I can't believe you would say such a thing!"

Carrie shrugged and avoided Mica's eyes. "These things happen, but not between friends."

"Carrie. I didn't tell you all this so I could have Zane for myself. I care about you, and I don't want to see you get hurt. I don't want Zane. Please believe me."

"Good. You have Kyle. One movie star ought to be enough for you." Carrie turned and walked away.

Mica was too astounded to speak. What had happened to the Carrie Graham she'd been so close to over the years?

From the corner of her eye, Mica could see the cast and extras getting in place for the next scene. She would rather have gone home, but she didn't have that option.

When she moved back to the edge of the crowd to await her cue, she noticed Zane standing not ten feet from her. He was staring right at her, and when he knew he'd caught her eye, he grinned and winked. Before Mica could look away, she saw Carrie step up to his side and put her hand on his arm to get his attention. He looked down at her and gave her his famous bone-melting smile, the one Mica now knew he used as the first of a series of maneuvers to get women into his bed. Mica turned away, trying to convince herself that Carrie was a grown woman and was free to make mistakes if she pleased, but her loyalty to their friendship demanded that she not give up on Carrie so easily.

Surreptitiously, she watched them exchange conversation and smiles, and although she could not hear them, she felt sure by Zane's body language that he saw an opportunity in Carrie. Moments later, Carrie was called onto the set, and she made it obvious that she was reluctant to leave Zane. It was as if Carrie was trying to prove that she, too, could catch and hold the attention of a movie star. As childish as such behavior was, Mica knew that Carrie was insecure in her relationships with men, and she could understand why she was doing this. Or at least, she thought she understood. Mica was sorry she'd said anything to Carrie about Zane, but at the time she'd thought it was the right thing to do.

Lost in her thoughts, Mica was unaware of Zane's approach until she heard him say, "I was sorry to see you go the other night. Shelley would have stayed only a few minutes." He stopped directly in front of her.

Startled and feeling hemmed in, Mica whispered, "Can't you take a hint? I don't want to talk to you. Frankly, I think it's a good thing Shelley arrived when she did."

For an instant his face bore an ugly expression. "That's not the way you acted at the time."

Mica caught her breath at his implication and anger flashed through her. Forgetting that others might hear her, she retorted with increasing volume, "Just leave me alone.

Do you understand? Whatever impression you got was clearly erroneous. I'm not interested!''

"No? I don't believe you. I've seen women play hard to get, but in the end, you're all alike.'' He winked at her and sauntered away.

Mica tightened her hands into fists to keep from charging after him and telling him exactly what she thought of him. "He's not worth it!'' she told herself through clenched teeth. She had rarely been so angry in all her life. Suddenly she realized that several of the extras standing close by were staring. Embarrassed, but feigning nonchalance, Mica stepped into a concealing shadow a few feet away. It was somehow surreal that she was standing here in the dark in downtown Sedalia, watching a movie being filmed, fuming over Zane Morgan's attempts to seduce her. Never in her wildest fantasies had she ever envisioned this. Struggling to calm herself, she looked back toward the lights as Kyle moved into place and started his lines with Shelley. She hadn't spoken with Kyle since the morning she'd woken up in his bed and left his house in anger, but she hadn't stopped thinking about him. She knew she was falling in love with him and seemed powerless to stop herself. What future could she possibly have with Kyle? In a few weeks, he would be gone forever. She pressed her fingertips against her temple, hoping she could ease the throbbing pain brought on by her anger toward Zane and the frustration of her hopeless love for Kyle.

By the time Mica heard her cue to go before the cameras, she had regained control of herself and her headache had eased. She had to act as if nothing had happened, finish her scenes as quickly as possible and go directly home to get away from everyone long enough to think. However, as she stepped before the bright lights, the glare aggravated the ragged edges of her headache and the pounding pulse in her temple returned. She took a deep breath in an effort to calm herself, but the headache reminded her of her anger, and she had to expend much more effort than usual to get into character for the scene.

Shelley glared at her until the cameras began to roll, then she magically turned into Deborah Stinson, Angie Dillon's friend. Even as distracted as Mica was, she never ceased to be amazed at how Shelley was able to completely mask her own personality and step instantly into her role. Shelley was beautiful in her expertly applied makeup, and Mica was familiar enough with the cameras to see how she turned herself instinctively to present her best angle to the film. Her delivery of lines was another story, however.

Shelley had clearly not spent any time studying the lines, and she failed to give Mica the cue for hers. Mica found herself standing in silence and waiting for the words from Shelley that would cue her response. Shelley waited with a placid expression on her face while the cameras rolled. Mica felt she should do something, so she said her lines, but without the proper cue lines, they were meaningless.

"Cut!" Greenberg shouted. "What's going on?"

His assistant held up the script and pointed at the error. Shelley glared at him. "I can't act with amateurs," she snapped. "She's just trying to make me look bad."

Greenberg scowled at her. "Do it again. Do you need to hear the lines read first?"

"Of course not." Shelley jerked her head around and glowered at Mica. "You had better watch your step, schoolteacher. You're playing with the big girls now."

Shelley's threat had been delivered with such a ridiculous choice of words that Mica smiled in reflex. Shelley looked as if she was ready to attack, cameras or no cameras. Mica turned away and went back to her mark for the beginning of the scene. At the proper time, Kyle came on and delivered his lines to Mica. She found it even more difficult to act with him than it had been with Shelley. Kyle's character, Ryan, was in love with Mica's character, Angie, though Angie wasn't supposed to know it at this point. Mica found his eyes spoke too openly of love, and she had to remind herself over and over that he was acting. She couldn't allow herself to read more into his expression than was real. Kyle, like Shelley, was a consummate actor, and that had to be all there was to it. She was glad when the scene was over and she was able to escape back into the darkness.

Miss Nelly and her two friends were waiting for her. "Did you see the way Kyle was looking at you?" Miss Nelly said, nodding to emphasize the truth in her observation. Buford and Birdine nodded.

"No," Mica protested. "He was only acting. Ryan is supposed to be in love with Angie."

"Not at this point in the film."

"Then you must have imagined it or Greenberg would have had us do it over." She looked back to where Kyle and Zane were being filmed standing next to some vintage cars from the sixties. "He's good at his profession."

"I've been around a long time," Buford said. "Zane Morgan and Kyle Spensor are both watching you the way a canary eyes birdseed."

Miss Nelly added, "You want to watch that Zane. I don't trust him."

"Neither do I," Mica agreed as she rubbed her eyes, then remembered her makeup. "Did I smear the liner?"

Birdine studied Mica's face, tilting her head first one way, then another. "You're all right. I still say Kyle is interested in you. He's a real nice boy."

Mica had to smile. Anyone under the age of fifty was a boy to Birdine. "I agree. But any interest Kyle has in me is only because of the film. We have nothing in common."

Buford laughed. "That just makes it more interesting. Opposites have a way of attracting."

Birdine nodded to Miss Nelly. "That's so true. Do you recall how Harriet Beavis married that drummer? They was like chalk and cheese."

Mica looked back at Kyle. "I can't afford to believe that he cares for me. He'll be gone soon. I can't get attached to him."

"I don't know about that," Miss Nelly said. "Life has some odd quirks and twists if you ask me."

"It would have to be some odd ones, indeed, for me to have a future with Kyle Spensor." She watched as Kyle moved confidently in front of the cameras. She wished Miss Nelly and her friends were right.


SHELLEY WATCHED Mica pass out of the lights and head away, presumably in the direction of her house. She had no liking for Mica at all, and she didn't care who knew it. If everyone in this hick town stopped going to see her shows, Shelley wouldn't feel the loss in her bank account. She only had to be nice to the ones who counted.

She recalled the scene she had interrupted in Zane's apartment. Zane would have had that little nobody undressed and in his bed in a matter of minutes. Not that Shelley cared what happened to Mica. But Zane was another matter. She had determined to have an affair with him and Mica stood in her way. For a moment she wondered if she had been wrong to interrupt Zane's seduction. Once he had bedded Mica, he might have lost interest in her; she had seen it happen that way before. Shelley promised herself that she wouldn't interfere next time.

She went back to the makeup trailer for a touch-up before her next scene. Calula could work wonders with makeup.

"How's the filming going?" Calula asked as she put aside her magazine and joined Shelley at the mirrors.

Shelley sat down and leaned back. "Slow, as usual. You can't do anything with amateurs on the set. Greenberg must be out of his mind."

Years before, Calula had gone to Hollywood in search of her own career in acting. Although she was an exotic-looking beauty, she had soon come to grips with the fact that she had little or no acting talent. She had settled into the job of makeup artist, and if she had any regrets, she never voiced them to Shelley.

Calula nodded in commiseration but offered no opinion. That was another thing Shelley liked about Calula. She never forgot who the stars were and always treated them as such. When Shelley was around, Calula rarely talked at all.

"I only hope I can save the film from being a box-office bomb." Shelley tilted her head to study her eye shadow from a different angle. "I'm going to fire my agent for talking me into this."

Calula nodded as she reached for the tray of eye shadows and started working on Shelley's eyes.

Shelley stared at her reflection. This picture was telling on her in terms of stress, she decided. Her eyes had fine wrinkles radiating from the corners, and the skin on her forehead could use some firming. Even Calula's talent couldn't hide these minor flaws forever. That meant she would have to take time off for another plastic surgery. Silently she calculated how long it would take for the bruises to go away after surgery and tried to remember whether her agent had anything in the works for her to do immediately after this film. "Do you know what Bennie wanted me to do? That little worm."

"Your agent? What?"

"He wanted me to play the part of the mother in some remake of *Little Women*. Can you imagine such a thing? You'd have to plaster makeup on me an inch thick." She laughed a bit nervously.

"It could be an interesting role," Calula said in a neutral voice.

"I know I could play it," Shelley said coldly. "I was referring to the age of the mother. I could never be believable in the role of a woman old enough to have grown children. The very idea of that man! He was serious, too!"

Calula surveyed her art in the mirror and added a concealing color beneath Shelley's eyes. "How does that look to you?"

Shelley frowned. "I need more powder. I can't go before the cameras shining like this."

Without an argument, Calula reached for the face powder.

"Me! In the part of the mother," Shelley spat out as she stared at her image in the mirror. "As if I'm starting to age. I have no intention of taking character parts for years yet."

Shelley waited for Calula to agree with her, but the woman seemed to be preoccupied with applying her powder. Shelley refrained from frowning again. When she frowned the lines in her face were too obvious. When Calula was done, Shelley got out of the chair and, without a word, went back outside. She was more afraid of aging than she was of the most dreaded diseases one could imagine. There might be a cure for a disease, but there was none for getting older. Shelley walked briskly back to where the lights made the street as bright as day. She wasn't ready to be put out to pasture yet, and to prove it, she would have an affair with Zane. She had always been able to choose her lovers from the top echelon, and to do so would assure her that the years weren't stacking up so fast. She put on her best smile and tossed her hair as she had when she was young and the most popular star in Hollywood.

BUFORD SHOVED his hands into his back pockets and looked down at the square of concrete at his feet. "You say you want this dug up right here?"

"That's right," Mayor Graham said. "The city council has authorized a flower bed to be put here and in front of all the stores downtown. We're putting in petunias and moss rose."

Buford rubbed his chin thoughtfully. "This is right in front of the drugstore. I reckon Greenberg will be het up over it if you do it right now. He's still filming, you know."

"Of course I know. That's why we need to get after it. Can your men do it or not?"

"Sure. We can do it. We've dug up bigger things than this sidewalk. Have you talked to Greenberg?"

"I don't need to. The city council met in regular session last night. Jack Murray brought up the suggestion that had been made to him about putting flowers downtown, and the council agreed that it was a good idea."

"Are you sure it's a good idea to do this without telling Greenberg first?"

"That's not for you to worry about. That's Jack's job, but he's sick today. He called me this morning and said he was home and staying in bed."

"Yep. You're the boss." Buford had a feeling Jack was sick over having to tell Greenberg that the mayor was determined to dig up the sidewalk and put in flower beds. "Who's going to tend these beds once they're planted?"

"The individual merchants will be responsible for the flowers in front of their stores. It'll give them incentive to spruce up. Nobody wants dead flowers in front of their place of business."

Buford looked down the street. "And you say you're putting in petunias and moss roses?"

"It was my wife's idea. The council approved it."

"Yep." Buford had learned long ago it was easier to make an affirmative sound than a negative one, especially when dealing with people who weren't going to listen anyway. "Of course now, petunias tend to get stringy looking toward the end of summer, and moss roses don't ever do much of anything as far as I'm concerned."

Graham gave his hearty politician's laugh. "Well, I have to admit I don't know one flower from another. I just do as' I'm told."

"Yep." Buford kicked at the concrete and squinted as he peered down the sidewalk. "Yep," he repeated. He didn't want to lose the job, but he knew for a fact that Greenberg would be fit to be tied if he came downtown and found a backhoe digging up the sidewalk. "You know, Harry, I believe I saw Greenberg going into the grocery store a while ago. Why don't I just drive back over there and see what he says about this?"

Graham frowned. "I don't see any reason to do that, Buford. After all, he's not a resident of this town, and he doesn't have anything to say about the way it's run."

"Yep, but I'd hate for him to decide to pull out and finish the filming somewhere else. Like in Kilgore, for instance." Buford waited for Graham's reaction.

"Kilgore! He's mentioned moving to Kilgore?" Graham's voice rose into a squeak the way it always did when he was upset. "Sedalia and Kilgore have been rivals for years! You know that. Our football team and theirs have had a feud going since we were in school!"

"I know it, but the fact is, Kilgore looks pretty much like Sedalia, and they haven't been painting all their storefronts like we have. Greenberg likes that. I heard him say that he's of a mind to pull out." That wasn't exactly the truth, but Buford had learned from Whit Rodgers that Greenberg had gotten wind of the flower beds and had been trying to get the merchants to talk some sense into the mayor. Whit had said he figured it was between Greenberg and the mayor to work all that out, and neither he nor any of the other merchants wanted any part of the feud. Buford, on the other hand, could see that someone with good sense needed to do something. He wasn't certain his scheme would work, but he'd thought it was worth a try.

"He can't pull out! We have a contract!"

"Yep, but he may do it anyway."

Graham glared at the concrete, as if it were somehow responsible for the conflict. "What would we tell the town if that happened?"

Buford scratched his stomach as he thought. "I don't rightly know what you'll tell 'em."

Graham glared at him. "This movie business has been more trouble than it's worth, if you ask me. If it wasn't for the publicity, I'd let them move on." He scratched his head. "I can't disappoint the folks, though."

Buford nodded. He saw no point in telling Graham that in the movie script the town was called "Cane's Landing." The only place Sedalia would be mentioned by name would be in the credits. Birdine and Miss Nelly wanted to be in this movie, so Buford didn't want to mess that up.

"Shoot," Graham said in disgust. "This sidewalk's got cracks all over it. Look there. Ironweed's growing through in front of Buttons and Bows."

"Yep." Buford had known Graham long enough to know that if the mayor was far enough along in his thinking to say "shoot," he was about at the end of the argument. He waited patiently for the time to come.

"I guess there's no way to fix it up," Graham said with another glare at the sidewalk.

"We can do it right after they pack up and leave. There'll be plenty of time before the movie comes out. Think how surprised and pleased the tourists will be when they arrive and find petunias and moss roses instead of cracks."

Graham's face brightened. "I guess that'd be good enough, wouldn't it? After all, the tourists will come back year after year if they like it here."

Buford could see no reason in the world why a tourist would set foot in Sedalia even the first time, but he nodded. He and Birdine and Miss Nelly had emptied more than one coffeepot while trying to figure out why Graham thought this would draw tourists to Sedalia. They had come to the conclusion that either they didn't understand the first thing about tourism or Graham didn't have sense enough to scratch where he itched.

Graham made a few important-sounding grunts, then moved away down the sidewalk in the direction of the courthouse. Buford watched him for a few seconds, then got into his truck and drove to the grocery store parking lot and stopped next to the car Greenberg had rented. He got out of his truck, went around back and let down his tailgate to make a seat, and waited. He didn't have to wait long.

"Hidy," he said in greeting as Greenberg approached.

"Buford," Greenberg said in reply. He went past and unlocked the door of his car.

Buford watched in amusement. He never could understand why somebody would lock up a car when there wasn't a single thing in it to steal. "You don't know it, but you owe me a thank-you."

"I beg your pardon?"

"Harry Graham was about to dig up the sidewalks downtown." He watched the blood rise in Greenberg's face. A vein in the director's forehead popped up and began to throb, then his eyes glazed over.

"Mayor Graham is doing what? I'll kill him! I'll sue!"

Buford waited to see if the director would faint dead away, but instead the man tossed the sack of groceries into the car and stomped around to the back of the truck where Buford was sitting.

"I said he was fixing to bring in a backhoe and dig up the sidewalk and put in flower beds. Petunias and moss roses, to be exact. But he ain't doing nothing now."

"Why did he stop?"

"I reckon it was 'cause of what I told him," Buford said. "If he asks you, tell him you're going to move everything to Kilgore if he keeps interfering."

"What's Kilgore? What in the hell are you talking about?"

"It don't matter. All I'm saying is that I told Harry that you may change locations, and that kept him from doing something else stupid. If he says anything to you, just tell him the same as I did."

Greenberg took his handkerchief from his pocket and wiped his forehead. "I never saw anything like this town."

"We never had no movie shot here before, either. We're still learning how to do it and all." Buford examined a screwdriver that had somehow wound up in the back of the truck. "I've been wondering where this went." He put it in the pocket of his pants.

Greenberg stared at him. "Tell me about this Kilgore place."

Buford shook his head. "You don't want to know about that. Of course, it's just my opinion, but if you think we're crazy here, you never saw them. Besides, it'd mean moving all your people, and they're just getting settled in good."

"True." Greenberg sighed. "Will you do me a favor? If that...mayor...gets any other wild ideas, will you come tell me before he has a chance to mess up something else?"

"Sure as shooting."

Greenberg gave him a look as if he still didn't quite comprehend it all and went back to his car.

Buford was chuckling as he slid off the tailgate and slammed it shut. As Greenberg left rubber in the parking lot in his haste to get to wherever he was going, Buford grinned. He hadn't had this much fun since the time Old Man Mobley's milk cow was penned inside the bank by teenage pranksters. He was glad the summer was only just beginning.

# CHAPTER NINE

MICA KNEW she was wrong to care so much for Kyle, but it was as if her thoughts couldn't be parted from him. To give her mind a new road to take, she picked up her copy of the revised shooting script and stretched out on her couch to read. Two days before, she had memorized her lines for the scene to be filmed next, but had discovered that the writers were constantly rewriting the script and she never knew when her lines might be changed at the last minute. The script fell open to a scene between Kyle and her. Mica touched his character's name on the page. She could almost hear him saying the words, and she knew how his eyes would smile into hers and how his hair might ruffle in a breeze. Although they had met only weeks ago, she knew his smallest movements, the exact timbre of his voice, the sound of his laughter.

She let the script drop to the floor and rubbed her eyes. She knew it was a mistake to care so much for Kyle, but she couldn't stop. Why was it that he was always on her mind? The answer was obvious. No one else was quite like Kyle Spensor.

At the sound of the doorbell, Mica sighed. Hoping it wasn't Norma Mobley wanting to do another inspection of her property, Mica went to the door. She wasn't sure she could bear the woman's innumerable questions and snooping today.

To Mica's surprise, it was Kyle on her doorstep. For a minute she didn't know what to say. "Kyle," she said at last.

"Hello." She tried in vain to quell the excited flurry in her stomach. "I didn't expect to see you today." She'd invited him for supper on Saturday, but this was Friday. "I'm not supposed to be on the set, am I? Did I misread the schedule?"

"Not that I'm aware of. I have the day off, too."

"About the things I said the other morning at your house, I'm really sorry. I—"

"No, no. No need to apologize. I was probably out of line. I'd rather we forget all about that." He looked around as if he had come to admire the view.

"Then why did you come?"

"I wanted to see you. Am I interrupting something?"

"No. No, of course not." A wave of relief washed over her. She'd been anxious about whether his feelings toward her had changed as a result of their spat. Realizing she hadn't invited him in, she quickly stepped aside as she opened the door wider and motioned for him to enter.

She preceded him into the living room. "I see you've been studying your lines," he observed.

She picked up the script and put it on the coffee table. "I wanted to be prepared for tomorrow's shooting."

"It's a shame Shelley isn't that professional."

Mica laughed. "As if I'm more professional than Shelley Doyle. Right."

"You know she seldom knows her lines until the third or fourth take. You, on the other hand, are always prepared. I admire that."

"Thanks," she said as she looked into his eyes to be sure his compliment was sincere. It was. "Coffee?"

"No, thanks."

"I don't see how you stand up to the grind. I'm exhausted at the end of the day."

"So you have no aspirations to be a star?" He smiled, but he seemed to be paying close attention to her answer.

"I love being in this movie. At times I can still scarcely believe it. But no..Real life for me is teaching twelfth-grade English at Sedalia High School."

He sat beside her on the couch, and unexpectedly, she became keenly aware of his nearness. The scent of his cologne brought to mind the passionate kiss they'd shared, and unwittingly she longed for another—and much more, as well. The sound of his voice broke her reverie, and she looked away so he wouldn't see the flush that was rising in her cheeks. "You don't fit my image of an English teacher. My tutors were all older than a rock and about as interesting. I don't know if I was a difficult student or what, but learning was hard for me when I was a kid."

Surprised by his admission, she turned back to him and said, "That's too bad. It probably would have been easier if your tutors had made it fun for you."

"I'm sure you're right. To me, the acting was fun, and I learned a lot about this business at an early age. It was also a real trip as a kid to be earning more money than most adults. Fortunately, my mother was more honest than some and put the money into a savings account for me. She'd give me a weekly allowance, but she never let me squander any of it. I was friends with child stars whose families relied entirely on them for financial support and who never saw a dime of their own money."

Again, Mica was struck at how dissimilar their childhoods had been. "Didn't you ever play?"

"Of course I did. I played practically all over the world, and my friends were—and most still are—household names." He leaned closer. "What were your school days like?"

"Oases," she replied before she thought. "I mean, they were good. I've always enjoyed the experience of learning. I love to read."

"I can't imagine you as poor. You're so confident."

"I am now. But I was painfully shy in school. I was always a little surprised that Carrie Graham was my friend. Her father was mayor then, too, and my parents never knew what to make of that." She paused as she thought of Carrie. "Her marriage to Marvin and their divorce changed her. We're still friends, of course, but she's different."

"Everything changes." He laid his arm along the back of the couch and touched his fingertips to her hair.

Mica felt the caress as if her hair were laced with nerves. "Not around here," she said in an effort to hide her response to his touch. "That's part of the problem with teaching here."

"Oh?"

"For as long as anyone can remember, the required reading for twelfth-grade English classes has been *The Catcher In the Rye*, *Huckleberry Finn* and *The Grapes of Wrath*. Not that those aren't great books—they are! But so are some others."

Kyle's fingertips brushed the back of her neck, and she felt it throughout her soul. She talked faster. "I think it's important to change things around from time to time. I've told the school board I want a change in my curriculum for next year. I want my students to read *The Mayor of Casterbridge* and *Tom Jones*. And something more recent, like *Gone With the Wind*. Unfortunately, they're balking."

"I don't see anything wrong with those books." His voice was soft and gentle.

Mica swallowed the lump in her throat and refused to look at him. Her pulse skipped, and she thought he must surely be able to tell that his nearness was affecting her. She made a greater effort to appear normal. "They said *The Mayor of Casterbridge* was unsuitable because it's nothing but a story about a city official who sold his family, and they said *Gone With the Wind* is racist! And that *Tom Jones* is too difficult for a high school senior to comprehend!"

"I read it when I was younger than that."

She looked at him. "You did?"

"I like to read, too. Did you think I never tackled anything more difficult than scripts?"

"I didn't know. You said that learning was difficult for you."

"Learning what my tutors were trying to teach me was. Maybe that was just stubbornness on my part."

"There's so little I know about you."

"I guess that's true. I keep forgetting that."

Mica forced herself to look away. "I've been thinking of offering the board a compromise. Maybe *Pride and Prejudice, Wuthering Heights* and *Far From the Madding Crowd,* but I expect they'll balk at those, too, because none of them is by an American author."

He shook his head in commiseration.

"But I haven't given up. I suppose they'd find something objectionable about any book other than the ones that have been taught in that class for aeons. Even *Huckleberry Finn* has been under the gun lately in some places. I tried to argue that by changing the books from year to year, the students wouldn't be tempted to spend time looking for copies of book tests from years past to study and instead might read the books themselves. They said standardized book tests made a teacher's job easier, and changing just for the sake of changing was ridiculous."

"Seems a bit closed minded."

"More than a bit. I think it's the boards' creed." She sighed as he moved his hand away. "I sound as if I'm not satisfied with my job, but that's not it. I only want more flexibility. I can understand not being able to teach just anything that pops into my head, but I feel teachers deserve more leeway."

"I agree. Especially teachers who are experienced, as you are."

"I may have six years behind me, but as I said before, only two of them have been here in Sedalia. I'm just glad the probationary period for me is over. Until my renewal contract was signed at the end of May, the school board could have fired me for almost any reason. Now, finally, my job is more secure. It's never guaranteed, but the justification for firing a teacher or not renewing a teacher's annual contract after the probationary period must comply with state law, not just the school system's whim."

"That's good, then, that your job is more secure." His voice wavered, as if he wasn't being completely truthful about his feelings.

"I had to bite my tongue, but I managed to hold off my request for a curriculum change until they signed my contract. They're not happy that I asked for a change, but now they can't dismiss me as a 'troublemaker' or for being 'disruptive of the system.' They may not grant my request this time, but I'll bring it up again soon and stay after them until they give in. I have good ideas for improvements, and I'm sure they'll recognize that one of these days and be glad I'm teaching here."

Kyle put his forefinger under her chin and gently drew her face around so she met his eyes. "Even with all the difficulty you're having with this school board, you'd rather stay here and fight it out with them than leave?"

Mica made herself laugh. "I have no intention of leaving here. This is my home. You asked me that once before. Is there more to your question than you're saying?"

He looked as if he wanted to explain, but after a moment, he said, "I've just never known many people with such dedication. I admire that."

Mica was puzzled by the tone with which he'd delivered the compliment. "Thanks. You seem to be pretty dedicated to your career, too."

Behind his pleasant smile, Mica thought she could see an expression of regret.

"Do you want to go for a walk?" he asked.

She didn't particularly want to, but she nodded. She was finding him too irresistible in the intimacy of her house. "I'll get my keys."

She put her house key in her jeans' pocket and made sure the door locked behind her. "So far Mrs. Mobley hasn't mentioned the change in locks," she said as she walked with him down the sidewalk. "Maybe she hasn't noticed."

"More likely she was aware that she had no right to come in while you weren't home and knows not to force the issue." He glanced up and down the street as they crossed. "I've enjoyed being here in Sedalia this summer."

"Have you? Summer is my least favorite season. It gets so hot here."

"How are the winters?"

"We see snow occasionally, but for the most part the winters tend to be mild. We're far enough north to get fall colors and far enough south to have an early spring. It's just about perfect here if you ask me." She smiled. "Of course, I'm prejudiced. Carrie doesn't agree at all. She would love to move away." She sobered as she remembered her last conversation with Carrie.

"Would she love to move to Hollywood?"

"How did you know?"

"She mentioned it to me. She was asking me how hard it would be for her to get a part in another picture after having been in this one. I'm afraid I had to burst her bubble. Acting is a difficult profession to break into, even with *The Last Wildcat* under your belt."

"I'm glad you told her that. I don't know what she's thinking of. She's in love with a man here who loves her and wants to marry her, and she's talking about throwing all that away for a chance to be in another movie."

"I gather you wouldn't be so fickle with a man who loved you?"

Mica gazed down the familiar street, intentionally avoiding looking at Kyle. "No, I wouldn't. Not if I loved him in return." She was silent for a moment as she wondered what it would be like to be loved by Kyle. Realizing the tangent her thoughts had taken, she said, "Jake really does love Carrie, and I thought she loved him."

"Sometimes people don't realize what they have until they lose it."

She looked up at him. "Is that personal experience talking or mere observation?"

"I've seen it happen more than once."

She remembered he was divorced and wondered if he was referring to his ex-wife. She didn't ask. Mica didn't want to hear Kyle admit he was still mourning the loss of Tamara Nolan.

As if he had been reading her thoughts and knew he needed to clarify what he had meant, he said, "Tamara called me after her divorce. She said she was through with the man she left me for and wanted to know if she could come back." After a moment's pause, he added, "That sounds like a country-and-western song, doesn't it? I wonder if I could set that to music."

"What did you tell her?"

"I said no."

"Just like that? Just 'no'?"

"Somewhere during the five years we were married, the love between us died—if it had been love in the beginning. I told her I wished her the best in life, but I also assured her I wasn't willing to try again. She hung up on me."

"How sad."

"That she hung up on me?"

"No. I meant it was sad that the love died."

"Under the circumstances it was inevitable." He glanced at her but made no further comment. After a few steps he said, "Do you hear what I hear?"

Mica listened. "All I hear is the bell on the ice-cream truck."

"Exactly. There it is," he said, pointing to the far end of the block. "I'll race you." Without waiting to see if she would accept his challenge, he took off running.

"Hey, no fair." She ran after him, but she was no match for his long stride. He reached the truck first and was already buying ice cream for the two of them by the time she got there.

"I hope you like chocolate," he said as he handed her the ice cream on a stick. "It's the flavor *du jour.*"

"As if there possibly could be another flavor." She accepted the ice cream and began to peel the paper away. "I haven't done this since I was a child."

"I've never done it except in movies," he said with a laugh. "The real thing is better."

They walked along eating the ice cream quickly before it melted in the heat. Mica found even his silence to be companionable. She risked letting herself pretend he wasn't only here for a few more weeks and that she could allow herself to fall in love with him. It was all too easy to see how she could. Mica wasn't sure she wasn't in love already.

"I got an interesting phone call this morning," he said. "It was from someone who called himself Brother Malcolm Stout."

Mica almost choked on her ice cream. Swallowing quickly, she said, "Brother Malcolm called you?"

"It was more of a warning, actually. One of those 'get out of town or else' calls."

"Do you get calls like that often? How can you be so calm about it?"

"Easy. I'm acting." He grinned at her and winked. "I phoned Greenberg and reported it. He says he'll take care of it."

"I can't believe he actually called you and told you to get out of town!"

"His exact words were 'Get out of town and stop corrupting our young people with your film from Satan.' I don't know who his writer is, but his script needs work. First of all, there is no one under the age of twenty-one in this movie unless you include the kids in the crowd scenes, none of whom has a speaking part, and second, we aren't making a movie that's in the least questionable. It'll have a G rating and is aimed at the family market. He hasn't done his homework."

"How can you be so calm about it? I'd be terribly upset. I *am* terribly upset."

Kyle shook his head. "We get cranks from time to time. This isn't as bad as the incident in Seattle when a man called to say he had planted a bomb in my room."

"How awful! How can someone say a thing like that?"

"It was true. He had confused me with Mark Spenser, who does the political-intrigue movies. The bomb didn't go off, however, and no harm was done."

"I don't see how you can be so easygoing about things like this. Of course Brother Malcolm won't plant a bomb in your room, but he could cause some unpleasantness."

"We won't be here much longer and then he'll calm down."

Somehow that didn't make her feel any better, and her ice cream lost its flavor as she thought how quickly the time was passing. They turned down a quiet street, one of Mica's favorites, which was lined with crepe myrtles in varying shades, the result of a neighborhood beautification project from several years back.

"This is beautiful," Kyle said. "Is it always this quiet around here?"

"Are you kidding? This is turmoil for Sedalia. Sometimes the quiet is almost too much, even if I do love this town. There's not much to do here, but I know practically everyone, and there are few surprises."

Suddenly Kyle stopped and shaded his eyes from the midafternoon sun as he stared at a house with a For Sale sign in the yard. The house was typical of the neighborhood, neat and trim, sitting behind a beautifully landscaped lawn. Crepe myrtles, dogwoods and redbud trees surrounded it, but the dominant feature was a huge oak that hovered protectively over the front yard. "This is a great house! It's got both character and charm."

"The owner's been transferred to a branch of his company in Chicago. I know his wife quite well. They hated to leave, but it was go or switch jobs."

"I wouldn't have wanted to have to make that decision."

"Me, neither. If I could afford it, I'd buy it." She gazed at the house. "You should see it in the spring when the other trees are in flower. It's one of the prettiest houses in Sedalia. I'm afraid it may be for sale for quite a while, though."

"Overpriced?"

"No. Not many people move here. The housing market is slow. The ones who already live here have their own houses already, and we don't do much moving from house to house around here. It hasn't been vacant long, but I suspect it will be."

"That's a pity." He narrowed his eyes. "Houses go to pieces if they aren't lived in."

"I know. Why do you suppose that is?"

He grinned and said in a fair imitation of Bela Lugosi, "They are the living dead. They feed on their occupants while they sleep."

Mica laughed. "That's terrible."

"Now you know why they always cast me in comedy roles."

She matched her steps to his. "I haven't said the words before, but I want you to know I really enjoy spending my time with you."

He reached out and took her hand; it fit perfectly into his. With a charming smile, he said, "I already know that. It shows."

Mica felt the warmth of his smile all the way through her soul. His hand was warm and strong, and he held hers firmly, as if he was constantly aware of her skin against his. She regretted turning the next corner and seeing her house ahead. She wished the walk could go on forever.

"What do your parents think about you being in a movie?" he asked as they crossed her lawn and mounted her porch steps.

"They can't believe it. I talked to Mom last night, and she's fascinated about the movie being shot here. They were wishing they could come down to see it for themselves, but Dad's got a bad back and it hurts him to ride in the car for more than a few minutes at a time."

"Sounds like you miss them. I miss having a family, too. A real one, that is. Now that Mother is dead, I don't have any family ties." He grinned down at her and said in jest, "I'm all alone except for a hundred of my closest friends, as they say in Tinsel Town."

"I suspect you have more friends than that." She opened the door. "Would you like to stay for supper? I know this is a day early, but I bought the hamburger meat this morning. If you'd rather wait until tomorrow night as we'd planned, that would be all right with me."

"Tonight's fine," he said, then as his grin broadened, he added, "As long as you promise to burn them."

"For you? Anything."

"Good. That means you'll let me help. All hamburgers cooked on a grill have to be burned in at least one spot or they aren't properly prepared."

"I thought it was supposed to be sophisticated to eat meat half-raw," she teased. "You're the only one I know who likes it the way I do."

"Save the raw for sushi. If it doesn't rock on the plate, it's not done."

Kyle followed her into the kitchen and took the hamburger meat from her as she closed the refrigerator door. "This looks like more than we'll need."

"That's one of the tricks I've learned about living alone. I seldom want to cook just for myself, so when I do, I cook enough for at least two meals and eat leftovers the next day or freeze the food for later."

"Homemade TV dinners. What'll they think of next?"

She handed him a box of matches and asked him to go out back and light the gas grill. As she was gathering up the other ingredients for their meal, she glanced out the kitchen window. Kyle was lighting the burner on the grill, and she was suddenly moved by how domestic he looked. A tenderness stole over her and her eyes grew misty.

By the time she had the lettuce and tomatoes ready, Kyle had succeeded in his mission and had taken over the job of cooking the meat. She sat on the back porch steps, watching Kyle cook.

Kyle appeared deep in thought. Glancing over at her as he turned the meat, he said, "I'm curious about something you said a while back. What is it about teaching that makes it so special for you?"

"I've always liked kids, especially teenagers. I know they can be difficult, but I like working with them."

"I don't think I'd be a good teacher. I'd be forever going off on tangents."

"What makes you think I don't? Kids learn best when they stay alert. I like to surprise them and make them think." She paused. "As I said earlier, the school board is a problem, though. And not just for me. It isn't written down anywhere, but the board has made it clear to the teachers that they are not welcome at board meetings. Unless they have been called to appear before the board. If I were on the board, I'd want teachers there."

"I'd always assumed that teachers might be required to attend the meetings."

"Just the opposite. We never know what decisions are being made about our careers until they're carved in stone. I don't know if it's like this in all small towns, but it wasn't that way in Dallas, and I think it's wrong. After all, how can we attract qualified people to teach if they are poorly paid and treated as menials?" She smiled. "Sorry. You hit a raw nerve."

"It's good to see someone who cares so much."

Mica brought out the buns and the lettuce and tomatoes, and they ate at the picnic table under the shade of her pecan tree. Mica thought how pleasant it was to do such simple things with Kyle. She couldn't remember an afternoon she had enjoyed more.

After clearing away the meal, they sat outside at the picnic table, talking about everything and nothing until the shadows began to lengthen. "You lead an exciting life," she said. "Teaching is fulfilling, but no one could call it 'exciting.'"

Kyle reached across the table and took her hand and stroked it with his thumb. "You know, I've spent so many years being everyone else but me, I sometimes wonder who I am."

She tried to keep her voice light, even though his caress was making her pulse race. "I may not know much about you, but I know who you are. You're Kyle Spensor, one of Hollywood's finest actors.''

He smiled, but his eyes were touched with sadness. "Can't you ever forget that part of me?"

For a moment, she was silent; then, with her voice low and laced with tenderness, she said, "Seriously, Kyle, when we're together like this, I have to remind myself that you don't belong here and that you won't stay, that in a few short weeks you'll be gone and I'll never see you again." Although she'd tried to keep her voice from breaking, it had quivered.

Kyle met her eyes, but he didn't answer. His hands cradled hers with gentle strength, and he studied her face as if he was memorizing her features. "Leaving Sedalia is going to be very hard for me," he said at last.

Mica was too choked up with emotion to respond.

As the sun dropped lower, they stood and walked to the gate. "It's about time for me to go," he said with reluctance. He looked at the red-and-gold sky as if he wished he could slow the sun's progress so the time for him to go would never come.

"You don't have to leave this early."

"No, but I should." As he gazed down at her, she saw how tempted he was to stay. He reached out and touched her cheek with the backs of his fingers. "I always meet people on location, but I don't have a woman in every town like some men in this business. I usually stay pretty much to myself so I don't have any entanglements."

"Am I entangling you?"

He nodded. "I'd be lying if I denied it. You aren't like anyone I've ever met before."

He stepped nearer and she swayed into his embrace, her breasts mounding against the firm wall of his chest. Their bodies fit together perfectly. When he put his fingers under her chin and tilted her face up for his kiss, it seemed to Mica to be the most natural thing in the world. His warm, moist lips claimed hers, and as before, she found herself losing track of time. The world seemed to center in his kiss and the desire he instilled in her. She wanted nothing more than to feel his flesh against hers, to make love to him with reckless abandon. He was drinking in the essence of her as a woman, and she wanted it to continue forever.

After the longest, most sensual kiss she'd ever experienced, Kyle slowly drew back and gazed silently down at her. His hazel eyes searched her face as if she was a treasure he had discovered. Mica had so much she wanted to say to him that she couldn't say anything at all.

"Mica, I must go," he said, his voice husky with his own pent-up passion. "It wouldn't be right for me to stay."

Mica wanted to tell him to stay, to somehow convince him that it didn't matter that he thought it wouldn't be right, but instead she said nothing.

Kyle stepped back and unlatched the gate. "I'll see you on the set tomorrow."

"Goodbye."

He shook his head. "I don't want there to be any goodbyes between us."

She watched him go, and it was as if he was taking a part of her with him. Was it possible—this thing that was happening between them? How could they have any future together? Would it have been worse if he had stayed and they had made love? She didn't think it could possibly be worse for her. But what about him? Only Kyle could answer that— and apparently he had. She watched him walk away until he was out of sight, and only then did she turn and go into the house.

WHEN MICA SAW Carrie coming toward her across the lot, she slowed her steps. Since their argument the week before, they hadn't spoken. Mica had kept her distance, not wanting to risk saying or doing anything else that might push Carrie toward Zane or farther away from her. She hoped Carrie was in a conciliatory mood, but all she could tell from her face was that Carrie didn't appear still angry. "Hello," she said as Carrie drew near.

"Hi." Carrie seemed equally apprehensive about talking.

"Looks like the rain may hold off until the day's shooting is over."

Carrie glanced up at the gray sky. "Maybe. I hope so."

"I'd hate to see the river of starch that would wash out of these skirts," Mica said with an attempt at lightening the strain.

Carrie smiled. "No kidding." She glanced away and back again. "Look, I was way out of line with what I said about you trying to keep Zane and Kyle all for yourself."

"I'd never do that, and I'm sorry I gave you that impression. I'm sorry we had words."

Carrie nodded but still avoided eye contact. "Me, too. I'm so confused lately."

To make conversation, Mica said, "I heard that Diane King's supposed to get here any day now. What do you think she'll be like?"

"She couldn't be worse than Shelley. She never says a civil word to me off camera."

"I guess she's insecure," Mica said, automatically offering a reason to excuse Shelley's ugly behavior. Although Mica always tried to see people in a positive light, she wasn't blind to reality. With a smile, she added, "Or maybe she's a malicious, spiteful, domineering egotist."

"I'm betting on the second."

Laughing, they walked toward the costume trailer where they would change for the next scene. Mica knew they were both pretending that everything between them was back to normal. She prayed that, in time, it would be. Hoping for another safe subject, Mica asked, "How is Jake? I haven't seen him in days."

"He's all right," Carrie responded, then fell silent for a moment as she looked away. With a hint of sadness in her eyes, she said, "But things between us are kind of shaky. Jake's wanting me to spend all my spare time with him. He's tried to bring up the subject of marriage, but I've told him I'm not ready for anything like that. You know how I feel about marriage. But he keeps pushing."

"Yeah, I know." Mica wanted to sing Jake's praises to Carrie, since she knew both of them and felt he'd be good for her. But because her truce with Carrie was still too new, she said nothing.

Carrie continued. "I don't want to do anything I might regret years from now. If I did marry Jake, wouldn't I always wonder if I could have made it in the movies?"

Mica hedged the question. "Or it could be the other way around."

Carrie was silent for several steps. "Maybe all this confusion means I don't love Jake and never did. I thought I loved Marvin when I married him, but it didn't take long for me to realized I'd made a mistake. It was a while, though, before I was willing to accept it. I was trying to figure out how to leave him, when he found someone else and left me first."

Mica wisely said nothing more. She knew how hurt Carrie had been over Marvin's unfaithfulness.

"Maybe I'm just not cut out for marriage."

"You know better than that. You just weren't suited to be Marvin's doormat."

Carrie pointed to where the cameramen were setting up for the next scene. "Can you look over there and honestly say you don't feel a rush of excitement about all that?"

"Of course I do. Being in this movie is the most exciting thing that's ever happened to me. But it's not my real life. I wouldn't want it to be. Next fall, I want to be in front of a new class of students, inspiring them to see a bigger world than Sedalia. If I can convince one student to reach for his full potential, it'll be worth it."

"But what about you? Don't you want to be a part of that bigger world? I do. Maybe you've reached your full potential, but I haven't."

Mica glanced at her. "Are you saying you plan to leave here when the cameras do?"

"Maybe. I don't know."

Mica sighed. She could no longer refrain from speaking her mind. "You'd better level with Jake. He deserves to know."

"I know it, but it's not easy."

"No, it wouldn't be. He really loves you."

"In a way, I wish he didn't," Carrie admitted. "I don't want to hurt him. I really don't."

"We're running out of time to talk now, but if you need to talk more—or if Jake does—I'm here for you both."

"Thanks, Mica. I'll keep that in mind." They walked in silence the remaining distance to the trailer.


CARRIE LEANED against the inside of the passenger door of Jake's car as she stared moodily out at the night. She hated to argue with Jake, but that seemed to be all they did lately.

He was leaning against the opposite door, his muscled forearm resting on the steering wheel. "You're talking nonsense." He was tense, but he was trying to hide it.

"Why is it nonsense for me to want to make something of myself?" she snapped.

"I'm not saying I don't want you to make something of yourself. I'm saying that it's foolish for you to try to become a movie star."

"I never thought you'd be the type to try to hold me back. I really expected more of you."

Jake gripped the wheel as if he would like to break it in half. "Carrie, be sensible. You're thirty years old."

"That's not exactly over the hill," she said in stinging tones.

"It is out there. You'd have what, maybe ten to twelve years of your prime? Then what would happen? I've read enough to know there are more out-of-work actors there than stars, and I'll bet most of them can sing and dance as well as act!"

"Go on! Put me down. Would you like to kick me, as well?"

"Carrie, somebody's got to talk some sense into you. What did your parents say about this?"

"Mother is all for it. Daddy isn't."

"And of those two, who would you say has the most common sense?"

"Jake Farrell! Don't you dare talk about my mother like that!"

"I like your mother just fine. I always have. But in a case like this, you ought to listen to your father."

"I'm a grown woman, Jake. I can make my own decisions without advice from anyone."

"Okay, then. What's it going to be? Hollywood or me?"

"I haven't decided yet. I need time to think. I don't want to rush into anything."

"Rush?" He stared at her in disbelief.

"Besides, it doesn't have to be a choice, does it?"

"I can't leave my store and go to Hollywood with you."

"You wouldn't have to go. We could—"

"Wait a minute, Carrie. You want me to put my life on hold for a few years while you go traipsing off to Hollywood? That's what you're saying, isn't it? What do you take me for?"

"Why are you putting all this pressure on me? I haven't decided for sure that I'm going. It's just an idea. A dream."

Jake turned to her and put his arm along the back of the seat behind her. "Listen, Carrie, I love you. I've loved you for years. When I heard you and Marvin were getting a divorce, all I could think of was that I'd have a chance with you. Now you're saying you could leave me behind while you try to get into movies. I don't know what to think. Do you love me?"

She looked down at her hands, clasped in her lap. "I'm all confused, Jake. I think I'd better go home. I need to think."

"Does that mean you don't love me?"

"Jake, you're not giving me a chance."

"What about you?"

Carrie closed her eyes and bit her upper lip, trying to control her mounting anger.

Impatiently Jake asked, "Well?"

Carrie's eyes sprang open and she glared at Jake. "All right! I've made a decision. All my life I've done what other people thought I should do. This time I'm doing what I want to do." Before she could change her mind, Carrie jerked open the car door and hurried away into the night.

# CHAPTER TEN

"REPENT!" The loudspeaker blared from atop the car rolling slowly down the street. "Repent and turn away from Satan. Send the evildoers among us back to Hollywood where they came from."

Mica and the others on the set faltered in their lines. "Cut!" Greenberg shouted. "Who the hell is that?"

The car continued down the street at a snail's pace, its speaker blasting out the gospel according to Brother Malcolm Stout. At the end of the block, the car turned the corner and the sound faded.

"All right, everybody, back in place," Greenberg said. "Let's try it again."

Mica turned back to Kyle, and as the camera started rolling again, she tried to smile convincingly as she delivered her lines. Kyle was Ryan Colby as he responded, making words that sounded ordinary on paper come out humorous. Mica wondered how he could so unerringly do that. If she had been reading the same words, she had a feeling they would have fallen flat. Kyle gave them more depth than the writer probably had intended. The most difficult part of her job these days was to pretend to be Angie, who had only a passing interest in Ryan.

The muffled sound of Brother Malcolm's loudspeaker grew louder as his car retraced the path it had taken only moments before.

"Cut!" Greenberg shouted again. He turned and glared at the offending car. "Where the hell is that sheriff?"

His assistant looked confused. "The sheriff?"

"He swore to me there would be police cars out to prevent an interruption of our work."

"I think you want the chief of police, not the sheriff," the assistant said doubtfully.

"Whoever the hell I mean, get him!"

The assistant ran to obey. Mica turned to Kyle and said, "We have police protection these days?"

Kyle nodded. "Harve told me that there have been a number of threats from Brother Malcolm concerning the various ways he intends to prevent the movie from being made."

"He can't do that—can he?"

"Not legally. I'm surprised the chief of police hasn't done more to stop him."

"I'm not. Nothing ever happens around here that requires police protection. He probably didn't take the threats seriously."

Kyle smiled at her. "You look pretty today."

Mica felt pleasure wash over her. "It's the makeup lady. She can work wonders."

"Makeup has nothing to do with it."

"Well, aren't we full of compliments today?" Shelly commented as she came to stand beside Kyle. She glared at Mica before turning to Kyle. "Could you help me with something? I'm not sure the camera is at just the right angle."

"I'm not a cameraman," Kyle said.

Mica could tell Shelley was trying to take Kyle's attention away from her. She considered remaining where she was, but she knew from experience it was easier to work with Shelley if Shelley was appeased. Yielding to the pressure, she walked away and took refuge from the sun under the shade of a nearby pecan tree.

Zane discovered her almost at once. "Hello there," he said.

"Hi. Looks like it's going to be a hot one." She wished the shots could be accomplished inside where there was air-conditioning.

"In more ways than one." Zane leaned against the tree trunk as though he were posing for a publicity still. "When are you coming back to see me?"

"I'm not."

Zane looked frankly amazed. "What do you mean? I'm asking you out."

"Oh? I was under the impression you were asking me in. I'm not that naive."

"I have no idea what you're talking about. Didn't you have fun the other night?"

"I have to go over my lines." She gave him a smile of cool dismissal. He didn't take the hint.

"You know what I think? I think you'd like to come by my place, but you're afraid I'm not serious about the invitation."

"You know what I think? I think you're wrong." Mica looked back to where Kyle was talking to Shelley and pointing at a camera. Shelley was all but draping herself over his arm. Mica wanted to tell the woman to keep her hands off Kyle, even though she knew she had no right to feel so proprietary toward Kyle. He wasn't and never could be hers.

Zane grinned. "I see you're still playing hard—"

Mica interrupted him, saying through clenched teeth, "Not hard to get. Impossible. I'm not interested in playing your game."

The stunned expression on his face was gratifying. "Who do you think you are?" he demanded before he thought. Then his professional grin snapped back in place. "Don't kid me. I'm really excited by you. I've even thought about asking you to go back to Hollywood with me.''

Mica had never felt so exasperated. "Zane, I've heard some unbelievable lines in my life, but that one takes the cake. You're no more seriously interested in me than you are in this tree. Give it up." She turned and walked away.

Carrie had been standing nearby, and once Mica had stepped away from Zane, she moved in to take her place. Not giving any indication that she had overheard the exchange, she smiled and said, "Hi, Zane. How's it going?"

Zane was glaring after Mica, but when he found a woman beside him, his hormones took over. "Well, hello there."

"I hope I'm not interrupting you." Carrie smiled at him.

"I like being interrupted by pretty women. You know, you're doing an awfully good job." He was gratified to see she was hanging on to his words. "You ought to consider going into movies full-time."

"To be honest, I have considered that. Do you think I'd have a chance?"

"Are you kidding? You'd have them eating out of your hand!" He made his blue eyes wide and truthful in appearance. "Do you have an agent? No, you wouldn't, since you're a local and this is your first movie. Well, that won't be a problem."

"You could help me find an agent?" Carrie gasped. "You'd do that for me?"

"Sure, baby." Zane could do that easily enough. He had a list of agents, and it was only a matter of choosing a name and giving it to her. "Of course, now, you mustn't mention my name or say I sent you."

"No?"

"No, agents are funny about that. They like to think they discovered the talent on their own."

"That's odd. I'd have thought your name would carry more weight with them than a call from me, who they wouldn't know at all."

"Not know you? After *The Last Wildcat*? Why, agents will be searching for you." He watched her face light up, amazed that she was so gullible. He knew that she and Mica were good friends, and because Mica had become wary of him, he had assumed Carrie would have been wary, too. But he was wrong. She would be convinced the sky was green if he told her it was so. "I'll tell you what, you come over to my apartment tonight, and I'll help you decide which agent to go with."

Carrie's mouth dropped open. "To your apartment? Tonight?"

"Unless you have other plans." He pretended that the prospect that she might turn him down would cut him to the bone.

"No. At least, I don't have any plans that can't be changed. Okay, I'll be there. What time?"

"How about around eight? That should give us plenty of time to get to know each other."

"Eight o'clock. I'll be there."

He grinned as she hurried away. She hadn't even needed to ask what apartment he was staying in. That was more proof she wouldn't require much prompting to tumble into his bed. He looked back at Mica. He didn't care about her personally, but now she was a challenge. He was determined to have her, too, before he left Sedalia.

THAT EVENING, Carrie was as nervous as a schoolgirl as she rang Zane's doorbell and waited for him to answer. It was as if fate had stepped into her life at precisely the right moment. Only two evenings earlier, Jake had left her no choice but to break up with him and pursue a career as an actress. The next day had been hard for her, because once she was no longer angry with Jake, she began to miss him. It had been hard to set aside her emotions and focus her thoughts on how she could get the breaks she needed, but she had managed. And it had taken her three trys before she'd managed to initiate a conversation with Zane, but persistence was already paying off.

"Hello," he said as he swung the door open. "Come in."

Trying to appear more confident than she was, Carrie stepped into the apartment and looked around. Her first reaction was disappointment that the decor wasn't more lavish. But then she remembered that Zane was merely renting the place, and even though these were Sedalia's best apartments, they were nothing special.

"This place isn't much," Zane said as if he had read her thoughts. "Too bad you can't see my place in Hollywood."

"What's it like?"

He went to a cabinet and took out a liquor bottle. As he poured each of them a drink, he said, "It's Spanish. About the size of a football field." He handed her a generous glassful of bourbon.

Carrie took the glass and sipped it. She was reminded of Mica's visit here, but she quickly put that thought out of her head. "This is good."

"Only the best." He sat on the couch and patted the cushion beside him.

She sat down next to him and wondered what to say. Zane was even more impressive when alone in his apartment. "So," she said brightly. "What's your agent's name?"

"Hey, you cut straight to business, don't you?" he said with a laugh. "We have plenty of time to discuss that later." He put his hand on her nape and pulled her closer.

Carrie was surprised and more than a little flattered. Zane Morgan wanted to kiss her?

"Besides, I've been thinking, and I believe I know a better agent for you. Morey is fine for me—we're old friends and I look after my people—but you need a new face in the business. That way the two of you can rise to the top together.'' He leaned over and began kissing her neck.

A sigh escaped Carrie, and as she started to let her emotions take control, she was hit by a twinge of guilt. ''There's something you should know.''

''What's that?'' Zane's lips moved to her ear.

''Mica Haldane and I are really good friends, and I've been dating—''

''Baby,'' Zane said in his sexiest voice, instantly cutting off the rest of her sentence, ''don't you think I know all that?''

''You do?''

''I've been watching you for weeks. I figured anybody as sexy as you must be married. I saw you with that guy, and I said to myself, 'Damn! She's taken.' Then I asked around and found out he's just a boyfriend.''

''Who did you ask?''

''I forget. The point is, where I come from, if a woman isn't actually married, she's fair game.''

Carrie willed herself to move away, but couldn't budge since he was kissing her temple and hairline. ''But I don't want you to think that I'm...''

''Easy?'' Zane supplied. ''Baby, I'd never think that about you. I respect you too much.'' His hand slipped inside her blouse.

''You do?'' Carrie was finding it hard to think, let alone to speak.

''Look, we only go around once in life. Right? So we owe it to ourselves to make the most of it. I want you and you want me. What could be simpler?''

Carrie knew she should object, but Zane was kissing her eyelids and his fingers were setting her nerves to strumming. With a sigh, she put her arms around him and let him lay her down on the couch.

THE NEXT DAY at the grocery store, Mica saw Carrie in the produce department and went over to talk to her. "Hi," she said as she stopped to put a head of lettuce in her basket. "Would you like to come over later?"

Carrie looked startled, as if her mind had been far away. "Mica. I didn't see you come up."

"That's me. I move like a shadow. Is something wrong?"

"No. What could be wrong?" Carrie moved away and dropped some tomatoes into a plastic bag without examining them for bruises.

Mica tilted her head thoughtfully. Carrie wasn't making eye contact, and she was moving in jerky motions. "Hey, come on. This is me. Your best friend. Remember? I know you well enough to know something's bothering you."

Carrie frowned at her and glanced around to see if anyone was near. "I have no idea what you're talking about."

"Did you and Jake have another argument?"

"I don't see how that's any of your business," Carrie snapped.

Mica abruptly stopped examining the bananas. "I'm sorry. I didn't think that would upset you. I was only concerned."

"Look, Mica, we aren't high school buddies anymore. I don't have to confide every thought to you and have you analyze it for me." She tossed the sack of tomatoes into her grocery cart and stalked away.

Mica stared after her. She considered following Carrie and demanding to know what had upset her, but she refrained. If Carrie was as distressed as she sounded, confronting her in the grocery store wouldn't be the smartest move. The last time they had talked, Mica had gotten the impression that things between them had smoothed out. Evidently, that was not the case.

As Mica puzzled over what had just happened, it occurred to her that at first Carrie had looked worried; then, when Mica had asked about a possible argument with Jake, she had become angry and defensive. That was it! Carrie was angry about something to do with Jake. Suddenly Mica remembered that she had advised Carrie to let Jake know of her desire to move to Hollywood. She had assumed that levelheaded Jake would be able to convince her to give up the idea. As she finished her shopping and went home, she worried that she might have been wrong to suggest anything to Carrie.

She was putting away her groceries, when the doorbell rang. Mica hurried to answer it, hoping it would be Kyle, but instead it was Norma Mobley who was standing on her porch. "Oh, hello, Mrs. Mobley," Mica said, trying to hide the disappointment she felt. "Come in."

"Something's wrong with my key," Norma said, frowning at the door lock.

Mica had decided not to volunteer anything about having changed the locks, and so she didn't offer an explanation. She did, however, feel it necessary to be cordial to her landlady. "I was just putting some things away. Come on into the kitchen." She knew from experience that Mrs. Mobley expected to visit when she dropped by.

"You won't believe what's happened. I've never been so upset in all my life," the woman said as she dropped into a kitchen chair as if she planned to spend the rest of the day there. "Brother Malcolm has been fined for spreading the Lord's word to that bunch of Satan worshipers from California."

Instantly Mica changed her mind about placating the woman. "If you mean because he was broadcasting over that loudspeaker of his where we were filming, he deserved it. He was creating a nuisance." Mica stood on tiptoe to put the box of cereal on the top shelf of the pantry.

"A nuisance? Surely I didn't hear you right." Norma drew herself up and fixed her glare on Mica.

"Greenberg had asked that the street be kept quiet so we could do the scene while the sun angle was right. Brother Malcolm was driving up and down near the cameras and using that loudspeaker on his car to disrupt the filming. We couldn't block out the noise."

"Noise! You call spreading the Good Word noise?" Norma sounded shocked. "That's blasphemy!"

"The things he was saying about those of us involved in making the film were slanderous. Not everyone shares your religious views, and we shouldn't be subjected to hearing them if we choose not to. Especially when it disrupts work."

"Just listen to you! Your mama would be so put out with you if she could hear how you're talking. You ought to spend more time on your knees and less with that Hollywood trash."

Mica managed to control her temper, but it wasn't easy. "They aren't trash, Mrs. Mobley. Kyle Spensor is one of the nicest men I've ever met. Almost all the crew are friendly and easy to be around. They aren't any different from the rest of us."

"Speak for yourself. You won't catch me around people like that." She pushed at one of the grocery sacks. "Drinking and carousing around town! They'll all come to grief— you just wait and see. And to fine Brother Malcolm! I'll never vote for Harrison Graham for mayor ever again!"

"He had nothing to do with that incident."

"He's the one who talked the city council into hiring Everett Wilson as our police chief!"

"Chief Wilson was just doing his job. Now, if you'll excuse me, I really have a lot to do before I go to the set." She waited pointedly for Mrs. Mobley to go back to the front door and leave.

The large woman frowned at her, as if she had gotten the message but was considering staying anyway.

Mica simply waited, not giving the woman any option but to leave.

Finally Mrs. Mobley rose and strode to the door. "Mark my words. Those movie folks are sent by Satan! You'd best avoid them or you'll be blamed along with them! And you'll be sorry!"

"Goodbye, Mrs. Mobley."

Mica closed the front door behind her landlady as quickly as possible without hitting the woman's backside, and leaned against it with a deep sigh of relief. What had Mrs. Mobley meant by saying she would be sorry if she was to be blamed along with the movie company? She supposed the woman was referring to a judgment day, but she still felt uneasy. Brother Malcolm was making a lot of threats, and Mica wasn't as confident as Kyle that all the threats were idle. She decided this was a legitimate reason for her to find Kyle and talk to him.

Since Friday night of the week before, she'd had a lot of time to think—too much, actually—and she'd concluded that what Kyle had meant by it not being right for him to stay was that he didn't love her and couldn't stay and make love to her without feeling guilty. She had been crushed by the realization, but she blamed no one but herself. She had given herself over to the fantasy that he would return her love, despite the odds against their having any sort of lasting relationship. No one had forced her.

The second conclusion she had reached was that his not loving her had done nothing to diminish the love in her heart for him. Twice since that night, she had spent time with him on the set. They had talked privately but not intimately, as though they had mutually agreed it would be better that way. If her assumptions were correct, and she had no reason to doubt them, Kyle had great respect for her and enjoyed being with her. His feelings for her, however, stopped short of love. Whether that would change over time, she had no way of knowing. But that it might did give her a shred of hope—not that they could somehow share a lifetime of love, but that it might be a day, an hour or even a moment.

Kyle was relaxing in his backyard when she got there, and as she neared, he got to his feet and smiled in welcome. "Have a seat." He pulled a plastic lawn chair around for her.

Mica sat and squinted up at the sky, just visible through the canopy of leaves overhead. "It's so hot! Halfway here, I wished I'd taken the car."

"Would you rather go inside where it's cooler?"

"No, here in the shade is fine. I really prefer being outdoors in the summer."

"Me, too. There's even a breeze now and then." He pointed to a novel on the foot of the chaise longue where he had been resting. "I've been catching up on a little reading. You look tired. Is something wrong?"

"This hasn't been a good day for me. First Carrie tried to take my head off at the grocery store, then my landlady came by to tell me that everyone working on or near the movie is going straight to hell."

"I don't know where people get such screwy ideas."

"Neither do I. But I'm concerned. She's a front-pew member of Brother Malcolm's church, and I'm worried about his threats."

"Don't be. People who make so much noise about causing trouble rarely do. It's the quiet ones you have to watch out for. And from what I gather, neither your landlady nor her preacher is apt to become quiet. Just ignore them."

"I wish I could. Mrs. Mobley is upset because Brother Malcolm got fined for disturbing the peace. He's probably furious. And I got mad and told her I thought he deserved to be fined. I've never seen Mrs. Mobley so angry. She left in a huff. Well, actually, I asked her to leave. I suppose I shouldn't have told her how I felt. I'm afraid she'll stop renting to me.''

"She can't do that. What about your lease?''

"I had a lease for the first year, but since then it's been a month-to-month renewal.'' Mica gazed glumly at the trunk of the tree that shaded the yard. "I'd like to move, but the rent is so reasonable there, and it's close enough for me to walk to school.''

"Would it help if I talk to her?''

"No, that would only make it worse. As I said, she's convinced all you 'Hollywood sinners' have cloven hooves and horns.''

He sat opposite her. "Prejudice runs really deep in some people. The funny thing is that the public tends to either glorify actors as saints or denounce them as sinners. Speaking of actors, Diane King is supposed to join us tomorrow. It sure has been a pain trying to work around her absence.''

"I'm looking forward to meeting her. She seems so nice in her movies.''

Kyle grinned.

"Okay. So she's acting in her movie roles. Isn't she at all like that?'' Mica asked.

"Actually, she is. But she has a watchdog for a secretary. Una jumps to Diane's defense any time Diane is too shy to stand up for herself. Shelley's already throwing tantrums because of Diane. Sedalia may not have had a fireworks display on the Fourth of July, but if Shelley goes after Diane, there'll be fireworks enough for everyone.''

"Diane would have to be an angel compared with Shelley. I don't think I'll ever be able to see another Shelley Doyle film again—other than this one, of course.''

"Moviedom does lose some of its sparkle, doesn't it? Tinsel is only pretty from a distance, you know.''

"Do you mind if we go over some lines? I'm having trouble understanding the scene where you tell me Greg is in love with Deborah."

"Okay, let's go through it. Do you have the lines memorized?"

"Yes." She stood and mentally put herself into the role of her character. Knotting her fingers together, she said, "'Ryan, I've tried to make Greg notice me, but all he sees is Deborah. What am I doing wrong?'"

Instantly Kyle became Ryan. "'You've got to let go of that idea, Angie. Greg isn't the one for you.'"

"'How can you say that? I've loved Greg since grade school. I was sure he cared for me, until she came along.'" Mica ducked her head to demonstrate the misery she thought Angie would feel at that moment. "'I've done all I can to make him notice me.'"

Kyle came to her and put his hand on her arm. "'You've got to be true to yourself.'"

Mica's pulse quickened at his touch. She dropped her character and said, "This is the part I don't understand. If Angie loves him, isn't she already being true to herself by trying to show him?"

Kyle pulled back his hand and shook his head. "She's trying to be something she isn't."

"I know, but if she likes lacy dresses and hair ribbons, why doesn't she wear them? In the end Greg chooses Dawn, who is so feminine she's almost unbelievable. If Angie was herself, she might have a chance with Greg."

"And that's exactly what Ryan is trying to tell her. Even though he loves her, he is willing to lose her in order to let her have the man she wants."

"Okay, I understand now." She picked up Angie's character again. "'That's fine for you to say, Ryan, but if I quit pretending to be interested in the things he's involved in, I'll never see him. If I was wearing a dress, I certainly couldn't get close to him without ruining it. This way I can be with him.'"

"'Why should you have to change yourself in order to win him? Greg ought to appreciate you. I do.'" He reached out and took her forearm in his hands, and she looked up at him. "'Greg is a fool not to want you.'" His voice dropped to a husky level and his thumbs stroked the roundness of her arm.

"'Do you really think so?'" she whispered. Mica was struggling to remember this was all pretend.

"'I'm positive. If I were him, I wouldn't want any other woman but you. If I thought you loved me, I'd be the happiest man in the world.'"

Mica swallowed. It was difficult to remember this was Ryan talking to Angie and not Kyle's own words to herself. "'You're a good friend to say that, Ryan. Really you are. But I love Greg enough to go after him, whatever it takes.'" She gazed earnestly up into Kyle's face. Her lips parted and she saw Kyle's eyes drop to her mouth. For a long moment, they stood transfixed.

He turned away, and in a tightly controlled voice, he said, "I think you have the lines down all right."

Mica also turned as she tried to get her emotions in check. "It makes sense now that you've explained the motivation to me. Usually I'm not that dense. If I were Angie, I'd want Ryan and not Greg."

"You would?" He looked back at her, his hazel eyes unreadable.

"Of course. Anyone can see how shallow Greg is. All he cares about is winning that race and drilling for oil."

"He's supposed to be so virile that even a shallow thought is enough to make him irresistible."

"Then they picked the right man to play Greg." She thought about Zane and how he had no more interests than the character he was playing. He was handsome, true, but he never seemed to have a thought that didn't involve his body.

Kyle turned away again. "He's good-looking. No one can deny that."

"Are his teeth really capped?" she asked as she followed Kyle into his kitchen.

He reached into the refrigerator and took out two canned drinks. "I've heard they are. I guess only his dentist knows for sure."

"His dentist and the movie magazines. When we learned who was coming for this film, Carrie dug through some of the back issues of her movie magazines for information about all of you."

"Oh? What did you learn about me?"

She paused. "It said you were dying of a broken heart over Tamara and the divorce."

Kyle laughed. "As you can see, I've recovered."

"It also quoted you as saying you never intended to marry again."

"At the time I thought that was what I wanted."

"And you don't now?"

Kyle was quiet for a minute. "That all depends."

"I think you'd make a wonderful husband...for the right woman."

"You do?"

Mica realized she was probably saying more than she should. She turned away and sat in a kitchen chair. Kyle swung up onto the counter. "I'm worried about Carrie," she said to change the subject. "When I saw her at the grocery store today, she was acting very strange, as if something was wrong. At the time, I had no idea what it might be, but since then it's occurred to me that she may be upset with me because I told her she ought to tell Jake about this notion she's got about going off to Hollywood to become an actress. As serious as he is about her, I thought he ought to know.''

''And you think she may have taken your advice?'' He watched her brush the hair back from her face in a gesture that was unintentionally provocative.

''Right. And they probably got into an argument over it—and she blames me.''

''Even so, I think you gave her the right advice.''

''I don't know. It might have been better if I'd said nothing. It's like she has 'forbidden fruit syndrome.' I tried to get her to put the Hollywood thing out of her mind, but the more I reasoned against it, the more she seemed to be leaning toward it. Maybe I should call her. May I use your phone?''

''Sure. Do you want privacy?''

''No.'' She smiled at him and Kyle thought his heart would flip over. She dialed Carrie's number from memory and waited for her to answer.

Kyle had been in love before, not only with Tamara, but with another woman who was long gone from his life. The emotion wasn't new to him, but the intensity was, and all too soon he would have to leave town and leave this love behind. He reminded himself again that it was foolish of him to fall in love with a woman he could be with only now and then. Maybe, he thought, he, too, was suffering from ''forbidden fruit syndrome.''

Mica hung up. ''She's not home or she's not answering. I wonder if I should go over there.''

''If she doesn't want to talk, I'd give her some space.''

''You're right. Carrie doesn't like being pushed. I hope she gets over this. I'd hate to lose her as a friend.'' She sighed. ''We've tried to pick up the friendship where we left off in college, but you never can, really. We've both changed.''

"People do."

She stepped closer and leaned against the counter beside him as she looked out his window. He could feel the heat of her body, even though they were not touching, and he was reminded of the almost overwhelming desire he had felt for her the last time they had kissed. Had she moved this close to him intentionally? Did she have any idea how arousing she was? It was all he could do to refrain from reaching out and taking her into his arms.

Unwilling to trust himself so close to her, he slipped off the counter and got himself a drink of water from the kitchen faucet. When he turned back to her, he couldn't help but notice the way the sunlight through the window highlighted the hint of red in her dark hair and paled her skin. He wondered if she knew how beautiful she was. "Speaking of people changing, have you heard anything from the school board?"

"As a matter of fact, I called Mr. Hubbard yesterday. He said the board hadn't made a decision on my book request, so I offered him the alternative list of titles, the ones I was telling you about, and told him that I'd be happy teaching any combination of them. I reminded him that I needed a decision pretty soon, because I'd have to order the books and get my lesson plans developed. He said he'd pass the information along to the board, but he was even cooler toward me than before and he didn't sound very hopeful. He'll probably wait until the last minute and then turn it down."

"Why would he do that?"

"It's a game they play—at the expense not only of the teacher, but the students, as well."

"That sounds awfully petty."

"It is, but that's Sedalia Independent School District for you."

"Looks like Sedalia needs an alternative school."

She smiled wryly. "We do, but where would we get one? If we had a private school, the wealthier kids would go there, and the ones I'm trying to reach would be right where they are now."

"There has to be some solution to this."

"If you come up with one, I'd love to hear it."

Kyle pondered the subject for a few moments. "What about a school set up with an endowment to subsidize the tuition for those students who couldn't otherwise afford it?"

Mica thoughtfully bit her lower lip. "That might work," she said with hope lighting her eyes, then she shook her head. "But where would we get the endowment? No, I'll have to keep fighting the public school board until they listen to reason. At least they can't fire me now without just cause."

Kyle nodded his understanding, but resolved to look further into the matter.

## CHAPTER ELEVEN

DIANE KING ARRIVED in Sedalia midafternoon. By suppertime everyone in town was reporting to everyone else that, unlike Shelley, who looked hard and jaded off camera, Diane was even more beautiful than the cameras recorded. Like all the others, Mica could hardly wait until the evening's filming so she could meet the actress who some said would be as great a star as Marilyn Monroe.

No one on the set caught a glimpse of Diane until she emerged from the makeup trailer. As if she had rehearsed it, Diane paused in the doorway and smiled at her throng of admirers. Her light brown hair curled back from her heart-shaped face, and her eyes, a shade of blue not found in contact lenses, were soft and dreamy. Her smile was sweet, as was her expression, and her tiny waist looked as if it had been designed for the prettily ruffled dress she wore.

Mica and Kyle stood together in the throng. "She's so pretty!" Mica whispered. "How well do you know her?"

"Quite well," answered Kyle. "When she first made it big, we were rumored to be an 'item.'"

"Were you?"

"No, we're just friends."

Diane came down the steps and the onlookers surged toward her, but the crew ordered the crowd away from her. When the ropes were back in place, Diane walked close to her restrained admirers, signing autographs and smiling.

"I've never seen Shelley do that," Mica said.

"Shelley lives for the moment. Right now she's still in demand, but her clock is ticking. She sees women like Diane as threats. And she's right."

"That's sad. Couldn't Shelley play character parts?"

"She could if she would."

Diane left her admirers and went to the set, tiptoeing around and over the cables and power lines used by the crew. Mica followed her, eager to see how her favorite actress would deliver her lines. Her scene was with Shelley, and the older woman was glaring at her already.

Greenberg double-checked the cameras and said to Diane, "I want Dawn to enter as if she just came from the drugstore. Deborah, you've been talking to Greg and are heading down the street." Once the women took their places, Greenberg nodded to his assistant and the film began to roll.

Diane left the drugstore with her skirts swirling, looking as virginal and clean as if she were made of spun glass. She took two steps and tripped over an uneven place in the sidewalk. In the silence that followed, Shelley's laughter was all too clear. Diane glared at her and went back to her place. Taking a deep breath, she again became the misty-eyed Dawn.

Mica glanced back at the makeup trailer and saw a masculine-looking woman come down the steps. Her hair was slicked back and she wore slacks that could as easily have been worn by a man. Mica figured the woman had some connection with the film, because she'd been in the makeup trailer, but she had never seen her before. She nudged Kyle. "Who's that coming this way?"

Kyle glanced behind them. "That's Una Lundquist. I'm not too sure where Diane met her, but Una is her secretary—the one I told you about."

Una went to Diane and they conversed in low tones. Una reached out and straightened Diane's skirt and spoke to her again. With a faint smile, Diane looked in Shelley's direction. Una, however, glared at the older star, and didn't flinch when Shelley returned the look in kind.

Kyle said in an undertone, "It's a well-known fact that Una and Shelley hate each other. No one knows why. During one movie, the animosity between them got so bad that Una had to be barred from the set."

"She's not the sort of person I'd have guessed a shy person would hire. She looks intimidating."

"Exactly. She runs interference for Diane. She's very protective and guards Diane like a hen with one chick."

"They aren't...?" Mica wasn't sure how to phrase her question.

"Diane isn't. I don't know about Una. No, I think it's just that Una takes her job seriously."

Greenberg called for action again. This time Diane did the scene without a single mistake. Greenberg nodded his approval. As the assistant called for the next scene, Una went over to Greenberg and they shook hands like old friends.

"Una is more likable than Shelley, in my opinion," Kyle said. "She's direct, and if she likes you, she's a loyal supporter." He waved at Una and she waved back and nodded.

When the scene was over, Diane came in their direction. She seemed eager to speak to Kyle, but smiled shyly at Mica.

"Hello, Diane," Kyle said easily. He held out his hand and she shook it. "I'd like you to meet Mica Haldane. She's playing the part of Angie."

"Oh? We have several scenes together." She smiled at Mica as if she hoped for friendship but was too shy to assume that it might be possible.

"Yes. I've been looking forward to them."

Turning to Kyle, Diane said under her breath, "Can you believe he has me and Shelley in the same film? Una was beside herself when I told her."

"I'd have cast it the same way."

"Yes, but you do have a tendency to live dangerously. Has Shelley been causing trouble?"

Kyle said, "She's been on time the past few days and has been getting the scenes down faster."

"She could do them in one take if she wanted to," Diane informed her. "She just likes the attention."

"We all do," Kyle said. "Why else would we be in this business?"

Diane looked with interest at Mica. "I don't recall having seen you before. Is this your first movie?"

"I live here and teach at the high school."

"I liked high school," Diane said. "At one time I considered teaching, but went into acting, instead. My family worried about me becoming an actress. No security, you know. But it worked out well for me in the long run."

Kyle nodded.

Mica said, "I have to go. My scene is coming up."

"I'll see you later," Diane replied.

Mica hurried to her place. Glancing back, she saw Kyle laugh at something Diane said. They were both so handsome. Mica couldn't help but think Kyle belonged with someone like Diane. The thought made her ache.

Across the street, in the area where Miss Nelly and her friends were holding court with plates of cookies and candy, Carrie had seen Diane's entrance, and from that distance she had watched the filming of the subsequent scenes.

"I tell you, I heard that Shelley woman throwing a tantrum in the wardrobe trailer. I don't know how you missed it," Buford commented to Carrie as he poured another cup of coffee from his thermos.

"I remember when our youngest used to do that," Birdine replied. "Do you remember, Buford?"

"I sure do. Back then a spanking cured it."

Miss Nelly offered a cookie to one of the crew who was walking by. "These are from a recipe my family has handed down for generations," she said. "Take two." The man was glad to oblige.

Carrie saw Jake coming toward her, but she pretended she hadn't. Less than a week had passed since Jake had pressured her into choosing a chance at an acting career over him. That night when she had run from his car, she had decided that their relationship was over. He had left her no choice. And when he didn't call or come by the next day, she had concluded that he was through with her, as well. Before she could decide how to avoid him, Jake was by her side.

"I need to talk to you," he said.

"I'm busy."

"This won't take long."

Carrie didn't want to cause a fuss in front of Miss Nelly and her friends, so she motioned for Jake to follow her across the street. Hoping they would be less conspicuous there, she sat on one end of a bench and indicated for Jake to sit on the other end. "What do you want?" she asked.

"I want to talk. I miss you, Carrie."

"You should have thought about that the other night— before you backed me into a corner." She found it difficult to meet Jake's trusting eyes. One thing was for sure—he hadn't been with another woman. Guiltily she glanced across the lot at Zane.

"I was hoping you'd changed your mind."

Carrie finally looked directly at Jake and saw the pain in his eyes. She hated the certainty that he would be even more hurt if he knew everything.

Earlier, Zane had spoken to her as he'd passed and had given her that sexy wink that turned her bones to butter. What would Jake say if he knew she had been to Zane's apartment twice now? She had never before even considered being unfaithful to Jake, and she hated herself for being so weak.

Carrie shook her head firmly. "No, Jake, I haven't. I'm not ready to give up my dream."

"There you go about dreams again! Isn't there anything I can do to change your mind?"

"I'm sorry." She rubbed her temples, where a headache was building. "Don't be so understanding, Jake! Get mad at me and say you never want to see me again."

"I'd be lying." He crossed his muscled arms over his broad chest. "Nope, if anybody backs out, it has to be you. I love you, Carrie, and I'll be waiting right here when you give up and come home."

Carrie gave him an exasperated look. She felt guilty enough about Zane without Jake being noble. "Fine! You just stay here and wait! But I'm not coming back!" She turned and stormed away. Now how could she do anything but go to Hollywood to save face? She headed for Zane.

"Hello there," Zane said as she approached. "How's it going?"

She risked a glance back at Jake. "Just dandy," she snapped without thinking.

Zane's eyes narrowed. "Pull in those claws," he said in a voice that was only half in jest. "I don't like claw marks. Not when I'm on my feet, that is."

A couple of cameramen who were standing close by must have heard Zane, for they poked each other and grinned at her.

Carrie felt a blush burn her cheeks. These men couldn't know she and Zane were lovers, but it was evident from their behavior that they suspected it. Before long, would the whole crew be talking about her the way they'd talked about Wendy? She wanted to run back to Jake, but when she looked back, he was gone. Carrie lifted her chin in stubborn pride.

Greenberg was frowning at the scene in front of him. "Cut!" he shouted. "Morris, have you gained weight?"

Paul Morris, who was one of the stunt men, ducked his head. "I might have put on a pound or two."

"How are you going to double for Zane if you outweigh him by fifteen pounds?"

Morris thought for a minute. "I don't think it'll show. All I have to do is tumble out of the car. I'll be going pretty fast."

"You won't be going that fast." Greenberg looked at the nearest cameraman. "Harve, you're putting on weight, too. You all are! What's going on here?"

Morris grinned sheepishly. "It's Miss Nelly's cookies and the candy, I guess. I've always had a sweet tooth." Harve returned the grin and nodded.

"That does it." He turned to his assistant and pointed toward the elderly trio across the lot. "You go over there and tell them to stop feeding my cast and crew."

"Me?" the assistant asked. "I can't say that to Miss Nelly. She's too much like my own grandmother."

"Do it!" Greenberg glared at the man as he hurried off to do as he was told. "Morris, go to wardrobe and get someone to cinch you in. I haven't got time to put you on a diet."

Morris jogged toward the trailer. Harve shifted his weight and pretended to be checking the adjustment on his camera, his newly widened girth straining against his shirt. Greenberg, who had never cared for sweets, made a grumbling noise and slouched in his chair.

The assistant delivered his message as instructed, then added, "I'm sorry, Miss Nelly. I wouldn't have said it if Greenberg hadn't ordered me to."

Miss Nelly tilted her head back so she was peering down her nose in the director's direction. "He's a small man," she proclaimed. "He never eats my cookies."

"It's nothing personal. Greenberg just doesn't have a sweet tooth." The assistant added, "I like them a lot and so does everyone else. That's the problem. Between your cookies and Birdine's fudge, we're all gaining weight. That won't work in a film."

Miss Nelly exchanged a look with Birdine. "Very well. You may tell him we will make no more cookies."

"Or candy," the man prompted. "You have to agree about the candy, as well."

"Or candy," Birdine agreed.

As the man scurried back to report his success to Greenberg, Miss Nelly turned to Birdine. "Pound cake?"

Birdine gave a sharp nod. "The kind with real butter."

Miss Nelly turned back with a triumphant smile. "We'll show that little man. I won't have my friends being half starved so far away from their homes and families."

"I couldn't sleep nights," Birdine agreed. "The very idea!"

Buford grinned but didn't comment. He had learned to go with the flow.

The filming lasted well into the evening. As it drew near supper and TV prime time, the sightseers drifted away and left the cast and crew to their business. Mica was tired, but she knew she was giving a good performance. She rarely needed to be told more than once what Greenberg wanted, and she tried hard to please him. Diane was settling down and getting into her own performance, interspersed with private conferences with Una. Shelley was still causing trouble whenever she thought it would reflect poorly on her fellow actresses.

Zane had finished his scenes for the time being and had gone to his dressing room in the makeup trailer. Mica was glad to have him out of the way. Zane was still being too insistent on talking to her, and he did so in a way that Mica found too personal. She had never before needed help in discouraging an unwelcome suitor, but Zane was unusually persistent, and she was beginning to wonder if this might be a first time.

She looked around for Carrie as she waited for her next and last scene for the night, but she was nowhere to be found. Twice that day Mica had tried to get Carrie's attention to talk to her, but both times Carrie had deliberately avoided her. Mica was worried that Carrie was still upset with her.

The scene being filmed at the moment was between Kyle and Diane King. As she watched, Kyle smiled at Diane the same way he had smiled at her only that afternoon, and emotion knotted in Mica's middle. Whether it was reasonable or not, she loved him. And it hurt to think that he didn't love her. More than once since she'd reached that conclusion about his feelings for her, she'd questioned whether she had been right.

Out of the corner of her eye, Mica spotted Kyle's friend, Harve Giacono, drinking a cup of coffee near the door of the trailer that served refreshments for the cast and crew, and she went to talk to him. "Hi," she said.

"Hello. I figured you'd be over there watching Kyle."

"I thought I'd get some coffee." She didn't particularly like strong coffee, the only kind that was being served here, but she poured herself a cup to give her an excuse for standing there. "Kyle and Diane make an attractive couple, don't you think?"

Harve nodded. "I suppose that's true, but looks can be deceiving."

She sipped the scalding coffee. "Oh? I had heard a rumor that they'd been more than just friends at one time." She glanced at Harve.

The man chuckled as if he knew why she had come to him. "Rumors are nothing but just so much talk. Kyle's not like Zane. Not by a long shot. He keeps pretty much to himself. We're good friends, you know. My wife, Janet, has given up on finding him à wife.''

"Oh?" Mica tried to look only casually interested.

"No, I'd say he's shown more interest in you than in anyone since Tamara.''

Mica laughed. "I could hardly compete with Tamara Nolan.''

"No competition there. Kyle's been over her for a long time.'' He looked across the lot at the brilliant lights. "Yeah, I'd say I know Kyle about as well as anyone knows him.'' Harve smiled at her over the top of his plastic cup. "Kyle deserves more in life than what he and Tamara had.'' He shook his head thoughtfully. "I was amazed when I heard those two were married. It's a wonder it lasted a month, let alone years. He tried, but one person alone can't make a marriage last.''

"Is he over her? For certain, I mean.''

"Yeah," he said. "Kyle has her out of his system." He studied Mica. "It's none of my business, but he talks about you a lot.''

"He does?''

"We have breakfast together nearly every morning, and he always brings the conversation around to you.'' His sharp, dark eyes asked the question he didn't voice.

"I care for him," she said softly. "I care a great deal.''

Harve grinned. "Like I say, Kyle deserves more out of life than he usually gets. It's good to see him happy, even if it's just for the summer.''

Mica couldn't swallow past the lump in her throat. Putting her coffee down on the counter, she said, "I guess I didn't want this after all.'' Harve knew Kyle cared for her, but he was confirming the unpleasant truth that it would last only as long as the filming here in Sedalia. She asked herself what else could be possible. She had known all along they couldn't have a lasting relationship. But that hadn't stopped her from wanting him.

"I'd better get back to work before Greenberg starts cracking his whip," Harve said as he tossed his empty cup into a trash can. "Nice talking with you."

"Same here," Mica replied. With her thoughts tumbling, she headed back toward the lights and cameras. As she passed the cast's trailer, Zane came out. She tried to ignore him, but couldn't.

"Hello, baby," he said with a smile. "Were you looking for me?"

"Actually, no." Mica smiled so her words wouldn't sound rude, only truthful.

"I see Kyle is still tied up. That gives us time to be together." Zane looped his arm over her shoulders. "Tell you what. After our last scene, let's go to my place and unwind."

"No, thank you." Mica slipped from beneath his arm and quickened her pace toward the crowd working behind the lights and cameras.

As Zane followed her, the door of the trailer opened again and Carrie slipped out. Keeping to the darker shadows, she watched Zane walking away from the trailer as though he was trying to catch up with Mica. Surely he wasn't doing so for personal reasons. Mica had made it clear that she was not interested in Zane, and she had believed the reverse was also true.

She had become Zane's lover and wanted to be confident in her relationship with him, but doubt and suspicion were already creeping in. Only minutes before, when they had finished making love in his dressing room, he had seemed preoccupied and cool, and she was aware that he was pretending around others that nothing had changed between them. Of course, she didn't want him to publicly announce that they were having an affair, but she also didn't want to think that he was ashamed of his association with her. That afternoon she had called the agent Zane had recommended and his secretary had given her the impression that the agent wasn't interested in an unknown from Sedalia, Texas. Carrie had been told to send her portfolio, whatever that was, and when she admitted she didn't have one, the woman had become colder still. She had told Zane about that when she'd met him in his dressing room, but he'd shrugged it aside and said he would take care of it later. She hoped he wouldn't forget, but she had a sinking feeling that he didn't want to be bothered.

She skirted the various groups of people, avoiding contact with anyone, and went to where her car was parked. Once she was inside, she lowered her head to the steering wheel and closed her eyes. Had she made a terrible mistake? What would she do if Zane did lose interest in her? That was all too frightening to think about.

She sat up and squared her shoulders, trying to pretend she had more confidence than she felt. This had to work out. She had come too far to back out now. Steeling herself against thoughts of failure and embarrassment, Carrie started her car and drove home.

## CHAPTER TWELVE

"NEVILLE, THIS PLACE is an eyesore and the city council is ordering you to spruce it up," Harrison Graham said to the owner of the unsightly air-conditioning shop. Jack Murray was at the mayor's heels, as usual. Jack was pretending an interest in the used air conditioners displayed in the shop front so Neville Daws wouldn't turn his anger on him.

"I already told you, Harry. I ain't spending no more money on this place when it ain't necessary. My roof don't leak, my door latch works and I got all the business I can handle. New paint ain't necessary."

Graham drew himself up to his less-than-impressive height. "I expected you to say that. You'll be glad to hear you have a benefactor."

"A what? What are you talking about?"

"An unidentified man has come forward with the money to paint your building and to put a privacy fence around the equipment you need to keep in the back. The rest you'll have to haul away."

"Who was it? You?"

"No, and I was instructed not to give a name. The gift is to remain anonymous." Graham scowled at the man and added, "Not everyone in town has your lack of civic pride."

Daws shrugged. "I reckon I don't mind as long as it don't get in my way. When are they gonna start?"

"Immediately. Jack, call Perry's Paint Shop and tell them to get started on it."

Jack moved to the phone and made the call as Graham and Daws argued about how much of the junk in back was necessary for the running of his business. Graham was finally satisfied that the town's worst building would soon be improved, and they left.

On the sidewalk outside, Graham turned to his city manager. "Well, that's done."

"Daws can be a mean one. I never thought he'd agree, even if the paint and fence were donated."

"I know the man. I was pretty sure he wouldn't turn down anything free." Graham smiled at his town and patted his rounding stomach. "Things around here are starting to look really good, Jack. You'd think it was spanking new to look at it now."

Jack nodded. "You've done yourself proud. Next election, people will remember this. I just hope Greenberg doesn't get his dander up and move the filming to Kilgore like Buford Ponder said he'd threatened to do."

"Relax, Jack. He was only talking about the buildings downtown. Besides, I needed to show Daws who was boss."

GREENBERG ARRIVED at the site for scene number 72, expecting to see the cameras and lights set up, but what he found was his cameramen milling around and the equipment still on the trucks. For a moment he couldn't tell what was wrong. Then he looked at the building. His pace increased to a trot until he was directly in front of the only building in town he had considered dilapidated enough to use as backdrop for one of the movie's pivotal scenes. "What the hell happened to my building!" he demanded.

His assistant came hurrying to him. "When we got here the painters were just leaving. The head of the crew said someone had paid for the work. There's a wooden fence going up in back."

Greenberg muttered an oath and glared around him. "Where's that damned mayor?"

"It won't do any good to talk to him now," the assistant pointed out. "The damage is done."

"This is, but who knows what he'll do next! You find him and tell him if he touches *anything* else, we're going to scrap every foot of film we've shot here and start over in Kilroy."

"You mean Kilgore?"

"Kilroy. Kilgore. What the hell difference does it make? Just see to it that the mayor understands. I should have done this weeks ago."

He glared at the pristine white building that previously had been splotched with various colors, a result of its many layers of ancient paint flaking and peeling from years of neglect. To another of his assistants, he said, "Look at it. It's got as much personality now as a hen's egg! Maybe we ought to put it back like it was."

The other man eyed the building and shook his head. "You know what that'll cost. We're pushing our budget as it is."

Greenberg cursed again. He knew it was out of the question to have a scenery team fly out and make the building old again, though he was tempted to do just that to show the mayor that two could play this game. "You're right, and we're already behind schedule. I don't want to spend any more time in this place than is necessary." He looked over at the side of the building, where the sign his crew had prepared to cover the real business's sign was propped against the building. "Get me that sign."

As the assistant went to do the director's bidding, Greenberg motioned for Harve Giacono to come to him. He and Harve were friends, as well as having worked together often. "You rented a car?"

Harve nodded. "Sure did."

"Scout around and see if you can find me another place here in town that will pass for a body shop, some place that has a sign we can cover with our own."

As Harve headed for the parked cars, Greenberg stared up at the building and tried to quell the gripping pain in the pit of his stomach. He had hoped his old ulcer would lie sleeping, but the mayor of Sedalia seemed determined to drive him insane. His assistant, along with two other men, returned with the sign.

"Load that in the truck and follow Harve. He's looking for another building." He headed for the nearest shade to wait and think of all the ways he would like to throttle Graham.

AS THE ACTORS ARRIVED, they learned that the scheduled scene would be filmed in an as-yet-unknown location and were told to stay nearby. Mica and Kyle decided to wait in Dubois' Drugstore out of the heat and away from the angry director. They told one of Greenberg's assistants where they would be so they wouldn't be missed.

After seating themselves in a booth, Kyle ordered chocolate sodas for both of them. "I hope the weather holds," Kyle said to make conversation. "Otherwise we'll have to postpone some of the filming. That's the problem with using so many outdoor scenes on location. You can't have rain in one scene and it be mysteriously dry in the next."

"I never knew making a movie could be so complicated." She toyed with her straw, thinking of something else entirely.

"What's on your mind, Mica? You seem distracted."

"I probably shouldn't be talking about this, but I've been overhearing gossip that involves Carrie, and I don't know if I should tell Carrie or not."

"Gossip that involves Zane?"

"You've heard it, too, haven't you?"

"I'm afraid so."

Mica groaned. "I tried to tell her to stay away from Zane, but she didn't want my advice. I'm really worried that she's gone off the deep end and is going to regret it. There's no telling how Jake will react if he hears the rumors. I've got to think of some way to talk to her about this without making matters worse."

"You take your friendships seriously, don't you?"

"Of course I do. Carrie is important to me. We've been friends too long for me to turn my back on her now—just because she's doing something I don't agree with. You don't know how seriously Carrie is considering heading for Hollywood. She thinks she has a chance of becoming a movie star." She couldn't keep the exasperation out of her voice. "Going into this, she *knew* it was only for the summer. I don't know what's gotten into her."

"I've seen it before."

"I had no idea she'd get so carried away with this movie!"

Kyle didn't answer for several moments. "I could try to talk to her."

"Thanks for offering, but I don't think she'll listen to anyone. She's about as stubborn as I am sometimes. The saddest part is that I think she may lose Jake over all this and she'll really miss him." She fell silent for a moment; then, with her eyes filled with sadness, she looked up at him and said, "I'm going to miss you a great deal when the movie is over."

He said nothing for several moments. "I'll miss you, too."

"Of course, I'll write to you," she added quickly, her face brightening. "If you don't mind."

He had to smile at that. "No, I don't mind."

"But I should warn you that I'm not a very good correspondent. Some people have the knack of putting words onto paper and some don't."

"We could talk on the telephone."

"I guess we could do that. I don't know."

He gazed at her across the table. "What are you trying to say, Mica?"

Softly she said, "I'm saying that I'm going to miss you so much that letters and phone calls will seem trivial after being able to see you and talk to you." She reached out and put her hand over his. "And touch you."

Kyle wondered if she knew how much even a casual touch of her hand excited him. "I feel the same way. I could fly back out here from time to time so we could be together."

She shook her head. "You know that won't happen."

"No, I don't."

"You're so busy. You have your life to lead, and it certainly doesn't include trips to Sedalia."

"It could."

Mica pulled back as if she was uncomfortable with the conversation and suggested they had better get back outside so they wouldn't miss their call. Kyle agreed, and in silence they went back out to await word of the scene's relocation.

"THE CHAIR RECOGNIZES Malcolm Stout," Arlen Hubbard said in a serious tone of voice.

"*Brother* Malcolm Stout," the preacher corrected him as he rose from his seat.

"I'm sorry. Brother Malcolm. Now, what is it you wish to discuss with the school board?" Hubbard was a member of another church, but Brother Malcolm was no stranger to him. Brother Malcolm had shown up at other meetings over the years to object to matters ranging from sex education to the teaching of evolution.

"I'm glad you asked, Brother Arlen."

Hubbard gripped his ballpoint pen tighter. He detested his first name; only his mother and his wife were permitted to use it when referring to him.

"As you know," Brother Malcolm began, his voice lifting into stentorian preaching range, "there is a blight among us. An evil spawned by Satan."

A man sitting in the audience began to chuckle, but Hubbard fixed him with an intense stare and the man swallowed his laughter and wiped the smile off his face. Although Hubbard didn't subscribe to all the narrow beliefs of Brother Malcolm's church, he insisted that his meetings be conducted with decorum. Besides, a majority of the board supported the preacher, and Hubbard wanted to keep them appeased so he could maintain his position as president of the board. He cocked his head as if to listen more closely.

"I refer to those folks from Hollywood."

Hubbard shifted in his chair. "Brother Malcolm, with all due respect, I can understand a person objecting to the traffic inconveniences and so forth, but that has nothing to do with the school board. You need to take that up with Mayor Graham."

"Mayor Graham is already in Satan's snare. His daughter is in the film."

"Granted, but—"

"I figure it became the school board's business—" he drawled each syllable as if he had a congregation hanging on each word "—when one of your teachers got involved."

"That would be Miss Haldane. Neither our code of ethics nor our standards of conduct prohibit her from acting in a movie during the time she isn't teaching." Since this was a public meeting, Hubbard had to keep his personal feelings to himself.

"I wasn't referring to that, even though my congregation and I disagree with you. I was referring to the fact that she's fornicating with the actor, Zane Morgan." He reared back as a buzz of whispers ran through the room. "I believe the Blue Book you use addresses immoral behavior."

Hubbard's eyes grew large, and he sat up straighter in his chair. "I hereby declare this meeting suspended so that the board can meet in a closed executive session to discuss this matter. Will everyone except Brother Malcolm Stout please leave the room?"

Once the room was clear, Hubbard called the executive session to order. To Brother Malcolm he said, "This is a serious charge. I assume you have proof of some sort?"

"Proof? What more do you need than the word of a man of the cloth?"

"Please understand, Brother Malcolm, that I am not disputing your word, but we must know the basis for your allegation."

Brother Malcolm's eyes bored into Hubbard. "One of my flock saw Sister Mica's car parked in a visitor's parking space at the apartment complex where Zane Morgan is living. Knowing this man's reputation and Sister Mica's connection with him through the movie, I felt it necessary to investigate. I myself can testify that her car was there at sunset and at midnight, when I checked the second time. It was obviously there all night."

Hubbard frowned as he drummed his fingers on the conference table. He didn't like Brother Malcolm's influence, but the board was already having problems with Mica. She had some harebrained notion of changing around her curriculum and disposing of literature Hubbard himself had selected and approved. "Maybe she had some reason to leave the car there," he said in an effort to be fair, but choosing his words carefully so as not to offend the preacher.

"I can't think of but one reason. Can you?"

Hubbard looked to the board members seated on both sides of him, trying to read their thoughts. The majority, who had always before sided with Stout, were leaning forward with keen interest. Hubbard knew he was on thin ice. "Was she seen there personally?"

"As a matter of fact, she was." Brother Malcolm looked proud of his pronouncement. "The same sister of my congregation who called me happened to see Sister Mica get into her car and drive away the next morning."

"Is she willing to come here and tell us what she saw?"

Brother Malcolm smiled ingratiatingly. "The women of my congregation don't hold with public testifying." He bowed at the woman on the school board. "Begging your pardon, ma'am."

Hubbard twisted his mouth from one side to the other. "This is serious, indeed. It could cost Miss Haldane her job."

"It's better to learn to walk righteously by losing a job than to burn in Hell forever." Brother Malcolm drew himself up as if he thought Hubbard might dispute him.

"Is Miss Haldane a member of your church?"

"No, Brother Arlen, she's not. More's the pity. If she were, I could handle this on my own. Since I can't, I've brought it to you good men. And you, ma'am," he added belatedly.

Hubbard knew Louise Farley, the lone female board member, must be angry enough at the preacher's obvious disregard for women's rights to chew nails. Louise was an ardent feminist and was generally vocal in her beliefs. In order to keep the discussion from deteriorating into verbal warfare, Hubbard said, "We'll take this matter under consideration. Thank you, Brother Malcolm. This executive session is adjourned." He nodded to his secretary to open the chamber doors and readmit the public.

Hubbard paid little attention to the rest of the board meeting. The evidence Stout had against Mica Haldane was circumstantial at best, but he wasn't sure that she would know that. This could provide him with a way to solve the problem he had with her request for a curriculum change. If she thought she could be fired for a violation of the morals clause, she might back down on the other matter.

He had been against hiring her in the first place but had been outvoted. Her family was from the wrong side of the tracks, and her father had a reputation for being a trouble-maker, or so Hubbard had always contended. Hubbard's enmity toward the man actually stemmed from the day in junior high school that Hubbard had picked a fight with him and lost. Although Hubbard had never told anyone of the fight, Haldane had boasted that he'd whipped Arlen Hubbard and Hubbard had felt humiliated. He had never forgotten. Now he had to deal with the willful offspring of the man, and time had proven that Mica was going to be a thorn in Hubbard's side.

As if he would need the reminder, he wrote on his note-pad, "Call Miss Haldane re morality issue." He was look-ing forward to it.

MICA WAS EXHAUSTED after the day's filming. She had been able to see Kyle for only a few minutes after leaving the drugstore, and she had been almost glad. She hoped to be able to spend the evening alone to get her mind on a more logical track where Kyle was concerned. Unfortunately, the message light on her answering machine put an end to that hope.

In half an hour she was dressed in what she considered to be her teaching clothes and was ringing Hubbard's door-bell. "I'm sorry I'm late," she said as she joined the three people in the formal living room and took a seat. "We were filming late, and I didn't get your message in time to be here at seven.''

Hubbard exchanged looks with the other man and woman. "That's more or less what we want to talk to you about.''

Mica was confused. "I assumed this meeting was to discuss my request for a change in curriculum.''

"No,'' Miss Farley said, her lips prim and her eyes cold. "It's about your second job.''

"Now I'm really confused. I don't have a second job.''

"Are you not in this movie that's being filmed?'' the man, Irwin McKenny, asked in a tone that indicated he considered her to be deliberately misleading them.

"I'm in the movie, but that's hardly like a second job. It will be over in a few weeks.''

"As you must know, the school board met last night.'' Hubbard waited for Mica to acknowledge this. "Brother Malcolm Stout addressed the board, and he voiced some opinions that many of us shared.''

"Brother Malcolm? What does he have to do with me?''

"We—the school board, that is—feel it's not in the best interest of our students to have one of our teachers take part in this film.''

Mica jumped to her feet. "What? I've been filming for weeks! Why didn't someone say something to me before I accepted the part? And what business is it of the school board how I choose to spend my free time?'' She glared at each of them in turn.

"It's very much our business,'' Miss Farley said. "We can't and won't entrust our children to people who don't uphold our moral code.''

"What!'' Mica whipped around to face the woman.

Hubbard said, "Your car was seen parked all night in front of the apartment house where Zane Morgan is known to be living.''

Mica was too astounded to speak for several seconds. "That was several weeks ago!" She instantly realized her choice of words was a poor way to defend herself. "I wasn't in Zane's apartment all night. Who says I was?"

"Brother Malcolm saw the car. He hasn't said anything before now because he had to pray for the right answer," McKenny said. "I'm in his congregation," he added, "and I know this to be true."

"If he spent more time praying and less trying to run everyone's life, he'd be better off," Mica snapped. "Although it is none of your business, I was in Zane's apartment only a short while, then I went to Kyle Spen—" She cut herself off, realizing she'd made another mistake.

"Spensor, too?" McKenny asked. "What else do you have to say in your defense?"

"Since you're taking this attitude, I refuse to give you an answer," she said with all the dignity she could summon.

"Miss Haldane," Hubbard said with forced patience, "we aren't the gestapo. We aren't telling you that you have to quit the movie or lose your position in the school. Not exactly."

The words the man spoke were chilling. "No? Then what are you saying?" Mica asked.

Hubbard curled his lips into a smile. "We're only suggesting that you should make that decision for yourself."

"Mr. Hubbard, you don't seem to understand. I've done quite a few scenes already. If I were to drop out, not only would the scenes have to be shot over, but I could be sued for breach of contract."

"I assumed there must be a contract of some sort. Why don't you bring it by my office and let me look it over? There may be some loophole to get you out of the film."

"I don't want out."

"I don't think you should answer too hastily," Miss Farley said. "We could dismiss you for not living up to the contract you have with us. On a morals charge, to be exact."

"That's blackmail!" Mica exclaimed.

"Now, now," Hubbard said in a placating manner, "let's not put it like that." He gave Mica a fatherly smile. "You go home and think it over. Nothing has to be decided tonight."

Mica gripped her purse as she struggled to refrain from telling the representatives of the school board exactly what she thought of them, and walked toward the door.

"We'll be in contact," Hubbard said after her. "Have a good evening."

Exercising great restraint, Mica managed to leave without slamming the front door. A morals charge! Her? She had never had so much as a questionable mark against her before. She was so angry as she drove home that it was only by habit that she got there safely. A morals charge! She never should have been so foolish as to go to Zane's apartment for any reason.

She wanted to call Kyle and tell him what had happened, but refrained. She had to handle this herself. Instead she turned on the television and pretended to watch the flickering screen while her thoughts tumbled and stewed.

She didn't think the morals clause was the real issue. No, it had to do with how upset Hubbard had been over her assertion that the previous years' curriculum was worn-out. Miss Farley wouldn't have cared at all if her car was in Zane's visitors' parking lot, but she was passionate in her devotion to *The Grapes of Wrath*. Irwin McKenny was a member of Brother Malcolm's church, so he was no more than Brother Malcolm's puppet. She strongly suspected Hubbard was trying to bluff her. No one had any substantial evidence of any wrongdoing on her part. Granted, it would be terribly embarrassing for the truth of that evening to become public information, but she had done nothing wrong and couldn't let the board coerce her this way.

Why did it all have to be so difficult? Why even stay here at all? There were other schools, some of which she already knew were more liberal. There were poor students everywhere, not just in Sedalia. But this was her hometown. Her roots, such as they were, were here. Because Mica had never known financial stability as a child, she had developed a strong sense of place. She wanted to make a difference and she wanted to do it here.

Mica resolved not to knuckle under. She doubted the school board would open itself to scandal by making these flimsy charges against her public. Surely they were bluffing.

# CHAPTER THIRTEEN

SHELLEY WAS deep in thought as Calula was doing her face for the morning's shoot. Zane, for whatever reason, was finding it difficult to seduce Mica. Shelley had also seen him with Carrie, and she was almost certain that he was sleeping with the woman, but Shelley didn't care so much about Carrie. She wasn't as pretty as Mica, and she had the hero-worship look about her that she guessed would be gratifying to Zane for a while but would dull quickly. Zane would be tired of her before the summer was over.

Mica Haldane, however, could be a different matter. Naturally there was no chance of her having a career in the movies. Shelley didn't see in her that nebulous star quality that producers searched for. But Mica did have Zane besotted with her, probably because she was proving to be a more difficult target than his women usually were.

As Calula tilted Shelley's head back and started painting liner on her eyelids in the style used in the 1960s, Shelley saw Zane come into the room. He didn't speak but lowered himself into a chair to await his turn. She noticed his face looked puffy, and she wondered if he was drinking heavily again. His love of alcohol would soon become a problem to directors as well as to Zane.

"Good morning," she said, keeping her voice sultry despite the hour.

"'Morning," Zane said gruffly.

"Hangover?"

He glared at her in the mirror.

"I have some drops in my bag for bloodshot eyes."

Zane paused, then nodded. "Okay."

She watched Calula do her magic for a moment. "Only a few weeks to go, and we can leave this wretched place." She kept her face expressionless and perfectly still for Calula's sake. "I can hardly wait, personally."

The trailer door opened and Diane entered, followed as always by her faithful Una. Shelley and Una exchanged a look of pure hatred. Una sat in a chair and picked up a magazine. Diane perched on the arm of Una's chair and read over her shoulder.

"What do you think of that dress?" Diane asked Una as she pointed to a picture in the magazine.

Una gave it consideration. "You'd be beautiful in it. That model makes it look ponderous."

Shelley tried not to grimace. Who but Una would use a word like "ponderous" to describe a dress? She noticed Zane was smiling at Diane. Shelley recalled a time when Zane had given Diane the rush. Was he still interested? Shelley detested Diane's fresh beauty.

Zane really wasn't so bad, she thought as Calula started teasing her hair. Certainly he was handsome. He might be drinking too heavily, but it hadn't damaged his looks or body yet. Zane would ride high for years with the proper care. Shelley narrowed her eyes thoughtfully. If she were Zane's wife, she would ride along with him. At least she would be supported in fine style if her next movie proved not to be quick in coming.

Diane stared at her reflection in the wide mirror as she fluffed her light brown hair. "How would I look as a blonde? Or maybe a redhead?"

Una looked up from the magazine and studied Diane for a moment. "Never as a redhead. As a blonde? I don't think so. Blondes are a dime a dozen."

Shelley clenched her teeth. She was a blonde, as far as everyone knew. "I'd say it depends on the person," she said coldly. "I don't think Diane could ever carry it off."

Diane and Una exchanged amused looks. Shelley felt as if she had been baited and had fallen for it. She could hardly abide to be in the same town with Diane King, let alone in the same makeup trailer. She wondered what Greenberg could have been thinking of to cast them together. It was as bad as putting Bette Davis and Joan Crawford together in *Whatever Happened To Baby Jane?*

She turned her attention back to Zane. As his wife, she could watch over his career and be sure he took only the best roles. She knew his agent and had used him herself once, but had dropped him because she lacked confidence in his ability. Zane was such a hot item that any idiot could land him plum roles. As his wife, she could keep him from throwing away his life and talent on a bottle, and the higher she raised him, the better she would live. As Calula began to brush her hair, Shelley decided her best bet was not merely to have an affair with Zane, but to marry him.

As the call was an early one, the sun was barely up when the actors and crew gathered on Main Street. Mica patted her hand over her hair to be sure it was in place as she looked around for Kyle. He was across the lot talking to Miss Nelly and her friends. Despite the early hour, all three were there under Miss Nelly's distinctive beach umbrella. On the table beside them was a plate loaded with cinnamon rolls and doughnuts. Greenberg, who normally avoided Miss Nelly and her calories, was eating a cinnamon roll and pointing out the camera angle he wanted to his assistant. After seeing what Buford Ponder had done to help him, Greenberg had realized that not all the locals were his enemies, and had decided to show his appreciation by socializing with Miss Nelly and the Ponders.

Down the street, Mica saw Carrie drive up and park. She hesitated, then went to meet her. "Hi," she called out.

Carrie looked up and said, "Hi." She didn't sound particularly glad to see Mica.

"Would you like to have lunch together? We're in for a long day today."

Carrie didn't meet her eyes. "No, I already have plans."

"Jake is coming by? I haven't seen him in a while."

"No, he isn't. Jake and I aren't seeing each other anymore."

Mica stared at her friend. "You're not!"

"I don't know why you sound so surprised. You were the one who told me I should tell him that I was thinking about going to Hollywood. You're the one who's always saying people should try to reach their full potential."

"But I didn't mean you had to break off your relationship with him. I just thought—"

Carrie interrupted, saying, "Mica, it's really none of your business."

Mica was stunned and she stepped back. With a voice as cool as Carrie's, she said, "You're right. It really isn't any of my business." She turned and walked away, telling herself it was silly of her to feel like crying. She and Carrie had been friends for a long time, but few friendships lasted forever. She headed for the umbrella and Kyle.

"Good morning," he said cheerfully. "You look great in the morning, I might add," he said in a voice that wouldn't carry to other ears. "Not everyone can manage these early calls."

"I haven't had my makeup done yet. Calula doesn't want me until seven o'clock."

Shelley and Zane walked by on their way to the cameras. Zane wasn't speaking to anyone, and Shelley was watching him with a covetous expression. Carrie met them by the drugstore. Her attention was all for Zane, but he barely acknowledged her.

"Carrie and I had words," Mica said to Kyle as he handed her a cinnamon roll. "I don't think she wants to patch it up."

"Did you ever find out why she was upset?"

Mica nodded. "She and Jake have broken up. He may need to talk. Carrie and I have known each other most of our lives, and it's not like her to act this way. I feel as if I don't even know her these days."

Mica ate the cinnamon roll. It was one of Miss Nelly's homemade ones and was better than any from a store. "If this keeps up, I won't fit into this dress."

"I know what you mean. Harve said he had to let his belt out a notch already. His wife has sent word that he's going on a diet as soon as she gets him back home."

"It would be hard on a marriage with so much travel. How do people do it?"

"Most can't. Harve and Janet have dealt with it since they were married, however. I guess they're accustomed to being apart more often than they're together."

"I'd have trouble with that. If I loved someone enough to marry him, I'd want him to come home nights."

"I feel the same way."

She looked up at him. "But you were married to Tamara Nolan and you both must have traveled apart often."

"I've learned from my past mistakes."

"Oh?"

Kyle was silent for a minute. "Some marriage commitments are more important than others, it would seem. Some love is stronger. I think if a man and a woman are enough in love, they should give that first priority and everything else has to fit around it. That's not the kind of love Tamara and I had."

"You don't have to tell me this—it's none of my business. I've been told once today to tend to my own fences. I'm not prying." She watched Carrie, who was still gazing starry-eyed at Zane.

"I know, but I want you to realize that."

Mica gazed up at him. Why was he telling her this? "I would give it priority, too. When I marry, my husband and family will come first."

Across the street, Zane took his place and Carrie reluctantly backed off camera. Shelley looked at Zane and smiled. Greenberg nodded to his assistant to start the cameras rolling.

Kyle and Mica watched for a few minutes, and before long Shelley muffed her lines and the cameras were stopped. Shelley was reaching out and touching Zane's arm as if to beg his pardon.

With a grin, Kyle said, "We may be seeing motion-picture history in the making. Look at the way Shelley is behaving toward Zane."

Even at that distance, Shelley's eyes appeared limpid and imploring, as if Zane were the only interesting man within a hundred miles. Carrie crossed her arms and frowned at Shelley.

"I wish Carrie would be less obvious. She will be terribly embarrassed if she learns everyone has noticed what is happening between her and Zane."

"She won't be the first one he's treated like that."

The lines were said and Zane pulled Shelley into his arms. She gazed up at him, then slowly lowered her eyelashes as he drew nearer. He paused a breath away and then claimed her lips in a kiss that would sizzle on the screen. Shelley was supposed to push him away and laugh at him. Instead she held the kiss for a fraction too long and her rejection seemed false.

"Cut!" Greenberg went to them. "You have to push him away sooner. If you don't, the audience won't buy it."

"I know all that." Shelley gazed up at Zane. "But it's so hard to do."

"I don't care if it's impossible. Do it!" Greenberg went back to his canvas chair. He nodded at his assistant.

This time Shelley forgot her lines but remembered to kiss Zane briefly.

"This could take all day," Kyle said. He glanced at the sun. "If I know Shelley, she will continue to screw up until this scene has to be shot again tomorrow. Greenberg has to have this street scene filmed before the sun gets too high."

Mica looked back to where Carrie had been standing, but she was gone. "I have to go to makeup. Will I see you later?"

"Would you like to have dinner with me tonight?"

Mica smiled. "I'd love it."

"I'll come by your house after I've had time to shower and change."

"Sounds great." She hurried away with a smile.

LATER, AS MICA showered and shampooed her hair, she reflected how much she was looking forward to seeing Kyle tonight. Their schedules had kept them on the lot together all day, but they hadn't had time to talk after that morning. She admired his professionalism. When she had a scene with Kyle, she could be sure of not having to do it over and over to get it right. The same wasn't true of Shelley. She seemed to be working overtime to see how much trouble she could cause on the set.

Mica stepped out of the shower and wrapped a bath sheet around her. In short order, she dried her hair and tousled it with her fingers. It turned under naturally and fell into place when she brushed it. She had chosen this hairstyle because she washed her hair every morning and it was easy to fix.

Calula had approved of it, because with a clip above her forehead, the rest could be teased into a sphere exactly like the style worn in the sixties.

She put her towel on the brass hook and went into her bedroom. A glance at the clock told her Kyle would be here soon. She took a satin-and-lace bra and matching panties from her dresser drawer. They were deep rose as was the dress she planned to wear. Mica had splurged, buying them with some of the extra money she had made from the movie. They felt soft and silky against her skin.

She stepped into the matching slip, then went to the closet. As she took out the dress and held it in front of her at the mirror, she thought of Kyle. He had become an integral part of her life.

She sat on the bed and wondered what to do about that. What if the impossible happened and he asked her to go to Hollywood with him?

Not daring to follow that line of thought, she stood and pulled the dress over her head. It fell in graceful lines and the skirt swirled around her knees. Although it wasn't really silk, it felt as if it were, and the rose shade complemented her. It was the golden rose of sunsets, and it made her hair seem brighter with its reddish highlights.

She chose a scarf with a rose, cream and burgundy pattern and draped it around her neck, knotting it loosely so it would follow the vee of her neckline. Then she put on gold hoop earrings and slid a garnet ring on her finger. The ring had been her gift to herself for having completed college and was her favorite. Her shoes and purse were burgundy, and except for the lonely expression in her eyes, she looked quite nice, she thought.

The doorbell rang and she gave herself one last inspection in the mirror, then hurried to answer it. Kyle stood in the doorway, wearing a navy blue suit that made him appear even more handsome than when he wore casual clothes.

She had never seen him in a suit before, and for a minute she could only stare.

"Am I early?" he asked when she didn't speak.

"No, no. Come in." She stepped aside and closed the door after him. "You look wonderful."

"I was about to say the same about you. *Beautiful* was the word I had in mind."

Mica was suddenly touched by shyness. Kyle was not only handsome, but his charisma seemed to fill the room. She thought that in a room full of people, Kyle would stand out far above the rest. His shirt was cream, the same shade as in her scarf, and his tie echoed the rose, cream and burgundy.

"It looks as if we chose our clothes together."

She nodded. "They say that means our minds are on the same track."

"I certainly hope so." He grinned but didn't elaborate. "If you don't mind a half-hour drive, I thought we might go to Tyler. I know of a nice place to eat there."

They left a lamp burning and walked to the car. When Kyle opened her door for her, she was reminded of how much she had missed the simple courtesy of having a man do that. Lee Harris had never opened a door for her. "I'm glad you're old-fashioned about the important things," she said when he came around and got into the driver's side.

"I'm glad you are, too. I dated a woman once who was mad at me all evening because I opened her car door."

"How silly."

"Like I said, I dated her once." He started the car and it purred as he drove away from the curb.

Mica relaxed and enjoyed the luxury of being driven in a car that wasn't likely to stall at every stoplight. She needed to trade her car in for a newer model, but she had been reluctant to spend the money. Her salary didn't stretch far enough for expensive things like cars. That reminded her of the school-board edict that she should quit the movie, and she grimaced.

"Is something wrong?" he asked.

"I was just thinking about something that happened a couple of nights ago. I was called on the carpet for being in the movie."

"You're kidding. Why would someone object?"

"It's Brother Malcolm again. The man is like a poisonous weed. He's infiltrating the town. He convinced the school board that I'm not living up to the morals clause in my contract because he saw my car parked in front of Zane's apartment that night."

"But you were with me. I could talk to them."

"And tell them I was too drunk to make it home so I slept in your bed all night? No, thank you. I don't think that would help."

"I see what you mean. But nothing happened."

"I know it and you know it, but do you think they would believe us? I don't."

"They can't fire you over something like that, can they?"

"They suggested the choice was mine. I could quit the movie or I could quit teaching."

"Are you serious? Why didn't you tell me this before now?"

"I didn't intend to tell you at all. None of this is your fault, and it's not your problem."

"It may not be, but I care about how it affects you." Kyle drove in silence for a while, then asked, "So what are you going to do?"

"I can't walk out on the movie. There are too many scenes left to finish."

"But you enjoy teaching. No one has a right to keep you from doing that. Maybe I could get Greenberg to juggle the schedule so you could finish early and get the school board off your back."

"You'd do that for me?"

"Sure."

Mica looked at him through the darkness. "You really would do that, wouldn't you?"

"I care about you," he said simply.

"I really appreciate the offer, but please don't say anything to Greenberg. I need to handle this myself." Mica averted her eyes. This was more than she could bear without showing him how she felt. And she didn't dare do that. She didn't want either of them feeling obligated. It was better this way.

"Whatever you say. But if you change your mind, the offer is still open."

Quickly they were out of Sedalia and into the countryside. Above them the stars were bright, and the moon, fat and orange, was sitting on the horizon. Kyle broke the silence by saying, "I like it here."

"You do? Really?"

"I've told you that before."

"I know, but I thought you were just being polite."

"No. It's the truth. I find the serenity here very appealing. And that's not the only appealing thing here, either." He grinned and she saw his straight white teeth in the faint glow from the lights on the dashboard.

Soon they were in Tyler, and Mica gave him directions to the restaurant. By the time they'd reached the door, they were laughing about something that had happened that day on the set. Mica was thoroughly enjoying his company and wished the evening could go on forever.

The restaurant was nearly full, and as they were shown to their seats, Mica saw Arlen Hubbard and his wife sitting near the window. Hubbard also saw her and his frown was automatic. Mica pretended she hadn't noticed him.

She was seated in such a way that she could see the Hubbards in her peripheral vision. He had pointed her out to his wife, and they were both watching her and Kyle.

"You stopped talking."

She leaned forward. "Don't look now, but the large man over by the window is the president of the school board. He saw us come in."

Kyle leaned forward also. In a conspiratorial whisper he said, "Pretend to drop your napkin and we'll crawl out of here."

"Be serious. He's frowning."

"So what? He can't tell you who to date, surely."

"No, but if he sees me with you, he'll know I don't intend to leave the movie."

Kyle's eyes searched hers. "I don't want to cause any trouble for you. Maybe we should go."

Mica considered his suggestion, but only for a moment. She didn't want to leave. "No," she said as she lifted her chin. "I want to stay. I'm certainly not ashamed of being with you. Mr. Hubbard and his wife can stare all they want to."

"Are you sure?"

"I may even hold your hand," she said as she reached out and put her hand over his. Kyle covered her hand with his other one, sandwiching it between his palms.

"This may be risky, considering what you told me on the way here."

"Right this minute, I don't care." It was true. Holding hands with Kyle and gazing into his amused eyes was all she ever wanted to do. "I'll worry about them tomorrow."

"Whatever you say, Scarlett. I'm with you all the way."

Mica enjoyed being with Kyle, and his humor was infectious. After a while she forgot the head of the school board and his wife were in the same restaurant and was laughing at Kyle's stories. By the time they were through eating and ready to go, Mr. and Mrs. Hubbard had already gone, and Mica was able to leave with no nervousness.

"Let's go dancing," Kyle said, placing his hand over hers on the car seat.

"I haven't been dancing in years."

"Where would be a good place?"

Mica thought for a minute. "I'm not sure there is one. At least, not one that plays something other than hard rock. Do you like heavy metal?"

"Not particularly. I had a different kind of dancing in mind."

"I have tapes at my house."

"Perfect."

On the ride back to Sedalia, Mica thought how easy it was to be with Kyle. She had seen several people do a double take in the restaurant, having recognized him, but he was as down-to-earth as anyone she had ever known.

At her house, they walked hand in hand from the car to the porch, only reluctantly letting each other go so Mica could unlock the door. The living room lamp she had left burning for their return bathed the room in a warm glow that was cozy and welcoming. "My tapes are over here," she said as she led him to the stereo system on the wall opposite the sofa. "I have a little bit of everything."

Kyle selected one, and soon the soft strains of a love song drifted through the room. He turned to Mica and took her in his arms.

Mica loved to dance and she was good at it, but she had never felt as light on her feet as she did in Kyle's arms. Their steps matched perfectly as the music seemed to command their movements. Mica sighed. "You dance beautifully."

"I had good teachers. It's hard to fake being able to dance. Besides, I enjoy it." He grinned down at her. "You're good, too."

"You can thank Francine Dennis for that. And you should see me twirl a baton!"

"Were you a drum major or majorette in school?"

"No. Mrs. Dennis came to our school and taught everyone to dance as part of the physical-education program one year. Otherwise I couldn't have afforded the lessons."

"It's too bad I wasn't around then. I don't like to think of you ever having had to do without anything."

"I survived. Lots of kids do."

"I hear there's more to childhood than merely surviving."

"My childhood wasn't unhappy. We were a close family. That's something money can't buy. But I've led a rather mundane life. Until this summer nothing of any great interest had ever happened to me."

"Impossible. If your life really had been mundane, you wouldn't be so interesting."

"You find me interesting?"

"Of course. Did you think I've been seeking you out in order to be bored?"

She gazed into his green eyes and couldn't look away. "You fascinate me," she whispered. "I want to know all about you and I don't think I ever will. You're so complex."

"That's something else we have in common. You're a confusing lady."

"In what way?"

Kyle didn't answer for a few steps. "You make me think about things that I never expected to consider again."

She wanted him to elaborate, but he only held her closer and swept her around the room in a series of whirls. Kyle slowed and molded her body to his as the music came to a stop. As the next song began, they stood together, not moving, not needing to say anything. Mica felt her pulse hammering in her throat. He was so close and exciting. The lyrics of the love song spoke the words she wished she had the liberty of saying to him. Words she didn't dare voice.

Slowly Kyle lowered his head and his lips covered hers. Mica leaned into him and put her arms around his neck. The kiss deepened and grew in passion. When Kyle lifted his head, his eyes were hot with longing for her. Mica made a decision. She loved him, and whether or not he loved her made no difference. She didn't have the luxury of time to wait to see what might grow between them. Their time together was too limited and the end was too near. Without a word, she took his hand and led him through the house to her bedroom.

At the doorway she paused and looked up at him, her eyes filled with questions. Kyle smiled and gently touched her cheek. "Are you sure?" he said in a tender voice. "I don't want you to regret this in the morning."

"Will you?"

"No. Not ever."

They went into the room and Mica stepped out of her shoes. In her stocking feet she was considerably shorter than Kyle and she felt small and fragile beside him. She ran her hand up his chest and felt the beating of his heart. "I won't regret it, either. If I thought there was a chance of that, I wouldn't have brought you back here."

Kyle kissed her again, and Mica let her emotions run free. She might only have this one night to last her a lifetime. When she was dizzy from wanting him, she pulled back and started loosening his tie. Kyle laced his fingers through her hair and his eyes were questioning.

She divined his thoughts. "I want you because of yourself—not because of what you do for a living."

He smiled and relaxed. "I needed to hear that."

She smiled up at him.

He pulled the scarf from her neck and methodically began loosening the buttons of her dress. Mica's skin seemed to burn wherever his fingers grazed it. She had never wanted anyone so much. Her hands trembled as she opened the buttons of his shirt. His skin was smooth and firm, with hard muscles beneath. As she ran her hands over his chest and stomach, she felt the muscles tighten as if he was restraining himself. It excited her to know he was so eager for her. Her hands moved lower and unfastened his belt.

Kyle slipped her dress from her shoulders, and it shimmered to the floor, pooling about her feet. He caught his breath at the sight of her. Mica had always been self-conscious about undressing in front of anyone, but with Kyle, all her inhibitions were gone. To be with him was the most natural, the most exciting, thing in the world. After removing her slip, he sat her on the side of the bed and sensuously helped her out of her panty hose.

As he removed his shoes and socks, she stepped out of her discarded clothing and came to sit beside him on the bed. He reached past her and pulled down the covers. She kissed him and drew him back onto the pillows. Kyle paused only long enough to strip off his slacks and underwear.

Mica ran her hands over the sculpted beauty of his body. "It's too bad you don't do skin flicks," she teased. "You'd be a box-office smash."

"So would you."

She smiled, acknowledging his compliment, then nuzzled his cheek and kissed the warm pulse at the base of his neck. Kyle rolled onto his back, taking her with him. His fingers released the catch of her bra and he pulled it from her. "You're beautiful," he said.

Mica tried not to think about the fact that he had been married to one of the most beautiful women in Hollywood and had probably been to bed with more than one star. "I was afraid I might not... That you might be disappointed."

"I could never be disappointed in anything about you."

He raised his head and nuzzled her neck in return, nibbling on her earlobes, then leaving a trail of butterfly kisses down her neck and across her chest to her pouting nipples. For long minutes, he lathed her breasts with his hot tongue, teasing and tantalizing her by alternately suckling her throbbing nipples and rapidly flicking them with the tip of his tongue. Meanwhile, his gentle hands caressed her cheeks, her arms and shoulders, her sides, the part of her back that he could reach and the flat plane of her stomach. Moment by moment, her arousal increased far beyond anything she had ever known. And when his roving hands slipped beneath the legs of her panties and his fingers entangled themselves in the nest of curls there, she parted her legs and almost cried out as his exploration moved to the core of her femininity.

Kyle took his time and savored every inch of her. Mica had never been so excited or so thoroughly aroused. She didn't know if he loved her now or if he ever would, but she loved enough for them both. Although she didn't dare risk telling him, she showed her love in her caresses and responsiveness. Kyle matched her passion and eagerness with that of his own.

When they became one, Mica felt as if her soul touched his. Never had she felt such togetherness, such complete pleasure. When she reached her pinnacle, he was there to hold her and to give her the greatest pleasure she could attain. As she came back down the other side of the mountain, he began to move again, and this time when she reached the summit of passion, he was right with her, loving her and pleasing her to a degree she hadn't dreamed was possible.

Afterward, she lay contentedly in his arms. Kyle made no effort to leave, but seemed to need her continued love as much as she needed his. Mica tried to stay awake, to savor every moment of lying here beside him, but he had loved her so thoroughly, she felt herself getting drowsy and drifting off to sleep in his arms.

## CHAPTER FOURTEEN

WHEN MICA AWOKE, she thought she would find Kyle lying beside her, but as she reached out to touch him, she discovered only cool sheets and an empty pillow. She lifted her head. He was gone.

She sat up, the sheet pooling around her waist in the early-morning light. She heard the click of the front door closing and knew he was leaving. Barefoot, she went into the guest room that looked toward the street and parted the curtains. With his coat and tie slung over his shoulder, he was walking out to his car. As she watched, he got in and drove away.

Mica let the curtain drop back into place. He hadn't waited for her to wake up. Did that mean he regretted spending the night with her? She wrapped her arms around her body to dispel the sudden chill she felt and hurried into the bathroom. As she stared at her face in the mirror, she asked herself if she had given him too much of herself. How could they have made love through the night and Kyle not realize how deeply she loved him? The words had never been spoken, but surely her love had been obvious. At the time she had felt as if her love was welcomed and returned in kind, and that one night of loving him would be better than none. Now she realized one night had given her only a desire to spend the rest of her life with him. She had always prided herself on her common sense. Where was that ability to reason logically now?

As KYLE DROVE toward his house, down Sedalia's quiet streets, he thought of nothing but Mica. He still wanted her, even though they had spent most of the night making love. She excited him and pleased him more than he had thought possible, and he became aroused again at the mere thought of her. He had left without waking her in order to let her sleep; she had slept so little during the night. Also, he had wanted to get his car away from the front of her house before anyone saw it. He didn't want his having spent the night to cause her trouble. The school board was already trying to find reason to fire her.

He parked and went into his house, pausing to put on a pot of coffee before showering and shaving. He wasn't scheduled to be on the set until later that day, but he had been spending so much time thinking about Mica, he hadn't finished learning his lines. He couldn't remember a time in his career when he had been so slipshod in his preparation, and he was surprised to find he didn't even regret it. Being with Mica or even just thinking about her seemed more important than this or any movie.

He loved her and he wished he had been able to tell her, but he could see no way they could have a viable future together without her sacrificing her career, which was terribly important to her.

As he dressed, he began exploring ways he might be able to rearrange his life to fit hers. Not finding a solution to this dilemma was becoming more and more impossible to consider.

MICA WASN'T surprised to find Norma Mobley on her front porch, but she was amazed that Brother Malcolm was with her. The preacher was a large man in height as well as in girth. He held his worn black Bible in his right hand as if it were a weapon, and he wasn't smiling as Norma preceded him into the house. Mica said, "I have coffee. Would you like some?"

"I never drink caffeine," Brother Malcolm replied, his deep voice reverberating throughout the small house.

"Neither do I," Norma said, despite the fact that she always had a cup of coffee with Mica during her inspections of the house.

Mica led them into the living room and sat down with them. She thought she had a pretty good notion as to why Brother Malcolm had come, especially in light of the look of foreboding on Mrs. Mobley's face, but she couldn't believe it might be so. She hoped she was wrong and that their visit was unrelated to his objections to the movie in town. Nevertheless, she waited for one of them to speak first.

"I know you are not of my flock," Brother Malcolm began, "but Sister Norma is, and she has interceded on your behalf."

"I have no idea what you're talking about," Mica said with a glance at her landlady. "I go to Saint Matthew's. If you're here to convert me, I'm afraid you're wasting your time."

"Converts are my business, but this time I'm here for an even more desperate cause. I've never been to the church you mentioned, but I'm sure it frowns on sinning."

"Of course it does," she said as she tried to figure why her landlady looked as if she had been personally offended.

"I know what happened here last night," the woman said.

Mica blinked. How could her landlady possibly know about Kyle? She didn't live far away, but her house wasn't within sight of Mica's.

"Sister Norma happened to drive by last night and saw a man's car parked out front. This morning when she was out, she saw that it was still here."

"How do you know it belonged to a man? And even if it did, it's none of your business." Mica's anger was rapidly rising.

"It had a rental sticker on it, and I called the place and asked," Norma said coldly. "It's rented to Kyle Spensor. And it is my business as long as you're living in my house."

"You must know the wages of sin are death," Brother Malcolm intoned with rising volume.

"I think you had both better go," Mica said as she got to her feet.

Instead of following her lead and doing as she asked, Brother Malcolm and Norma Mobley fell to their knees. In loud and demanding tones, Brother Malcolm commanded Heaven to see the evil of Mica's ways and to put fear into her heart. As he droned on and on, Mica was at a loss as to what to do. She was a regular churchgoer, but she didn't feel she had done wrong. She had gone to bed with Kyle, but it had been an act of love, not one of carnal hunger.

Mrs. Mobley opened one eye to see if Mica had followed their lead and gotten on her knees. Mica glared at her and stood her ground. The woman closed her eye again and interspersed several "amens" to punctuate the preacher's prayer. After what seemed to be a very long time, Brother Malcolm brought the exhortation to a close and got to his feet. Norma Mobley did the same. Mica stood there, angry and silent, her arms defiantly crossed over her chest.

"I can see our prayer has fallen on deaf ears," he said in a voice that clearly indicated he had no hope for Mica at all. "I suppose I'll have no choice but to bring this matter of ur repeated indecent conduct before the school board."

Mrs. Mobley glared at Mica for a moment, then said, "We will continue to pray. In the meantime, I think it would be best for you to find another place to live."

"That suits me just fine. I don't want you, either of you, to come here and try to embarrass me again."

"See that the house is clean when you leave," Norma snapped. She stalked to the door with Brother Malcolm at her heels.

Mica shut the door after them and leaned against it. She was far more angry than embarrassed. Only days before, Brother Malcolm had gotten the school board stirred up against her, probably with a performance similar to what she had just witnessed. It was a good thing that her probationary period was over, although Brother Malcolm's allegations were not proof of misconduct. Of course, the board didn't have to have proof to fire her, and if they did, she would have to sue the school district for reinstatement of her job. She would win the suit, no doubt, but whether the board had enough collective good judgment to realize that beforehand was questionable. And such a suit would be costly to both sides. She doubted she had enough money in her savings to pursue the matter if they did fire her. Suddenly the reality that she might be fired and be unable to defend herself hit home. *It isn't fair!* her mind protested as a knot formed in her stomach. There was nothing she could do but wait to see what would happen.

In the meantime, though, she was going to have to find another place to live, and finding another house in her price range was going to be difficult. The selection in Sedalia was pretty limited. Most of the houses she knew about with rent as cheap as this one were in a part of town where Mica would feel uneasy coming and going at night.

For the first time in years, she wondered if she really wanted to continue living in Sedalia.

BROTHER MALCOLM'S unsettling visit was still raw on Mica's nerves that afternoon when she arrived downtown.

"Hurry, Mica. Greenberg's waiting," Kyle said.

Mica had lost track of time worrying and was embarrassed that she was late. Greenberg frowned at her and glanced at his watch, but didn't say anything. Mica took her place by Kyle and tried to avoid looking up at him for fear that he would notice she was upset and want to know why. The evening before at the restaurant, he'd expressed concern that Hubbard's having seen them together would cause more trouble for her, and he'd said he didn't want to be the cause. She didn't dare tell him about Brother Malcolm's castigations and threats because he might feel responsible and pull away from her in a misguided attempt to protect her—if, in fact, he wasn't already wishing he hadn't stayed and made love to her.

The cameras started rolling, and Kyle, whose voice was now so dear and familiar to her, began his lines. It was the scene where Ryan was telling Angie he loved her. Mica had to look up at him. When she did, she saw the questioning in his eyes and all her lines fell from her head.

After an awkward pause, Greenberg called, "Cut. Try it again."

Once more Kyle spoke the lines that cued her response, but again, when she looked up at him, she couldn't get the words past her throat. The words he was saying were too close to what she wanted to hear Kyle say in reality. As the silence grew long between them, tears gathered in her eyes, and she shook her head and looked beseechingly at Greenberg.

"Cut," he said again. He motioned to Mica and they walked a few paces away. "All right. What's wrong?"

"I . . . I don't know."

"It's not like you to miss a cue. I want to know what's bothering you."

Mica opened her mouth to speak but had no idea what to tell him. At last she said, "I've had words with my landlady. I'm looking for a new place to live."

He studied her face. "That's all there is to it? I got the feeling there was a problem between you and Kyle."

"Kyle?" she asked too quickly. "I have no idea what you're talking about."

"Have it your way. Can you do the scene now?"

Mica nodded. She wanted to do it perfectly for Greenberg in appreciation for his not yelling at her. She saw now why Kyle said he was a great director. Greenberg knew instinctively how to handle people.

This time Mica was able to say her words and to make them convincing.

Carrie was in the next scene with Mica, but didn't carry off her part quite as well. Fortunately, the camera angle overlooked the expression on her face. Mica glanced in the direction Carrie was looking and saw Zane and Shelley talking together. They finished the scene without a problem.

As soon as the cameras stopped, Kyle started toward Mica. "Are you all right?" he asked.

"Sure." She gazed up at him and tried to smile. Making love with him had been the most wonderful experience of her life, and she was trying to keep that thought uppermost in her mind, but she was afraid he could see through her.

"If you're okay, I'm the pope."

"Don't make fun of me," she snapped. Her nerves couldn't take any more.

Kyle dropped his arm. "I wasn't. This was my last scene today. See you tomorrow." He turned and walked abruptly away.

Mica wanted to run after him and tell him she loved him and hadn't meant to upset him, but she couldn't. He wouldn't be upset with her long over something so slight, or at least she hoped he wouldn't. And in the meantime, she had to find someplace else to live.

That evening, after a fruitless search for another house to rent, she sat on her back porch, noticing how empty the house was without Kyle in it. Even her backyard seemed too vacant. Her life was empty, as well, and she was tired of being alone.

She heard footsteps on her drive and turned to see Kyle coming toward her. For a moment she considered going into the house, but she knew he had already spotted her. She waited for Kyle to speak to determine if he was still angry with her.

"I want to see you," he said in a gentle tone after a pause. "I think we need to talk."

"I'm glad to see you," she said carefully. She had no idea what he was thinking and feeling.

"Are you still upset?"

Mica looked away. "Not as much."

"Was it wrong of me to stay with you last night? I had the impression you wanted me to be there."

"I did. You know I did." She couldn't look at him. How could she explain all she was feeling?

"I'd hate to see the results if you ever got *really* happy."

She frowned at him. "How can you joke at a time like this?"

"Look," he said, "I know you must have heard all the stories about actors sleeping around, and you must be thinking all sorts of terrible things, but I'm not like that."

"What are you saying?" If he said he loved her, everything else would be bearable.

Kyle paused as if he was choosing his words carefully. "I'm saying that last night wasn't some casual fling for me. Was it for you?"

"Certainly not. How can you ask me that?"

"What else can I think?" he countered. "Last night was great, but today you've barely spoken to me. You're obviously upset."

"I'm just confused about everything. Can't you understand that?"

"I'd have a better chance if you told me what's wrong."

She had no choice but to tell him what had happened. She paused to try to get her thoughts in order. "My landlady saw your car out front last night and this morning."

"Damn! I thought I'd moved it before anyone was up and about."

"She brought Brother Malcolm over to pray over me this morning."

"I beg your pardon?"

"I've never had a preacher say such things to or about me. It was terrible! Then Mrs. Mobley said I have to find another place to live."

"Why didn't you throw them out?"

"It's not that easy to toss out your landlady and a man the size of Brother Malcolm. I was beginning to think they were going to stay right there in my living room on their knees all day."

"On their knees? Sounds like they put on quite a show."

"Brother Malcolm described me as a jezebel and a harlot."

Kyle took a step forward. "He said that about you? I'm going to go and have a talk with him!"

"No, don't do that. It will only make matters worse. You don't know what it's like to live in a small town."

"Is he going to the school board with this, too?"

"I don't know," Mica lied, hoping to lessen the impact.

He came to the porch and climbed two steps. "I'm sorry this happened."

Mica met his eyes. "I don't regret anything about last night. That's one reason I was trying to avoid telling you about their visit."

Kyle looked away. "I didn't mean to cause you problems of any kind. I don't want you to be in trouble because of me."

"I don't regret having made love with you. Not at all," she said softly. "I could never regret what we shared last night."

Kyle gazed into her eyes. "What are we going to do about this?"

She shook her head. "It doesn't matter. Not really. You'll only be here for the time it takes to wrap up this movie, then you'll be long gone. That's the only way it can be. So we'd better stop seeing each other now before it's too difficult—"

"I can't stand the thought of your being hurt because of me. I'll talk to the school board and Brother Malcolm."

"No, Kyle. Don't do that. If we just leave this alone, maybe it'll die down on its own. You're not responsible for this."

Kyle's face was drawn. "If it hadn't been for me, you wouldn't have been thrown out of your house. And your job may be in jeopardy. I think it's best for me to stay away from you and not make this worse than it already is." He turned and started walking away.

He turned back, and in the fading light of the evening she could see his face was filled with pain. "I'm sorry, but it has to be this way."

As she watched him go, her tears began to flow. She knew this parting was inevitable, but that didn't make it any less painful.

# CHAPTER FIFTEEN

SHELLEY WATCHED as Diane batted her eyelashes at Zane in a way that was flirtatious and at the same time innocent. Even though they were filming in direct sunlight, Diane's face was smooth and clear. She looked so young. With a lift of her chin, Shelley turned and stalked away. She was more than worried; she was frightened. How would she look on the screen in contrast to Diane? She was already cast as an older and too-worldly woman. Why had she ever agreed to take this part? Would she look foolish? She couldn't have that. Instead of going to the trailer, she headed for one of the crew she saw lounging around with nothing to do.

"I need a driver," she commanded.

He looked surprised, but pointed toward his car.

In five minutes Shelley was at the newspaper office, asking to see the editor. The office quickly turned into chaos as everyone there realized who she was and that she had finally agreed to grant the interview she had previously denied them. As the editor beckoned her into his office, she said to the crewman, "Wait for me."

She knew this would make her late for her scenes, but she didn't care. This was more important. She sat in the wooden chair offered her and crossed her legs, making sure her skirt slid high on her thigh. "I've decided I was wrong not to talk to you before, and I'm here to give you an exclusive interview."

It was gratifying to see the editor fumble around in his desk drawer for a tape recorder and notepad. She hadn't seen this much interest in her since her first crow's-feet had appeared and her career had begun leveling out.

"Where were you born?" he asked as he clicked the recorder on.

Shelley smiled and flirted with him. "That's been asked so many times. How would you like to know about Diane King?"

"Sure, if that's what you want to tell me."

"Well, I want to talk about myself, too. After all, you wanted to interview me, not Diane."

"Miss Doyle, you've been my favorite movie star since I was in high school."

He couldn't have chosen a more unfortunate set of words. She ran her eyes from the top of his balding head, over his paunch and down to where the desk hid his legs. "Yes. Well, as you know, Diane has just finished going through a divorce. It's amazing she was ever married at all."

"Why is that? I'd imagine Miss King would have her pick of suitors."

"Suitors are generally men."

The editor turned off the machine. "You aren't going to say anything that could get me into trouble, are you?"

She made her eyes innocent. "Why would I do that? I'm only telling you what everyone in Hollywood already knows. It's common knowledge that she travels around with a woman named Una Lundquist, and that Una is as butch as they come."

The editor paled and went to shut the door. "Miss Doyle, I can't print that! She could sue me for everything I own. Her fans would storm this office!"

Shelley sighed. She would have to be more subtle. "I understand."

He clicked the machine back on and said, "I understand she was married to Tony Burke."

"Yes, but they never actually lived together. It was what might be called a marriage of convenience. Then, while she was in Europe, supposedly to film a movie but actually for drying out, he found someone more interested in being his wife and divorced Diane."

"She made a film in Europe called *Drying Out*? I don't believe I've heard of it."

"Not a film. She was being detoxed. Alcohol and drugs are two of her greatest weaknesses."

Again he turned off the tape recorder. "I can't print that, either."

"Of course you can. Now that she's dried out, she has discussed waging a campaign against drugs. I hear she's even speaking to a chapter of Mothers Against Drunk Driving."

He turned the recorder back on. "You say Miss King is waging a war against drugs and is speaking to a chapter of Mothers Against Drunk Driving? Will it be a chapter in this area?"

Shelley couldn't believe anyone could be so naive. "No, she won't be here that long. She still has to check in with her parole officer from time to time in Hollywood."

The editor gave her a questioning look. "Parole officer?"

"Didn't you know? She was arrested on a charge of dealing in drugs. Of course, it was kept quiet. And her lawyer got her acquitted. Money does wonders. That was before she got religion," she added as an inspiration.

His eyes lit up. "Oh? She's found religion?"

She had almost forgotten she was in the heart of the Bible Belt. "I thought everyone knew that. That's why she doesn't mind having the information printed about her addiction to drugs and alcohol. That's why she went to Europe to break the habit."

"If she doesn't mind it being known, why was the press told she had gone to Europe to make a movie?"

"She didn't want it to be known until she could see if she would be able to break the habit. I've heard she met her secretary, Una Lundquist, at the hospital there. Una was an attendant or something. Have you seen her? She could restrain a woman twice the size of Diane."

It was so easy. Shelley was enjoying herself immensely. She was also aware that all work had stopped in the outer office and that everyone was openly staring through the glass panes of the editor's office at her. She ran her fingers through her hair with one of her characteristic gestures. "Now let's talk about me."

WHEN THE PAPER came out, at least a dozen people brought a copy to Diane for an autograph. At first she assumed the article was one on her arrival in Sedalia. Then, while an eager fan waited for her signature, her eyes happened to catch a sentence containing the words "detox," "drugs" and "alcohol." She snatched the paper back. Hurriedly she read the article and gasped in rage. "Oh, no!" Leaving the fan staring after her, Diane ran in search of Una.

"Look what she's had printed about me! It's on the front page!"

Una read the article and her eyebrows knitted over her nose. "It's libel!"

"How could the paper print such things? Is that editor crazy?" Diane paced her dressing room and glared at the paper. "What if this is picked up by one of the wire services?"

"We have to have a retraction printed. It even has *my* name in it!" Una reread it as if she couldn't quite grasp it.

"I'll have Shelley's head for this! I swear I will!" Diane launched into a tirade that spared no words. "I've never had a problem with drugs, and that incident with alcohol was years ago! How could she have ever heard of that? It even tells my real age! How did she know that? And look what it implies about you! About *us!*"

Una was silent for a long moment, then reread the damaging article. "I guess Tony told her about the drinking problem. He never did have good sense. I don't know why you ever married him in the first place. He was always beneath you."

"What am I going to do? Shelley did this for spite! I've never harmed her in any way. Why would she do this?"

Una shook her head. "Jealousy, maybe? You know how she is."

"But it's not true! At least, most of it isn't. You should be as mad as I am. Look what she has suggested about you. I'll sue her! I'll sue her for defamation of character. Then I'll sue the paper." Diane collapsed in tears.

Una was more logical and reasonable, but she didn't point out the fallacies. It was best to let Diane work out her anger in words. "You'll have to go to the newspaper and demand that they print a retraction. This is too damaging. The press will have a field day with you. Let's hope it hasn't already been picked up by the Associated Press."

Diane groaned and hid her face in her hands. "I should never have told anyone about my old drinking problem. Not even Tony. I'm past all that, Una. I have it under control now!"

"I know, but fans are fickle. They may not believe you. Maybe I should leave."

"No. That would make it appear as though there's some truth in this article. No, we have to ride this out." She bit her knuckle as she paced.

Una went to Diane and patted her awkwardly on the shoulder. "Help me remember all we've heard about Shelley. I can use it to our advantage."

Diane looked doubtful, but she nodded. Una was good at remembering gossip and at weeding out what was true and what was believable enough to pass as truth, and she had confidence in Una.

"It's sin! A hotbed of sin!" Norma Mobley wailed as she waved the newspaper at Brother Malcolm. "When I think of what that element has introduced into our town, I could cry!"

"I've prayed on it without ceasing." Brother Malcolm shook his head and glanced back over his copy of the paper. "Shameful! Thoroughly shameful!"

"They aren't full of shame at all. That's what is wrong with them! They need to have the fear put into them!"

"I've tried to reach some of them, but they ignore me or tell me to be on my way." He shook his large head. "It's always this way with men who are martyrs for their faith."

Norma felt her heart go out to him. "You try so hard. You really are a martyr, you know." She recalled the sermon he had preached the night before at the tent revival he had begun. "Your words last night were inspired."

"I like to think that's true."

"We have to drive those actors from this town!"

"You're right, Sister Norma. There's no telling what vice they are teaching our youngsters."

Norma shuddered. "It makes my flesh crawl to think about it."

He shook his head warningly. "We mustn't speak of the flesh. After all, we are alone in my office. It's not proper to talk of our bodies here."

She bowed her head in acknowledgment of what she considered to be proper discipline. "I'm sorry, Brother Malcolm. I forgot myself. It was just an expression."

"I know, but Satan is lurking everywhere."

She thought he must be right, because after his having said it was wrong to speak of her flesh, she found herself thinking that he was a nice-looking man, even desirable. She dropped to her knees. "Pray for me, Brother Malcolm. Don't let Satan get me."

He knelt beside her. "Don't worry, Sister Norma. He can't come in here. Not unless we let him. Fight back!"

Her eyes met his. When they were on their knees, he wasn't that much taller than she was. "I'm fighting hard." It was true. She found herself actually thinking of Brother Malcolm as a man and she wanted to kiss him. She clenched her eyes tighter and fought to get the carnal thought out of her mind. "I'm winning," she said after a moment. Her knees ached from kneeling on the hardwood floor and that was helping her to put her mind on proper matters. She opened her eyes. "I won. Satan has been repelled!"

He shook his head. "Don't let yourself become overconfident. That's one of his favorite tools."

She nodded. It was so hard to remember all the things that might give Satan power. It was no wonder it took a man of Brother Malcolm's stature to wage the war of salvation. Norma couldn't hope to do it all alone. She got to her feet. Lately her knees had been rebelling against so much kneeling, but she was sure Brother Malcolm would say that her discomfort was Satan at work again, so she didn't mention it.

"We have to drive those actors from our town," he said, as if the idea were all his own and original to the moment.

"Amen."

"I'm going to expand the revival. We'll meet in the tent every night until every actor is gone from our home place. We'll pray them out of here!"

"Hallelujah!"

He was on a roll. "We'll fight them in every way we can. I'll urge our brothers and sisters in faith to refuse to sell them goods and to speak to them. We'll wage a campaign to have the faithful talk to those residents who are in the movie and convince them not to pander to the wiles of Satan!''

"Amen," she said again fervently. She loved it when Brother Malcolm got worked up like this. She could almost smell the brimstone and see the fires. "We'll fight back!"

He put his large hand on her shoulder as if she was his comrade in arms. "Man and woman, we'll fight evil."

"As equals?" she gasped.

"Almost as equals," he amended. "We mustn't forget the natural order of things in our fervor."

"Yes, Brother Malcolm." She hoped he would keep his hand on her shoulder. It felt good there.

"We have to plan our campaign. Will you have dinner with me tonight?"

Norma's mouth dropped open. No other woman in her church had ever been shown this much regard. "I'd be honored!"

"Tonight, then. At seven."

Norma could only nod. She was too filled with awe to speak. She was to dine alone with Brother Malcolm! Already she was trying to decide what she would wear. Then she realized that thought was of the flesh, and she tried to think about something else.

"IT'S A GOOD THING this movie's almost over," Jake said to Mica as he bagged her box of light bulbs. "There's been talk all over town ever since the paper came out this morning. Brother Malcolm was in here, trying to convince me not to sell anything to the actors or crew."

"What business is it of his who your customers are? You don't go to his church."

"No, but my grandmother and one of my aunts do." He took the money she handed him. "He sounded like he was about to wage some holy war or something."

Mica remembered how frightening it had been to have Brother Malcolm and her landlady praying in her living room. "He can be pretty persuasive. If you ask me, he's a dangerous man."

"I agree." Jake glanced around to be sure they weren't being overheard and leaned over the counter. "He's the kind to try to stir up a mob, if you ask me. You be careful."

"I will be. And you're right. It won't be long before the movie is over." The thought of Kyle leaving so soon made her ache inside. To put her mind off him, she said, "Have you talked to Carrie lately?"

Jake frowned. "Not since we broke up. She's not herself, Mica. Have you noticed that?"

"As well as I can. She isn't talking to me, either. It's not like her to carry a grudge. She's changed in the past few years, but I hadn't noticed how much until lately."

"I know. You don't think she's, well, taking anything, do you?"

"You mean like drugs? Carrie? Never in a million years. She has more sense than to do that."

"I think so, too, but I can't imagine what else it could be."

Mica thought of how Carrie always seemed to be watching Zane, but she kept that to herself. Jake was already depressed. "It could be that she'll return to normal once our lives are back in the usual routine."

"I sure hope so. I still love her, you know. I guess I always have."

She patted his hand in a sisterly gesture. "I know. I hate to see you hurt."

"It's okay. I've waited for Carrie for so many years that a while longer won't make much difference."

Mica nodded. His devotion truly had been remarkable. "If you really want her, put out an effort and win her back. We have to hang in there. I don't want to lose her, either."

She picked up her sack and turned toward the door. "I'll see you later."

"Okay. Come back anytime."

She stepped out onto the sidewalk and nearly ran into Kyle. For a minute she was too flustered to speak. They had avoided each other for days. "Hello," she managed to say.

"Hello." He looked as if he found it equally awkward. "Been shopping, I see."

She gestured with her sack. "I ran out of light bulbs."

The silence threatened to grow. He said, "How's the house hunting coming along?"

"Not well at all. I've looked at a few houses, but all of them are either too expensive or in a bad part of town. I may be forced to move into an apartment."

"That would be a shame." He looked away for a moment, then looked back. "Listen, Mica, if there was any way I could—"

"Kyle, please don't blame yourself. It was my decision."

"But that doesn't change the damage that was done. Nothing can."

Mica didn't know what to say. Kyle clearly had his mind made up.

He seemed to want to say more, but instead he walked away. After a while, Mica turned toward home, but her steps were slower than usual, and she neither smiled nor looked to either side.

When she reached her house, the phone was ringing. Hurriedly she set her sack on the counter and went to answer it. For a brief moment she hoped it might be Kyle. "Hello?"

"Miss Haldane, this is Mr. Hubbard."

Her spirits sank. "Yes?"

"I've had a talk with some of the other board members and we think it's time to insist that you resign. It was bad enough when only morals were involved, but now that drugs are an issue, we—''

"Wait a minute! What's this about drugs?"

"It's become known around town that the actors are freely using drugs."

"There are no drugs being used. Whoever told you that was mistaken."

"It's in today's paper, and everyone's talking about it. The reputation of our entire school system will be ruined if we allow you to remain on our staff. So maybe it'd be best if you left...."

"Or you'll fire me?"

"I'm afraid I'll have no other choice."

"Yes, you do. You could take my word for it. You've known me all my life, and you should know I wouldn't be involved in something like drugs."

"You'll remember that drugs wasn't the original issue."

She tried to keep her voice calm. "I can assure you that I've done nothing to damage my reputation or to reflect poorly on the school. I want to keep my job, but I have obligations. I have a contract with the film company."

"Your first obligation should be to yourself," Hubbard said direly. "I've also had a call from Brother Malcolm. He says he has proof that Kyle Spensor was at your house all night and that his car was parked blatantly out front where your students and their parents could see it."

"It seems to me you and Brother Malcolm are working overtime to come up with reasons to fire me. I have a contract for that teaching job, you know. And I'm a good teacher! You don't seem to be considering my merits at all!"

"That's not entirely true, Miss Haldane. I'm just giving you the option of a peaceful resignation as opposed to a hearing in front of the school board. Will you resign?"

Mica was silent for a long time. "I need time to think it over." The movie would be finished in two weeks. Could she stall that long? "Can you give me until a week from Saturday?"

"I'm sorry, Miss Haldane. I have to have an answer by this Friday."

She gripped the receiver. "As I said, Mr. Hubbard, I have to think. I'll get back to you." He hung up in her ear, obviously angry, but she remained calm. She had to think. She knew what she wanted most. She wanted Kyle to love her. If he did, she could face anything, overcome any obstacle. Her *first* priority was no longer to have a job that she now knew wasn't all that secure. Should she throw all caution to the wind and call Kyle?

She had only three days to decide an issue that would have a tremendous impact on her life. Was fate pushing her toward Kyle? She had never particularly believed in fate, yet here she was about to lose her job on top of being unable to find another place to live. But Kyle had never once suggested that he wanted her to go away with him. She could lose everything she had worked so hard for in exchange for only two more weeks with the man she loved. But two weeks in Kyle's arms might be a fair exchange.

KYLE WAS GLAD to reach his house. He hadn't expected to run into Mica. On the set, when he knew she would be there, he could steel himself ahead of time and pretend that the sight and sound of her wasn't driving him crazy. The chance meeting had left him shaken.

He got a soft drink from the refrigerator and went out back and sat on the porch steps to think. Now that he knew Mica, what would life be like without her? He had never believed a person could fall in love so quickly and so completely as this. But what was she feeling? If she loved him, why would she have asked him not to see her again?

Unfortunately, the answer was obvious. He could see her point. He didn't have the right to cause her to lose her job and be publicly embarrassed by this crazed preacher. He couldn't upset her world and go waltzing off, leaving her in the muddle that once had been her chosen life. That meant he either had to tell her how he felt or never see or speak to her again.

He knew he loved her. That much he had been certain of for weeks. If it were up to him, they would never be apart again. Money was no issue. Kyle had invested his earnings wisely and had enough for them to live well for the rest of their lives. After a life spent in front of the cameras, maybe it was time to consider retiring, he thought, or at least cutting back on his projects. If he did, he could pick projects that would be filmed during summer break so Mica could travel with him. It would be so simple if he knew she loved him. Even the issue of her wanting to teach underprivileged children could be resolved. But what did she feel for him?

He couldn't simply walk away from her. He loved her too much. On the other hand, how could he do anything else if she didn't love him? He couldn't struggle to win her in these last few days and fail, knowing her job would be forfeit for his efforts. Did she care more for teaching than she did for him?

He thought how few the days were that he would have in the same town with her. Right now he could go inside and phone her by dialing a local number, or he might see her by chance, as had just happened at the hardware store. But soon these things would be impossible. Hundreds of miles would separate them, hours of travel. The thought made him physically ache.

Kyle rubbed his eyes and wished he had never come to Sedalia and that he never had to leave.

CARRIE HAD NO REAL intention of going by the hardware store. She had told herself she was only going for a drive. But when Jake stepped out to lock up for the evening, she was parked beside his car. The sight of his tanned arms and face made her pulse quicken.

When he saw her, he paused, then walked to the passenger door and sat beside her. Neither spoke for several minutes.

Finally Carrie said, "Do you ever have one of those dreams where one thing leads to another, and before you know it, everything is out of hand and it turns into a nightmare?"

"Yes."

"Well, that's the way I feel these days. Like everything snowballed too fast, and I made some big mistakes."

Jake squinted back at his store and didn't look at her. "What mistakes?"

Carrie bit her lip. "I love you, Jake. I got carried away with the idea of going to Hollywood and becoming a star. I was wrong." It hurt her to admit it, and her voice trembled.

He turned to her. "Were there any other mistakes I need to know about?"

This was the question she had dreaded most. Her love for him was greater than her need for honesty. "There were none that you should know about. None that matter."

He was silent a long time. Carrie had suspected he must have guessed or been told that she was seeing Zane. Sedalia was a small, gossipy town, and she hadn't been particularly circumspect in her infatuation with Zane.

At last he said, "I love you, too, Carrie."

Carrie felt tears rise in her eyes. "I don't know how I could have been so foolish," she said softly. "I almost threw away everything."

He turned to her and put his hand on her nape. It felt warm and comfortable there. "I would have waited for you," he replied as he gazed into her eyes.

"How did you know I'd change my mind?"

He finally smiled. "Because I knew that deep in your heart you loved me." He leaned forward and kissed her.

Carrie put her forehead against his. "Mica must be awfully mad at me. I've been so rude to her!"

"She's worried, not angry. I'm pretty sure you can patch it up with her. What caused your change of heart?"

Carrie lifted her head and looked at the parking lot. "It was odd, really. I had made up my mind to leave and had even started packing. Most of my things are in storage, you know, so I didn't have much to get together. And Mom came in with some of my things she had saved for me from high school. I started looking through them and all at once I realized that I didn't want to leave, that some dreams are better if they're never acted upon."

"I had hoped you'd changed your mind because of me." His disappointment showed in his voice.

Carrie touched his face and smiled at him. "I made my decision when I found the silver football you gave me the year you made the all-star team."

"You still have it?"

She reached into the neck of her blouse and pulled out a small football suspended on a silver chain.

Jake kissed her and grinned. "Welcome back."

"We have a lot of lost time to make up for," she said hurriedly to ward off her tears. "Will you come over at seven?"

"Make it six."

She smiled and nodded. "Six o'clock." When he was out of the car, she drove away. There was one more stop she needed to make before all her mistakes were corrected.

She drove to Zane's apartment and knocked on his door. When he answered it, she saw a wary look leap into his eyes. "We're through," she said simply, then turned and walked away.

# CHAPTER SIXTEEN

"I DON'T understand it," Harve said as he sat in Kyle's living room and lifted his beer to his mouth.

"You don't understand what?" Kyle had never been a heavy drinker and he still held the first beer he had opened, turning the can listlessly in his hands.

"You act as if you want to stay here forever. Don't you miss being at home?"

"I don't have a Janet waiting for me the way you do. No, I don't miss it." He looked out the window at the softer colors of early evening. He could see a gentle breeze stirring the leaves of the crepe myrtles in his side yard and knew the air was cooling. "I wouldn't mind staying here."

Harve sipped his beer and studied Kyle for a moment. "How's Mica?"

Kyle threw him an irritated glance. "Mica apparently doesn't care if I'm here or on the moon. She's the most evasive person I've ever seen. She vanishes after work and won't answer her door or her phone. Obviously she meant it when she said she wanted us to stop seeing each other."

"Have you told her how you feel about her?"

"I don't have any idea what you mean. How many beers have you had, anyway?"

"Two, and you know exactly what I mean. If you ask me, you're both in love, and I'm never wrong about these things."

"You are this time. I'm not going to fall in love with a woman who doesn't care if she sees me or not."

"Why do you think Mica doesn't care? Did she tell you that?"

"No, but it's how she acts. She avoids me off camera. I can't get her alone long enough to find out how she feels or to tell her what I feel for her. She's as elusive as quicksilver! Does this sound like the actions of a woman who is in love?"

"I've seen her watching you. When you're doing a scene, she stands over by the statue of the man on the horse and watches every move you make. Then when your scene is over, she heads back into the crowd."

"You seem to be watching her pretty closely."

"I was curious. She's pretty, and I like the way she smiles. I think you ought to tell her how you feel. More important, so does Janet."

"You've been discussing me?"

"Janet called just before I came over here. Damn, but I miss her. I've been giving a lot of thought to retiring."

"Right. I've heard that before."

"I'm going to, one of these days. I'm going to quit being a gypsy and stay home with Janet like an ordinary husband. I could accept only local jobs. It's awful knowing the girls are growing up without me being there to watch. It does bad things to your mind. I blame myself when they misbehave or make bad grades. I should have *been* there."

"Yes, and I could live here in Sedalia."

"You could, you know," Harve said with studied nonchalance.

Kyle was silent for a moment. "You don't think that's a crazy idea?"

"Why not? Small planes fly in and out of here all the time. A lot of actors don't live in Hollywood anymore. You never have been one for the nightclub parties. Sure you could live here. I'm surprised you haven't thought of it yourself. You could even start one of those regional theaters for off-Broadway plays. You've often talked about that. Maybe I'll find a place like Sedalia and do that myself."

"I thought of it. I told myself it wouldn't work."

"Well," Harve said carefully, "you'd want to have a good reason to stay. Like Mica, for instance."

"I told you years ago that I don't want to fall in love again. I'd probably be foolish to retire at this point in my career. And even a few months of separation can play havoc with a marriage. You know that as well as I do. No, I'm not a good candidate for marriage. Tamara is proof of that."

"That was then and this is now. There are worse things than taking a risk in a commitment. Like loving a woman and letting her slip through your fingers, for instance. Like growing old and thinking you could have had it all if you'd just put out a bit more effort. Not all marriages are like the one you and Tamara had."

"Go home. You've had enough to drink."

"Two beers? I have one more with my name on it, then I'll leave."

"You can be a pain in the rear. You know that?"

"Yeah. That's what makes me such a good friend." Harve grinned at him over his beer can and settled lower in the chair.


"WHAT'S BEEN bothering you?" Zane said as he reached out to brush a strand of hair back from Mica's face.

She avoided his fingers with practiced dexterity and looked away. "What's keeping Calula today? I don't have my makeup on or my hair combed, and the trailer door is still locked."

He shrugged. "Shelley and Una are at it in there. Shelley just read the retraction Una insisted be put in the paper and Calula is having to referee." He smiled down at her, his face darker than usual with the makeup that gave him the appearance of having a more even tan. "Have you been missing me?"

"How could I when I see you every day?" She glanced over at the crowd around Miss Nelly's cinnamon rolls. She missed Kyle and she saw him every day. She looked away.

"You know, I've been thinking about you quite a bit. You ought to consider coming out to Hollywood."

"I have a job."

"Teaching jobs are a dime a dozen. You have talent. You could make it big in the movies."

"I'm not leaving Sedalia."

He ran his finger along the edge of her collar. "I could see to it that you stayed busy. I could even give you the name of an agent. You shouldn't tell him I sent you, though. They like to think they get all the bright ideas."

"I've told you before that I'm not interested. Besides, school starts soon." She didn't tell him the most recent phone call from the school board had been less pleasant than the previous ones. Now, however, they had pushed her too far and she had refused to quit. She was waiting to see if Hubbard was bluffing about firing her. She knew the board wouldn't give her a good recommendation at this point, and she felt she had nothing to lose by bluffing in turn. Jake had told her he would give her a job at the hardware store if she was fired. That would pay the bills until she could find another teaching job.

That presented another problem. She had to move in the next two weeks and she had nowhere else to go. She hadn't been able to find another affordable place in an area where she would be safe alone at night. Nor could she until she knew if she would be staying in Sedalia or searching for another job. The stress was almost more than she could handle.

Zane edged closer. "I could put in a good word for you with some directors."

"Look, I've got a lot of problems right now. I may lose my job, I have to find another place to live and I need to be alone to think. Do you mind?"

"Not at all, but I think you need a shoulder more than you need anything."

She looked up at him in amazement. "Doesn't your balloon ever land?"

Zane followed up his lead. "I might not have any answers, but I can listen."

She looked over to where Kyle was eating a cinnamon roll and not so much as looking in her direction. "I don't think so. Thanks anyway."

He put his hands on her shoulders and turned her to face him. "Do you think you're the first girl who's fallen in love with a movie star?"

"What?" she gasped. "How did you know that? I never said anything to you about me falling in love." She would have guessed that Zane wasn't perceptive enough to figure out anything that hadn't been spelled out for him first.

"I wasn't born yesterday."

She wondered what he would do for conversation if he couldn't use a cliché. "So what do you recommend that I do about it?"

"Just go with the feeling, baby. I care about you, too."

"What?" She looked up at him in an effort to follow his meaning.

"Look, I can't propose to you yet, but if you come to Hollywood—"

"What on earth are you talking about?"

"Why, us. I've fallen in love with you, too."

"For heaven's sake, Zane, I didn't mean you. And we both know you aren't in love with me."

"Don't say that. You don't know how often I think about you. If I were free to marry you, I'd ask you in a minute."

Mica sighed and turned away. Zane was so completely egotistical, he could convince himself of anything.

"Look, I'll break my rule and take you to see my agent. With my connections, I can get you into a movie in no time. Stick with me, baby, and together we'll go straight to the top."

"That's a line from *When She Was Good* and who knows how many other movies. Give me credit for having some sense."

"The words might have been used before, but what words haven't? I mean them when I say them."

"And I'm Shirley Temple. Zane, don't you ever care about anyone but yourself?"

He looked wounded. "I just said I love you. Didn't I say that?"

"What you meant was that you want me to sleep with you. The answer is still no." She had turned him down on several more creative propositions already. It was getting to be a habit. She looked over at Kyle and caught him looking at her. He averted his eyes.

"Okay, you drive a hard bargain, but I'll marry you. Of course, I have to wait a few months. It's one of those divorce red tapes and so forth. I agreed to wait at least a year before I remarried, and I can't go back on my word. But as soon as the year is up, it's you and me to the altar, baby."

"Do you really think I'm that stupid? I may not know about divorce laws in California, but even if I wanted to marry you—which I don't—I'm too smart to fall for a line like that." She turned and walked away.

Zane had not been turned down by a woman since he had become a star, and he didn't like it. In his opinion, Mica was only playing hard to get, and he was determined to bed her at least once. He was scheduled to leave in three days, and he knew it was time for him to make the kill.

The door of the wardrobe trailer opened and Shelley stepped out as if she was making a grand entrance. On seeing Zane, she smiled and winked. Shelley was giving him a lot of attention these days. It was gratifying to his ego, and she looked better than she had a right to, given her age and fast life-style. He had no intention of giving her any encouragement, but there had been times lately when he'd had fond memories of their time together. It was a pity her star was on its way down. Otherwise he might have been willing to try rekindling the old flame. But it was on its way down, and Mica was much more interesting.

He watched Mica doing her last scene with Shelley. Mica had an arresting beauty. She fascinated him, particularly since she seemed unattainable. He wasn't sure how he'd do it, but he was determined to get her into bed before he left town. Stars had vied for his attention, and he wasn't about to let a small-town teacher reject him. What if word got to one of the gossip rags and made it into every supermarket? He would be a laughingstock.

Zane considered his options as he watched her. She hadn't fallen for the ''I'll make you a star'' line or even the one about him being so lonely in Tinsel Town. For some reason, most women were ready to believe he might be lonely, but he had not experienced anything even close to that since girls had discovered him in high school. Mica, however, hadn't believed it for a minute. She had even been impervious to his statements of having fallen in love with her in spite of himself. That one had never failed before. For some reason women loved to think a man had tried not to love them but couldn't resist. Zane had never understood this reasoning himself, but Mica had actually laughed the first time he'd told her this.

Zane didn't like being laughed at. He was determined to seduce her and be the one to laugh when he left her behind to grieve over her loss. Leaving broken hearts behind him

was Zane's hallmark. The girl in Georgia had almost been
his undoing, and his agent had ended up paying her off to
keep the matter from going to court, but that didn't deter
him. There was one ploy he hadn't tried. Zane grinned and
waited for the precise moment.

Kyle was also watching Mica. He wanted her so much he
ached. Seeing the sun in her hair and hearing the music in
her voice was like an exquisite torture. In a few days he
might never see or hear her again. He looked over to where
Harve was adjusting his camera for the next shot. Harve
made a motion that meant Kyle should get the lead out and
talk to her. Kyle looked away again. That was easy for Harve
to say.

All last night he had thought about her and wondered
what she would say if he went to her house in the middle of
the night and asked her to marry him. He thought it was
likely she would call the police and have him removed. That
was all that had kept him from going to her house and
banging on her door until she let him in. When it came to
Mica, he seemed to have no pride and no good sense.

When the scene was over, he watched her thread her way
into the crowd and disappear. She didn't even glance his
way, though she probably knew he was there beside Miss
Nelly and her friends. Kyle wished it were possible to stay
with her when the filming was completed. This wasn't the
first time he had noticed that a movie's fiction had an edge
over truth. Since he couldn't see Mica any longer, Kyle
ducked under Miss Nelly's umbrella and sat beside her.

"You ought to go after her," the old woman said.

"Who?" Kyle was always amazed at how much Miss
Nelly saw and understood.

"You know who I mean. Mica Haldane is a stubborn girl,
always has been. It runs in her family. I once saw her
grandmother drive a horse and buggy downtown and park
it in one of the spaces in front of the emporium just be-

cause the mayor told her she had to stop obstructing traffic. When I taught her daddy in school, he had to clean my blackboards for a week because he refused to apologize to another boy after they had a fight.''

"Maybe he was in the right.''

"Possibly, but back then we cared more for discipline in the classroom than who might have been right in a fight. I gave them an equal punishment, but he drew the line at apologizing. The point is, Mica is so stubborn, she may be willing to cut off her nose to spite her face.''

Kyle smiled at her. ''In English, please.''

"Go after her. Anybody can see you want her.''

"No, that seems to be limited to you and Harve Giacono.''

"That nice man who runs a camera? You ought to listen to him. Why are you letting pride stand in your way? I'm an old woman and I've been around long enough to have figured out some things when it comes to affairs of the heart.''

"Why, Miss Nelly, I thought you never married.''

"I didn't. I never found a man that was as smart as I was.'' She nodded her chin at him and gave him a hint of a smile. "My unmarried state doesn't make me blind, however. What are you going to do? Wait until it's time to leave and regret it from then on? At least speak to her.''

"I've tried. She doesn't want to talk to me.''

"Well, I never! I never in my life saw two such stubborn people. If you're dead set on breaking your heart, don't say I didn't tell you so. By the way, I heard Arlen Hubbard is talking about firing her.''

"What? She's going to lose her job? She mentioned something about that, but I decided she must have been exaggerating.''

"No, it's no exaggeration. Those Hubbard boys are all alike—a mean lot. You can tell because of their eyes being so close together. It's a family trait.''

Birdine nodded. "They're smart enough, but mean hearted."

"I'll go talk to him. I can't stand by and see Mica lose her job."

"I knew you were a nice boy the first time I set eyes on you. Mica could do worse than to pick you." Miss Nelly smiled.

"Mica hasn't chosen me. We don't have a future together."

"Now don't you go getting closed minded on me. You can work it out, two smart people like you and Mica. Give it a try."

Birdine nodded vigorously in agreement.

Kyle didn't answer. He wished it really were as simple as Miss Nelly seemed to think. It might have been possible when Miss Nelly was young for a man to override a woman's objections and court her anyway, but he had a feeling Mica would put him in his place before he could get out the words to say he loved her. He might love her, but he didn't understand her.

Meanwhile, Zane was ready when Mica came in front of the cameras. This was his last scene with her, and while there were no lines written between them, he knew it was his last chance to score big with her. He waited until Greenberg told them what he wanted out of this scene, then Zane turned to Diane and started saying his lines. He never memorized them verbatim, and he could see the confusion in Diane's eyes as she mentally scrambled to find a way to respond and still have her own lines make sense.

Zane maneuvered himself between the camera and Mica's usual exit. He didn't know where she disappeared to between shots, but he was determined to head her off.

"Cut! Zane, you're moving out of range." Greenberg motioned for him to come in closer. "Weren't you listening when I told you where to go?"

Zane hadn't been. He had starred in more movies than Greenberg had directed, and he had paid only a token amount of attention to his instructions. He ambled back into place.

Mica was looking past him, and he turned his head to see Kyle still sitting with Miss Nelly. Apparently Kyle was having no more success with Mica than was Zane. This helped his ego. Zane didn't want to be cut by a second lead. He caught Mica's eye and winked. Behind her, he saw Carrie but pretended not to notice her. Since she had knocked on his door with the announcement that they were through, Zane had ignored her.

As Zane said his lines, or his version of them, he thought about what would get Mica's attention. He had a plan, but he wasn't sure how to put it into motion. Her reaction to it would determine whether he followed it with a public rejection of her or whether she would end up in his bed. Either way, Zane would save face.

The scene seemed to take forever. Diane was upset over his not delivering her cue lines as they were written, and Shelley was standing within Diane's range of vision, making her more nervous still. Zane didn't care about how Diane felt, but he was tired of doing the scene over and over. Zane liked being paid to be a star, but he didn't care much for working.

At last the scene pleased Greenberg, and he shouted for a wrap-up. Before Mica could get away, Zane was by her side. He pulled her to him in the masterful way he had used in a dozen films. Her expression was at first startled, then angry. Zane didn't care. He lowered his head and kissed her with the expertise that always thrilled female fans.

Mica shoved against him, but he held her firmly, her hands trapped against his chest. He was aware that all movement around them had stopped, and he would have laughed if he hadn't been otherwise occupied. He could feel her struggling, even if no one else could detect it. As soon as he released her, he would say something scathing, then walk away. He was planning exactly what words to use, when she managed to break free.

He opened his eyes and was forming his grin, when she drew back and slapped him as hard as she could. For an instant he was stunned. This was no stage slap and it caught him full on the jaw. His skin burned and stung and he knew the imprint of her hand must be clear. Suddenly the unbelievable happened—the crew started to laugh.

As Mica stalked away, he heard the applause. She had bested him! Zane glared after her and, hoping someone would hear him and he would thus be able to save face, he muttered, "I never liked that girl in the first place. Did you hear her? She asked me to kiss her. She set me up!"

As if she had rehearsed the scene, Shelley was suddenly by his side. Her eyes flashed with righteous anger, and she said in a voice keyed to carry far and wide, "I saw what she did! She set you up and kissed you just so she could humiliate you! The nerve of that nobody! Who does she think she is?"

Shelley firmly linked her arm in Zane's and they walked away together. Zane hadn't been so grateful to a woman since his earliest days in show business. He put his arm around Shelley and hugged her.

## CHAPTER SEVENTEEN

KYLE HADN'T BEEN there to see Mica slap Zane, but he heard about it soon after Harve shut down his camera. "She slapped him?" he exclaimed. An incredulous grin spread over his face.

"He had the imprint of her hand on his cheek when he walked by me. Then he went stalking off in the direction of his apartment and... Hey! Where are you going?"

Kyle didn't pause long enough to answer. If Mica had slapped Zane in front of everyone, she must be terribly upset. She might need him. By the time he reached her house, he was running. He pounded on her door.

"Who is it?" she demanded without opening it.

"It's Kyle. Open up."

"No. Go away."

"I heard what happened between you and Zane. Let me in."

"I guess by now everyone has heard. Are you all going to come over here and laugh at me? Get off my porch."

"No one is laughing at you. Everyone has wanted to see Zane put in his place for a long time now." He hit the door again. "Will you open this damned door so we can talk?"

"No. Go away. I don't want to see you."

"Open the door, Mica." He didn't expect her to do it, but there was a click and the door eased open. "May I come in?"

As she stepped aside, he noticed the remnants of tears on her face. "Mica? Have you been crying?"

"No," she denied, but she wiped at the tears with the palm of her hand.

Tenderness stole over him, and he knew he had been right to come. Without speaking, he drew her into his embrace. After a brief hesitation, Mica put her arms around him and held him close.

Over the top of her head, he saw several cardboard boxes. "You're moving? You found a house?"

Mica nodded.

"I thought you said you couldn't find a place."

"I've rented a place on Shirley Lane." She pulled away and wiped at her tears again. "It's not too far from the house I lived in when I was a child." She avoided eye contact with him.

He went into the living room and looked around. Her books had been removed from the shelves and were stacked against one wall. "Have you heard any more from Brother Malcolm or the school board?"

"No. Not from Brother Malcolm." She turned away and busied herself by wrapping newspaper around a bookend and placing it in one of the packing boxes. "I'm going to call Mr. Hubbard and appease him by saying I'll relent on which books I'll agree to teach. After all, teaching something is more important than teaching nothing. As for the morals issue, I've done nothing I'm ashamed of and it's none of their business anyway." She tried to keep her tone light but failed.

He saw she was too proud to tell him she was about to be fired...or was Miss Nelly exaggerating? "What about Brother Malcolm?"

"What about him? He has no proof of anything, and he doesn't own the school board. I'm hoping the board will overlook him if I agree to everything else. After all, nothing happened between Zane and myself." Her hands slowed and she glanced back at him, her dark eyes sad.

"What about us?" he asked gently. "Something happened between us, Mica." He was thinking how terrible it would be if Mica had to face a panel and defend her relationship with him. He couldn't stand by and let that happen.

She closed her eyes. "I know."

"Do you regret it?"

Her eyes opened as if she was surprised he could even ask such a question. "No. I could never regret that." For a long moment, their eyes held. "But I know all I can have is a memory, not you. I'm not asking for or expecting more than that. You have your life, and I have mine."

"Is it as simple as that?"

She shoved her hair back from her face in an exasperated gesture. "It has to be."

"Does it?"

"Kyle, you're making this too difficult. I've told you I'm not asking for more than we had that night. It was beautiful. Perfect, even. But you don't belong here, and I don't belong anywhere but here. Can't you see that?"

"No, I can't. I'm trying to figure out what you want."

"Nothing! I don't want anything!"

"Mica, I'm trying to ask if—"

She snapped her head around and glared at him as she said, "Will you just leave?"

He was more perplexed than ever. "Okay. If that's the way you want it." He turned and headed for the door.

He didn't want to leave her, and he had a terrible feeling that as soon as he had pulled the door shut behind him, she had started to cry again. But what else could he do?

It took him longer than usual to walk home, but he was so absorbed in his thoughts that he found himself inside his house with no recollection of the trip. For a long moment he stood in the middle of his living room, becoming increasingly aware that the house was as silent and lonely as he was.

Suddenly he was galvanized into action. Grabbing the telephone directory, he hurriedly thumbed to the *H*s and was relieved to find only one Hubbard listed. Rather than telephone, he memorized the address and headed for his car.

He found two cars parked in the driveway of Arlen Hubbard's house and went to the front door and rang the bell. A middle-aged man opened the door and stared suspiciously at Kyle. "Mr. Hubbard?"

"Yes."

"I'm Kyle Spensor."

"I recognized you."

"May I talk to you?" The man merely glared at him in silence, but Kyle recognized the man's power ploy and waited him out. He could see how Mica might be intimidated by such a large and unfriendly man.

At length, Hubbard stepped aside and allowed Kyle to enter. The house was much nicer than Mica's but lacked warmth. It could have been a furniture-store showroom for all the personality it exhibited.

"Well, what do you want to talk to me about?" Hubbard asked when they were seated in the living room.

"Mica Haldane is a friend of mine. I'm here on her behalf."

"I thought as much. I'm afraid it will do no good, however. The board will meet tonight, and frankly, I'm going to recommend we let her go."

"But she needs that job."

"She should have thought of that earlier. She knows not to do the things she's been called to account for. Brother Malcolm is certain to be there, and if I don't call for her dismissal, he will."

"Doesn't it matter that she's a good teacher and that she genuinely cares about her students? All she's trying to do is teach!"

Hubbard gave him an ingratiating smile. "It's not quite that simple. The approved curriculum must be followed. If we let all the teachers teach whatever they pleased, we would get into trouble with the state board of education. We can't have that."

"Then you'll at least let Mica explain why she chose one set of books over the other?"

"I'm afraid we discourage teachers from attending the school-board meetings."

"That's ridiculous," Kyle said flatly. "She's on trial here. She should be allowed to defend herself."

Hubbard chuckled mirthlessly. "We aren't a court of law, Mr. Spensor. Far from it. We bear no ill will, per se, to Miss Haldane."

"Then you'll give her a good recommendation so she can find a job elsewhere?" Kyle tried not to glare at the man.

"No," Hubbard said with a shake of his large head. "No, I'm afraid we won't be able to do that. Miss Haldane has already given the board the impression that she's a trouble-maker over this book issue. No, she'll be fired on the morals charge."

"She wasn't at Zane's apartment all that night or any other night. She was there for a short time, but she left. I know that for a fact."

"You know firsthand where she was the entire night?" Hubbard's small eyes glittered. "Exactly how do you know that?"

Kyle sighed and stood. "Never mind. You certainly wouldn't take my word on that. Will it do any good if I come to the board meeting and speak for Mica?"

"No good whatever, but it might do some harm. Why make waves, Mr. Spensor? We don't like waves around here."

"No, I can see that." Kyle turned and left without a goodbye. Mica had lost the battle and just didn't know it yet.

He drove to a service station and asked directions to Shirley Lane. The street was narrow, and abandoned cars littered a number of grassless front yards. The houses were small and run-down. Only one had a For Rent sign in the window. Kyle waited for a handful of barefoot boys to sidle out of the street, then pulled into the red dirt driveway. He presumed this was the house Mica planned to move into, and the sight of it knotted his stomach. Not only did the porch sag on one corner, but the whole house looked as if it had been in need of paint for some time.

Slowly Kyle backed out and drove back the way he had come. He couldn't let Mica move to a neighborhood where she wouldn't be safe, and this street had all the earmarks of a high-crime district. He could no longer tell himself that he and Mica could step back into their former lives and be none the worse for their encounter. Now he had a reason other than his own broken heart to give him cause.

Kyle drove to a telephone booth and looked up Malcolm Stout in the phone book. With the address in hand and directions from a nearby gas station, he found Stout's house without much trouble. It was nicer than Hubbard's had been, and it wasn't difficult to see that Brother Malcolm had no qualms about living well.

Kyle parked out front and went up to the porch and rang the doorbell. He was sure someone must be home because the lights were on and there were cars in the driveway. But no one came to the door, so he rang the bell again. Still no answer. Thinking Brother Malcolm might be in the backyard and unable to hear the bell, Kyle went around to the rear of the house.

The backyard was empty, but Kyle could hear sounds coming from the glassed-in back porch. He went up to the door and was about to knock, when he happened to look into the room.

Brother Malcolm was there and so was a woman who fit the description of Norma Mobley. They were on the couch, engaged in an activity that he was sure the members of Brother Malcolm's flock would have been shocked to see. Kyle was taken aback, as well. Then a slow smile spread across his face. With new confidence he knocked on the door.

The naked couple on the couch jumped and the woman shrieked when she spotted Kyle standing out on the porch. He grinned and waved at them through the window. Brother Malcolm pushed Norma away and grabbed his pants as he struggled to his feet. Norma was scrambling to cover herself with the afghan that had fallen to the floor. Brother Malcolm strode to the door and yanked it open.

"Good evening," Kyle said pleasantly. Turning to the woman cowering on the couch, he said, "Your name's Mrs. Mobley, isn't it?"

"What the hell are you doing here?" Brother Malcolm demanded. "You have no right spying on me through my windows!"

"I didn't look in on purpose. But I'm glad I did. I believe this gives us something in common."

"What's that?" Brother Malcolm demanded.

"We both know something that will interest the people of Sedalia."

Mrs. Mobley finally found her voice. "You can't tell anyone you saw us! You won't dare do that!"

"No one would believe him anyway," Brother Malcolm snapped. "Especially not when they find out he's done the same thing with Mica Haldane."

"Now, see? That's what we need to talk about," Kyle said in a perfectly reasonable voice. "I'm willing to bet that just as many people will believe me as will believe you. Want to risk it?"

Norma spoke up. "Malcolm, you can't—"

"Shut up," Brother Malcolm interrupted. "Let me handle this."

Kyle leaned against the doorjamb. "The way I see it, you want to keep preaching in Sedalia as much as Mica wants to keep teaching here. I believe we can work out a trade. You take the pressure off Mica, and I won't tell what I've seen here today."

"That's blackmail!"

"Yep, that's exactly what it is." Kyle glanced over at Norma gathering her strewn clothing. "The other shoe is over there, ma'am."

Norma glared at him.

Brother Malcolm looked as if he was in danger of losing control completely. "I'm going to call the sheriff and have you arrested!"

"No, you won't. You're going to call Hubbard and tell him you were wrong about my car being at Mica's all night. Then you're going to tell him that you personally recommend that he keep Mica on the school staff." Kyle's voice stayed calm, but his eyes were as cold as steel.

Brother Malcolm looked as if he was about to refuse, then he wavered. He glanced back at Norma, who still clutched the afghan around her body. Without another word, he went to the telephone and dialed Hubbard's number.

MICA ANSWERED the phone and felt a cold dread when she recognized Hubbard's voice.

"Miss Haldane," he said in grave tones, "I'm afraid I owe you an apology."

"I beg your pardon?"

"I just received a call from Brother Malcolm Stout, and he says he made a mistake about seeing Kyle Spensor's car in front of your house all night. He even said there's room for doubt about your car in the parking lot being proof that you were with Zane Morgan a while back.''

''Brother Malcolm said that?'' Mica was so amazed her mouth dropped open.

''In view of all this, I don't believe we have charges to bring against you after all. And regarding the curriculum change you asked for, the other board members feel we may be able to approve the alternative list of books you proposed, seeing that you were willing to compromise with us. I don't think we will have any more problems.''

Mica couldn't think how to answer for a moment. She had expected to be publicly embarrassed, then fired. ''Yes. Yes, that will be great.''

''Fine.'' She could almost see Hubbard beaming over the phone. ''Then we have no more ill will between us?''

''I guess not.''

''Great. 'Bye, now.''

She slowly hung up the phone. Brother Malcolm had recanted his allegations against her! What on earth would have made him do such a thing? she wondered. Hubbard had even agreed to let her change books for next semester. Her relief was so deep, she felt light-headed. She wanted to call Kyle and tell him the good news, but she refrained. Her miracle didn't extend that far.

THE NEXT MORNING, Mica went to the wardrobe trailer for the last time. As she was buttoning her skirt, Carrie came in.

For a minute Carrie hesitated, as if she wasn't sure what reception Mica would give her. ''I tried to call you last night, but your phone was busy.''

''I guess you must have called while I was talking to Hubbard.''

''Did you get things settled with the school board?''

Carrie had no idea what Mica had been through with Hubbard over the past few weeks, and this was hardly the time to fill her in on the details. "They've agreed to let me teach from different books." Mica took her belt off the hanger and put it around her waist. "All that's left is to finish packing and move to my other house."

"I wish you'd reconsider this move. That neighborhood has gone downhill since you lived there last."

Mica smiled sadly. "No, it hasn't. It was always that bad. But I won't be there forever. I'm only agreeing to a month-by-month rental contract. As soon as I find another place, I'll move again." The truth was that she didn't care about a job or where she would live if she couldn't have Kyle.

"Mica," Carrie said hesitantly, "I miss you. I've done some really stupid things lately. I just want you to know I'm sorry for the way I've treated you."

Mica managed to smile. "That's okay. Everybody is entitled to go off the deep end once in a while. I just didn't want to see you get hurt."

"I appreciate that. I've got my head back on straight now. Jake and I even made up yesterday."

"I'm happy for you," Mica managed to say around the lump in her throat.

Carrie's smile faded as she searched Mica's face. "You haven't told Kyle how you really feel about him, have you?"

"No. How could I?"

"If you don't tell him soon, it'll be too late."

Mica shook her head and blinked back the tears. "It's already too late." She hurried to the door before her tears could spill over. "See you in a few minutes. Calula will be wondering where I am."

Mayor Graham was talking to Greenberg as the cameras were being positioned for the next scene. "I just wanted to come by and tell you how much we've all enjoyed having you in our town." He put on his best politician's smile and reared back in pride.

"It's been an experience." Greenberg hesitated, then extended his hand.

Graham shook it. "As mayor of Sedalia, I want to extend you an invitation. Come back anytime. Shoot as many pictures here as you like."

Greenberg stared at him for a few seconds. "Thanks, but I wouldn't want to disrupt the town again anytime soon."

"Tell your director friends. Sedalia will be glad to take in any of them."

"I'll tell them all about it, all right. Every detail. You can count on that."

"Good, good. By the way, I signed the papers this morning to start putting in new streetlights. We're putting up those turn-of-the-century models. The kind with the globe lights."

"You aren't starting today, are you?"

"As a matter of fact, we are."

Greenberg's face turned dark red. "You don't have plans to start on the part of the street nearest the drugstore, do you?"

"Why, we had planned to start on the opposite end, but I can have the crew change." Graham was obviously eager to please.

"No. Don't touch a thing near the drugstore. Don't touch anything until after we finish filming tomorrow. Then you can dig up the entire street for all I care."

"As a matter of fact, we have discussed removing the pavement and going back to the brick streets. You know, there are brick streets under all of downtown. You might mention that to your friends, as well."

"I will. I certainly will." Greenberg put his fists on his hips and frowned at Graham. "Now I have to get to work."

Graham clapped him on the shoulder. "We all do." He gave a hearty laugh. "See you around."

Greenberg thought it was to his credit that the mayor walked away unharmed.

Graham ambled on down to where Miss Nelly and her friends were holding court. "Everything going well, Miss Nelly? Birdine?" He grinned and nodded a greeting at Buford, who nodded back.

"Quite well, indeed." Miss Nelly opened an address book and motioned for Harve Giacono to come over. "Young man, I've seen how you like my cooking. If you put your address here, I'll send you a pound cake or some cookies from time to time."

Harve grinned and picked up the pencil. "I'd like that. I've told my wife about your pound cakes, but she thinks I'm exaggerating." He patted his middle. "I'm going to have to go on a diet as it is."

"Nonsense. Young people think they have to be skin and bones these days."

"True," Birdine agreed. "I recall my grandmother saying the same thing when I was a girl."

"Birdine, your grandmother was talking about our generation, not this one," Miss Nelly said, pointing to the cameraman.

"She would have been talking about this one, too, if she was still alive, God rest her."

Buford nodded. "It's true. She would have."

Harve wrote his name and address in Miss Nelly's book. "Send me a price list, and I'll order some cookies for Christmas."

Miss Nelly and Birdine exchanged a surprised look. "We never considered selling what we cook," Miss Nelly said.

Birdine put her head to one side. "Surely we couldn't ask for payment. Not from all of you. Why, we're like family now. I'll miss cooking for everyone on the set."

Miss Nelly nodded. "But we might see ourselves clear to sell a few cookies now and then."

Harve grinned at them. "Maybe this will be the beginning of a new line of work for you."

Buford chuckled. "Son, you may have just created a monster. You don't know what may happen when these two get started on something."

Graham grinned proudly. "If Miss Nelly and Birdine go into business, they will have my backing all the way."

Miss Nelly ignored the mayor's gratuitous offer of support, obviously giving Harve's suggestion genuine consideration. "Birdine, what do you think we could charge for cookies?"

They put their heads together and started planning their business venture.

"Now, you'll need a grease trap and one of those special hoods over your stove," Graham warned. "And neither of you live in an area zoned for a commercial business."

"You're too late," Buford said complacently. "They've already started."

"Now, Miss Nelly," Graham said in a placating tone, "do you really want to do this? You're looking at a lot of work, you know."

"Harry Graham, will you just go on about your business?" Miss Nelly said.

"But you have to have certain appliances and fixtures and meet certain conditions of the city codes if you're going to start a cooking business," Graham insisted.

Harve was laughing as he strolled away. He would put money on Miss Nelly over Graham's restrictions any day. He suspected their cookie-and-pound-cake business would be prospering by the end of the year.

"What are you so happy about?" Kyle asked as Harve joined him.

"I just saw Miss Nelly and the mayor lock horns."

Kyle grinned. "I wouldn't want to cross her about any-thing."

"It was my fault, really. She asked for my address so she could send me cookies from time to time, and I suggested she and Birdine start a mail-order cookie-and-pound-cake business."

"I'll give her my address before I leave." Kyle sat on the grass and leaned back against a tree. "Greenberg is getting a late start this morning." He searched the faces of people milling about, but didn't see Mica. Did she know yet?

"I saw her go into the costume trailer."

Kyle looked back at Harve with a guarded expression. "I don't know who you're talking about."

Harve squatted beside him. "Are you going to let her slip away? I'd have said you're a smarter man than that."

"It's more a matter of her telling me to shove off. She's not interested. She told me so yesterday." It hurt him to say that.

"Man, have you got rocks for brains? She does care. I know it as sure as I know I'm standing here."

Kyle didn't answer. He had spent the night thinking about Mica and trying to figure her out. As he watched the trailer where costumes were kept, he saw Mica come out and look around. Their eyes met across the lot, and she didn't look away for a long moment.

"See? See that look? That's how Janet looked at me be-fore we were married."

"Do you see her coming over this way? You're wrong."

"So she has to get her makeup on. I don't understand you."

"I don't understand me, either, if it's any consolation." It was true. If any other woman had avoided him in this way, he would have been more than happy to let her go her own way. With Mica it was different. His world seemed to revolve around her, and he wasn't sure when that had started. Looking back on the summer, he couldn't recall a time when he had fallen in love, but he also couldn't recall not feeling something for her, even from the first. He had known her such a short time, yet it was as if she was a part of him.

"Look at Greenberg. He's steamed about something." Harve nodded in the director's direction. Greenberg was striding down the street to where several men in work clothes were standing and staring at the sidewalk.

"I'll bet Mayor Graham is behind it." Kyle laughed. "Watching those two has been an entertainment in itself."

"I wonder if they'll become pen pals," Harve said with a grin as Greenberg started waving his arms at the workmen and pointing from the sidewalk to the cameras.

"I'll let you be the one to ask him." Kyle sighed. "I need to look over my lines again. You know this will be my last scene with Mica."

"I know. Don't waste it."

Kyle watched him rise and walk away. He had no intention of wasting the opportunity, but he was all too aware how adept she was at disappearing from the set. Kyle followed Mica into the makeup trailer. Calula glanced at him in surprise and said, "I've already done you."

"I know." He went to where Mica sat in the chair in front of the large mirrors. "I need to talk to you."

"Calula is about to do my makeup," she said without looking at him.

Kyle gazed in the mirror at her. Beyond her face, he could see the reflection from the opposite mirror, and their faces duplicated endlessly, smaller and smaller. "You have a way of disappearing."

"What did you want to talk about?"

Kyle was all too aware of Calula and the hairdresser. As he paused, the door opened and Carrie came in. Leon motioned for her to come to his chair. This wasn't the time or place to say he loved her, much less one to propose marriage. "May I see you after the filming?"

"I'd like to, but I can't. Mr. Hubbard called last night. He's had a change of heart, and I'm not fired after all. I have to start gathering my supplies."

"Gathering your supplies?"

"The fall semester will start soon. I have to order the books and sort through my desk. That sort of thing. And then there's the move, you know. I'll probably need to put down shelf paper, and I like to give a place a thorough cleaning before I move in." She was speaking quickly and a bit too brightly, and she still avoided meeting his eyes.

Kyle knew she was making up excuses to avoid him. "Okay. I'll be seeing you." He left before he lost control and said everything he was thinking. At least, he tried to console himself, his talk with Hubbard had helped.

Sitting in Calula's chair and staring at her reflection, Mica watched her eyes fill with tears. It hurt her to turn Kyle away, but she couldn't tell him the truth. She couldn't just blurt out that she loved him.

"Hey, you're washing off the makeup," Calula said. "It was your choice to let him go. I think it was a bad one, but what do I know?"

Mica stared into the mirror. She couldn't speak past the tightness in her throat.

"I've known Kyle for years," Calula said as if she were speaking to herself. "He usually makes friends wherever he is, but you don't see him coming on to women. You know what I mean? He keeps it platonic. Up until we came here, that is."

Mica glanced at her. "The summer is over. He'll be gone in a few days."

Carrie turned to face Mica despite Leon's protests. "Why did you tell him you're too busy to see him?"

"It had to end. Quick and clean is the best way for ending something that can't continue."

Calula's eyes met Carrie's as she turned Mica toward a blind wall. She jerked her head toward the door and Carrie nodded. As Calula bent closer to apply Mica's eye shadow, Carrie slipped out of the chair. Mica heard her leave, but she was too unhappy to question it. Carrie's hair never took long to comb.

Carrie ran after Kyle, half her hair combed and the other half askew. "Kyle! Wait!"

He paused and Carrie hurried up to him.

"I can't let you go without telling you this—I feel I owe it to Mica, as I've treated her poorly this summer. She wouldn't tell you, but she cares for you. If you ask me, she's in love with you."

"What? Then why...?"

"Mica has more than her share of pride. She thinks you don't care as much for her in return, and she's afraid of being hurt." Carrie made a discounting motion with her hand as she added, "And I don't know what she may have told you about this house she's moving to, but it's terrible!"

"I saw it."

"Look, I know it's none of my business, but Mica is my friend and I can't let her throw her love away like this. I had to tell you. What you do about it is up to you. At least now you know the truth." Carrie stepped back and touched her hair as if she hadn't realized how odd she looked. She turned and ran back to the trailer.

Kyle stood there for a minute as Carrie's words soaked in. Then he walked briskly toward the set.

Carrie stopped at the foot of the steps of the makeup trailer for a moment to catch her breath, then went back in, pretending nonchalance. As she got past Mica's range of vision, she surreptitiously winked at Calula. Calula opened her mouth to say something, but at that moment Diane and

Una came in from Diane's dressing room in the back of the trailer, noisily chatting between themselves. When Diane saw Mica she smiled. "I saw what you did to Zane yesterday. Congratulations. I wish I had been the one to do it."

"I don't know what got into me. I've never slapped anyone in my entire life," Mica said as their eyes met in the mirror.

"You couldn't have done better if you'd practiced all day." She laughed and Una joined in. "The expression on his face was priceless."

"I hope someone caught it on film," Una added.

"I never thought about that!" Mica's eyes widened. "Were we still filming? I didn't realize that!"

"He's had it coming for years," Diane said.

Una laughed again. "Maybe I can get a copy of that kiss and slap, and whenever I'm having a bad day, I'll just replay it over and over to cheer me up."

"All done," Calula said as she finished applying the blush to Mica's cheeks.

"Thanks." Mica left the chair and Diane slipped into her place.

Across the room, Carrie was watching Mica closely. "Are you okay?" she asked.

"Sure," Mica said, forcing herself to reply. Before Carrie could ask any more questions, Mica turned and left the trailer.

As Mica stepped out into the sunshine, she looked around for Kyle, but he was nowhere to be seen. A moment later, Carrie came out to join her.

"We'd better hurry," Carrie urged as she glanced at her wristwatch. "I think they're ready for us." They walked briskly to the drugstore.

When they turned the corner, Mica saw Kyle waiting for her by the door. Her steps slowed. How could she bear to let him go without ever telling him of her love? But how could she say the words, knowing he must not love her in return? At least this way she was left with her dignity, and broken hearts didn't show. A moment later she heard the call to places for her scene, and from the corner of her eye, she saw Greenberg walking briskly toward her.

Greenberg strode several feet past her and pointed to a spot on the pavement between them. "This is where I want you to start. Kyle will run to you, and when he gets close, you turn toward him. He will tell you he is no longer interested in Dawn, and as soon as he says that, you turn away again and start down the street. He'll jump in the car and follow you." He pointed at the 1960-model car, fitted with a camera on its front grill, that was parked at the curb. "Just keep walking as fast as you can. Make him keep pace with you. Got it?"

She nodded. As soon as Greenberg announced that the scene was a take, she intended to keep walking until she reached her house. She could bring back the costume later, at a time when she thought Kyle would be unlikely to be around.

"Now, Kyle, here's what I want you to do." As Greenberg outlined the scene, Kyle gazed at Mica, and she found she was no longer able to avert her eyes. She could only hope her longing wasn't visible to him.

Greenberg moved off behind the cameras, and when he shouted, "Action," Mica's heart jumped up in her throat. She could hear Kyle jogging up behind her, and when she knew he was close she turned back to him and delivered Angie's line: "'I think you're just awful, Ryan Colby. Here you are talking to me when you should be with Dawn.'"

"'But I don't care about Dawn,'" Kyle responded. "'She's in love with Greg and always has been. Don't you see? Now that Deborah is out of the way, there's nothing to keep them apart.'"

Mica tossed her head. "'I'm not taking anyone's left-over boyfriend.'" She turned and started stalking down the street at as fast a clip as she could manage. A few seconds later, she again heard running feet behind her and wanted to glance over her shoulder. Wasn't Kyle supposed to get into the car and follow? She thought she heard Greenberg shout "Cut," but she could still hear the footsteps.

Kyle caught up with her and grabbed her arm. "I love you, and I want to marry you."

Mica was lost. Had she memorized the lines wrong? "You're supposed to be in the car," she hissed. "Your line is 'I'm not anyone's leftover boyfriend.'"

"Forget the lines! I love you. Mica, will you marry me?"

She tore her eyes away to look back at the cameras. Greenberg was gesturing frantically, and the whole cast and crew were on their feet, edging toward her and Kyle for a better view. "Are you crazy?"

Kyle caught her face gently in his hand and pulled her around to face him. "Mica, I couldn't say this in front of Calula and everyone, and because you're so adept at avoiding me and since I'm scheduled to leave early tomorrow, I thought this might be my only chance to say this." He paused for a breath, and when she opened her lips to speak, he closed them gently with his fingertips. "I love you, Mica. I want to marry you."

She heard his words, but she was so amazed she couldn't answer.

"I know you haven't said you love me," he continued, "but will you give me a chance? I don't have to be on that plane tomorrow. All you have to do is ask me to stay. Otherwise I'll go and never bother you again." He waited for her answer.

Her lips moved silently for a few seconds before she was able to speak. "Don't go," she finally managed to say.

He gazed down at her. "You mean that?" He glanced back at the others. "They can't hear us from back there. You don't have to say that unless you mean it."

"Not mean it? I love you! I've loved you forever, it seems."

He lifted her off the ground in a hug that whirled her around. "Mica, are you sure? You won't change your mind?"

She shook her head. "I love you, Kyle."

He bent and laced his fingers through her hair. As he kissed her, she could hear the shouts and applause of the onlookers, but she didn't mind. Another miracle had happened.

When he lifted his head, he said, "We can stay here in Sedalia. I've been in movies all my life, and I think it's time I retired."

"I have a better idea. I'll go with you."

"What? How can you do that? All you've ever talked about is teaching in Sedalia."

"A lot has happened this summer. I'm not as enthralled with Sedalia as I used to be. I didn't expect the problems I've had with the school board, not to mention Brother Malcolm. I think I need some time away from here." She smiled up at him. "I definitely need some time with you. Like the rest of my life, for instance."

"You're sure? You're not saying all this because of the problems you've had?"

Mica shook her head. "Mr. Hubbard called me last night and said Brother Malcolm has dropped his allegations against me. He even apologized! Otherwise I'd have felt I had to stay here and work through this. I couldn't leave with a stain on my record. But now there's nothing keeping me here."

"You really want to go with me? There's no telling where the next movie may be filmed. Some of those locations are pretty inconvenient."

"I don't care. You said something a while back that made me think. You said you mainly went to school on location with tutors and that they weren't very good in general. I think I could teach child actors and do it in a way that would make learning interesting for them. I really am a good teacher, Kyle."

"I'd say you're damn near perfect." He bent and kissed her again.

Mica let herself be lost in the magic of his kiss for a long moment, then she managed to pull away. "Greenberg is fit to be tied," she said with a nod toward the others. "We have to get back to work."

He smiled down at her. "We'll have to film this scene again, you know. None of this is in the script."

"I know. Maybe I'm starting to act like Shelley, having to film a scene over and over."

"Trust me. You're nothing like Shelley." He put his arm around her and they walked back to the cameras.

"Okay," Greenberg said. "We'll keep the kiss. I'll have to do some close-ups. Somebody find the writer and have him change the ending to include the kiss. Now, Kyle, you get into the car and do the scene as we discussed it. Stop at the elm tree over there. Take it from 'I think you're just awful, Ryan Colby.'"

He looked back at the cameras where Harve and the others were grinning and laughing. Harve signaled that they were ready to film.

Mica started down the street, but she couldn't feel it beneath her feet. For all she could tell, she might be floating. Kyle loved her and wanted to marry her! She knew that from now on she would believe in happily ever after.

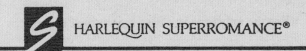

**When the only time you have for yourself is...**

STOLEN moments™

Christmas is such a busy time—with shopping, decorating, writing cards, trimming trees, wrapping gifts....

When you do have a few *stolen moments* to call your own, treat yourself to a brand-new *short* novel. Relax with one of our Stocking Stuffers— or with all six!

Each STOLEN MOMENTS title
is a complete and original contemporary romance that's the perfect length for the busy woman of the nineties! Especially at Christmas...

And they make perfect **stocking stuffers**, too! (For your mother, grandmother, daughters, friends, co-workers, neighbors, aunts, cousins—all the other women in your life!)

Look for the STOLEN MOMENTS display in December

STOCKING STUFFERS:

**HIS MISTRESS  Carrie Alexander**
**DANIEL'S DECEPTION  Marie DeWitt**
**SNOW ANGEL  Isolde Evans**
**THE FAMILY MAN  Danielle Kelly**
**THE LONE WOLF  Ellen Rogers**
**MONTANA CHRISTMAS  Lynn Russell**

HSM2

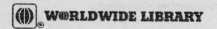

**WORLDWIDE LIBRARY**

**Where do you find hot Texas nights, smooth Texas charm
and dangerously sexy cowboys?**

### GUITARS, CADILLACS
#### Country music—Texas style!

Jessica Reynolds should be on top of the world. Fans love her music
and she is about to embark on a tour that will make her name a
household word. So why isn't her heart singing as loudly as her voice?
Could it have something to do with Crystal Creek's own sheriff?
Wayne Jackson is determined to protect Jessie from the advances of
overzealous fans...and big-time gamblers. Jessie can't help but hope
that his reason for hanging out at Zack's during her gigs is more personal than professional.

CRYSTAL CREEK reverberates with the exciting rhythm of Texas.
Each story features the rugged individuals who live and love in the
Lone Star State. And each one ends with the same invitation...

### Y'ALL COME BACK...REAL SOON

Don't miss GUITARS, CADILLACS by Cara West.
Available in November wherever Harlequin Books are sold.

Relive the romance...
Harlequin®is proud to bring you

A new collection of three complete novels every month. By the most requested authors, featuring the most requested themes.

Available in October:

# DREAMSCAPE

They're falling under a spell!
But is it love—or magic?

Three complete novels in one special collection:

**GHOST OF A CHANCE by Jayne Ann Krentz**
**BEWITCHING HOUR by Anne Stuart**
**REMEMBER ME by Bobby Hutchinson**

Available wherever Harlequin books are sold.

HARLEQUIN CELEBRATES
THE SEASON OF SHARING
AND FAMILY WITH

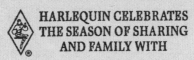

*Friends, Families,*
*Lovers*

Harlequin introduces the latest member in its family of
seasonal collections. Following in the footsteps of the popular
*My Valentine, Just Married* and *Harlequin Historical Christmas
Stories*, we are proud to present FRIENDS, FAMILIES,
LOVERS. A collection of three new contemporary romance
stories about America at its best, about welcoming others into
the circle of love.... Stories to warm your heart ...

By three leading romance authors:

KATHLEEN EAGLE
SANDRA KITT
RUTH JEAN DALE

Available in October, wherever
Harlequin books are sold.

*1993 Keepsake*

# CHRISTMAS

*Stories*

Capture the spirit and romance of Christmas with KEEPSAKE CHRISTMAS STORIES, a collection of three stories by favorite historical authors. The perfect Christmas gift!

Don't miss these heartwarming stories, available in November wherever Harlequin books are sold:

ONCE UPON A CHRISTMAS by Curtiss Ann Matlock
A FAIRYTALE SEASON by Marianne Willman
TIDINGS OF JOY by Victoria Pade

## ADD A TOUCH OF ROMANCE TO YOUR HOLIDAY SEASON WITH KEEPSAKE CHRISTMAS STORIES!

**Fifty red-blooded, white-hot, true-blue hunks
from every State in the Union!**

Look for MEN MADE IN AMERICA! Written by some
of our most poplar authors, these stories feature fifty of
the strongest, sexiest men, each from a different state in
the union!

Two titles available every other month at your favorite
retail outlet.

In November, look for:

STRAIGHT FROM THE HEART by Barbara Delinsky
(Connecticut)
AUTHOR'S CHOICE by Elizabeth August (Delaware)

In January, look for:

DREAM COME TRUE by Ann Major (Florida)
WAY OF THE WILLOW by Linda Shaw (Georgia)

**You won't be able to resist MEN MADE IN AMERICA!**